Cerulean Seas

Book Two in the Jessica Hart Series

A novel by Jenn Brink

HAPPY Reading :)
Jenn

Look for these novels by Jenn Brink

The Jessica Hart Series

Black Roses: Book One

Cerulean Seas: Book Two

Silver Bells: Book Three (Coming December 2014)

*Nail Polish, Push Up Bras & Pirate Ships
(Coming Spring 2014)*

*Tabula Rasa
(Coming 2015)*

For more information about Jenn Brink's novels, visit
www.JennBrink.com

The characters and events in this book are fictitious. Any similarity to real persons, living or dead, is coincidental and not intended by the author.

First Edition: November 2013

Brink Books
Fort Polk, LA 71459

ISBN-13: 978-1493671144

ISBN-10: 1493671146

For my friends, family, and eager Jessica Hart fans, both near and far, new and old, who have encouraged me to finish this work of words, I am forever grateful.

For the B-team, my amazingly talented friends who have selflessly volunteered your time to read, reread, edit, and contribute your suggestions to make this novel so much better than it would have been, you will never know how much I appreciate you.

Thank you.

One

My name is Jessica Hart, and my life sucks. It hasn't always been this way. A short lifetime ago, I was a happy, confident, contributing member of society. I'd give anything to be that girl again. Looking down at my hands, I could see where I had been biting my nails. When did I start biting my nails? It's hard to say, but I really need a manicure.

Looking up from my nails, I spied big green eyes frowning disapprovingly at me from behind the sink. The critical gaze moved to the freckles spilling across my nose and cheeks, then to my hair. My hair and I have a love-hate relationship fueled by the reality that I am barely adept with a flat iron or any other beauty torture instrument and its obstinate refusal to be stunningly perfect on its own. Some days it's wavy and some days it's straight. This morning it had been flat ironed, styled, hair sprayed, and held back with a clip. Then, I stepped outside.

By the time I arrived for my interview, without a minute to spare, it was in a sweaty mess sticking to my face and back. It wasn't pretty and it definitely wasn't giving off the professional vibe that I had been going for today. I sighed. No wonder the interview hadn't gone well. Pulling out a scrunchie and a brush from my purse, I gathered my long auburn locks into a quick ponytail.

"What?" I demanded.

Avocado colored eyes stared mutely back at me. For a moment I stared back, daring those eyes to say something, to voice their disapproval. Forcing a smile, I turned sideways, and proceeded to check out my form.

"What happened to you?" Disgust dripped from my lips.

Instead of answering, the girl in front of me peered critically down at my too tight waistband. I'm almost five-foot-nine inches, without heels. Three weeks ago I had had a rocking body. The kind of body everyone imagines a girl who is five-foot-nine should have.

What happened? Three weeks of my mother's down home cooking, mixed with a heavy dose of depression, had transformed my previously hot bod into the slack form reflected back at me. I poked myself in the gut. I could definitely stand to lose five pounds, maybe ten. With a sigh, I turned my attention back to the mirror and those disapproving avocado eyes surrounded by with thick black lashes (thank god for mascara).

I know what you're thinking. If I met me today I'd think the same thing. What a whiny, self-involved, loser. Honestly, I wasn't always this way. Okay, I've always been a little vain, but it wasn't that long ago that I was confident, in shape, and fun to be around.

"What happened to you?" I repeated quietly.

The girl in the mirror whispered faintly, "He happened."

Sparing a glare at the renegade in front of me, I quickly hurried into an empty stall, forcing back tears.

Today had started out just like all of the other days since my return home from Seattle; hot, dry and miserable. I sighed at the thought of the interview I had just left, knowing that there was little possibility of my prospects improving anytime soon. Taking a moment to get ahold of my emotions while pondering my fate, I contemplated just how I had reached this point in my life.

Four months ago, I'd had my own apartment. It was just a little one bedroom, but I didn't have to share it with anyone. I could use up all the hot water for my shower, let my laundry pile up, and eat ice-cream for breakfast. I had all but owned a five year old, sky blue, convertible Miata. And, I'd had a job. A job that I'd loved. A job with people who gossiped in the break room and talked about their kids. A job that utilized my education while allowing me to pay my bills on time, every month. There had even been a little extra in my bank account to go to the mall and Starbucks, as long as I didn't go too often.

Today, I didn't have any of that. I had quit my job, sold my pretty blue Miata, and everything else I owned, on what could only be called a whim. A rash decision to get married to the wrong guy and move across the country had changed everything. To say it hadn't worked out was an understatement.

Three very long weeks ago I had returned home, tail tucked between my legs in humiliation and one step behind the gossip mill. Once here, I'd had no choice but to move back into my childhood home, with my parents, in rural South Eastern Oklahoma. It was an unplanned change of life following a hellish week that I was working hard to forget, for many reasons.

Since my homecoming, I had been attempting to rebuild my life, starting with getting a job. After three weeks (that felt more like six) of interviewing all over Oklahoma and northern Texas, in the intense August heat, I was losing hope and my sanity.

With a heartfelt sigh, I exited the stall and began to gather up my things from the counter. Picking up my lip-gloss, I had to frown. I was out of the good stuff, reduced to using the stuff little girls use. The ones sold in packs of five at Wallyworld. To be honest, I couldn't even afford the cheap stuff. I'd found this one in the back of a dresser drawer a few days ago, left over from when I was a little girl.

"God, I need a job." Guilt followed the words from my lips. "It was a prayer." I awkwardly insisted to the girl in the mirror. In turn, she gave me the same look my mother does when I curse at the dinner table.

Just as I was finishing up my little invitation-only pity party, the door to my temporary sanctuary opened, revealing an impressively put-together woman in her mid-twenties. I could only presume she was the next applicant. I knew they would be interviewing all week, they had said as much.

As the professional looking twenty something beside me touched up her lipstick, with a lip liner not bought at Wallyworld, I slid my lip gloss into my purse, took a deep breath, straightened my shoulders, and headed out of the ladies room. I was leaving yet another interview for a job that I didn't want to take, with a company that I didn't want to work for, that paid less than I needed to make.

Opening the glass doors leading to the parking lot, the heat slammed into my body, causing me to once again reconsider moving back home. Hoping to avoid the worst of the heat, I moved quickly through the parking lot towards my daddy's twenty year old F250. By the time I reached the truck, sweat was pouring down my body, causing my clothes to stick uncomfortably to my skin. Yanking open the door on the old farm truck, I simultaneously cursed the blistering heat while congratulating myself on remembering to leave the windows down.

"Ow, Ow, Ow!" I squealed.

'The faded blue vinyl-covered seats seared my legs as I jumped up into the cab. Narrowing my eyes against the glaring sun, I glanced around the heat scorched parking lot with its prickly yellow grass futilely attempting to grow around the edges. According to the weatherman, we were on day forty-two in the triple digits without rain, with none in the forecast. It was August in Oklahoma, and the heat was oppressive, just like my life.

"Face it Jessie, you are depressed," I said to the empty cab.

"Of course I am. Look at me!" I answered, with a wave of my hand.

A man with fresh sweat stains under his arms gave me an odd look as he climbed into his car. I self-consciously gave him a weak smile as he drove off.

"Look at that! Complete strangers think I'm a nut." I shook my head. "Jessie, you have got to stop talking to yourself."

With a focused frown, I slowly turned the key in the ignition. "Please, start," I begged.

The truck always started for my dad, every time, without fail. Not for me. Daddy said there was nothing wrong with it. I was just in too much of a hurry. It's an old truck and needs finesse. That's what he says. "Yeah right, the truck just hates me. It's personal." I muttered to the empty parking lot.

Three times I turned the key. The engine didn't make a sound. The air wasn't moving. To make things worse, the sun-warmed plastic was making my butt cheeks, legs, and back feel as if they were on fire. Anger at myself and my life surged to the surface, focusing on the old farm truck.

"Stupid truck! Finesse this!" I shouted, hitting the gas as I jerked the key to the right.

The engine roared to life, bringing with it a new flood of hot air. A smile crept across my face as the extra heat forced a new sweat river to trickle down the valley between my breasts. With a heartfelt sigh, I cranked up the AC. Waiting for the cab to cool down, I took a moment to kick off the cream colored, professionally boring, half-inch heeled pumps that hadn't helped me get the job. A cursory glance at the parking lot told me that no one was paying attention to the old farm truck tucked into the back of the lot.

Without a second thought, I slid out of the matching grey silk pencil skirt and jacket that I had painstakingly put on this morning. Just as quickly, I began peeling off my hose. Once I was freed from the silk imposters, I inched into a pair of cutoff jeans. Next went the crème colored, sweat dampened, silk blouse. After quickly sliding a tank top over my head, I tossed my nice interview clothes into a heap on the passenger seat, took a deep breath, and manually rolled up the windows. The temperature inside the cab had cooled to the double digits signaling that it was time to start the drive back home.

A too familiar feeling of being watched moved through me, causing the skin to crawl on the back of my neck, or was that sweat? After a quick look around the seemingly deserted parking lot, I put the car in gear. Just as I turned out of the parking lot, my phone began to sing. I didn't have to look at the screen to know who it was.

Barbie is my cousin Margaret O'Grady from New York and my best friend since birth. She's two months older than I am, three inches shorter, two cup sizes bigger (thanks to her third ex-husband), and far worldlier than I will ever want to be. Her body is curvaceous, her hair is bottled blonde, and she's addicted to men and shiny stuff.

Not exactly in that order. I prepared myself to either sympathize or be excited, whichever the occasion should require.

"What's up, Cuz?"

"Are you at home?"

"Nope." I shook my head as I shifted gears. "I had an interview just south of the city. I just got into the truck to head home."

"Any luck?"

"No." I frowned. "My life sucks."

"Not anymore," she said excitedly.

"Do I want to ask?" I wondered aloud.

"You and I are going on vacation." I could hear her grin.

I shook my head. "I can't. I'm unemployed, borrowing my daddy's farm truck, and living with my parents, again. I can't afford a vacation." I looked down at my ragged nails. "I can't even afford a manicure."

"Yes, you can," she insisted. "I just got the divorce settlement from Jonathan. So, I have plenty of money, but I need someone to celebrate with me, and you need someone to cheer you up, and get you out of this funk that you've been in since you moved back home. So, you're going. My treat!"

Barbie didn't need this divorce settlement to have 'plenty of money'. On top of being the only heir to her parents' small fortune at the tender age of ten, she had made a very lucrative career out of marrying well. At this point, she had been married four, five, seven times? I couldn't remember. She stopped having large weddings several husbands ago.

Her newest ex-husband, Jonathan, was an independently wealthy advertising executive, until he met Barbie. They had only been married about fifteen minutes when she had walked into their Fifth Avenue townhouse to find him in their bed doing his secretary, Kyle, doggy-style while wearing her black leopard print corset and matching thong. The only things she'd let him keep after the divorce were the corset and thong.

Tempting as her offer was, I really needed to find a job so that I could move out of my parents' house. "Barbie, I'm really sorry, but I can't go."

"You can," she stated firmly. "There's nothing stopping you. You've got no husband, no boyfriend, no kids, and no job. You don't even have a goldfish."

"Don't remind me. I'm thirty years old and I don't even have a goldfish," I grumbled.

"Whatever." One thing about Barbie, she only has tolerance for her own melodrama, which keeps me grounded by default. "You're just barely thirty. It's been what, two weeks?"

"Three," I said, with a frown.

"What time is it there?" she asked, abruptly changing the subject.

"Nine-thirty and it's already horribly hot." I made a face at the sun.

"Great, if you hurry you'll have just enough time to get home, pack, and get to the OKC airport before your flight leaves."

"You already booked my flight?" Why was I surprised?

"Of course I booked your flight. You don't have any money."

The matter of fact way she said it didn't make it any easier to hear. "Why would you do that? If I don't go you'll lose the money that you paid for the ticket." I frowned into the phone.

"Well cousin, your flight leaves at three-ten this afternoon. I'd suggest you be on it." She wasn't taking no for an answer.

I could feel myself giving in as I asked, "Where exactly are we going on vacation to?"

"Fuck-It Island." I could hear her smile.

I sat up a little straighter in my seat. "You're joking?"

"Nope, it's a resort island off of southern Thailand. Our plane leaves from LaGuardia at eight am tomorrow. So, you better not miss your flight out of OKC." She spoke with the no-nonsense tone she usually reserved for telemarketers and ex-husbands.

"Fuck-It Island? Really?" I bit my lower lip. "How can I say no?" With a smile, I put my foot to the gas in the old Ford and hopped onto the highway.

"I knew you'd see it my way!" she squealed.

Catching myself smiling my first true smile in weeks, I had to admit that Barbie was right. I needed to stop wallowing in self-pity. Perhaps an adventure in Thailand was just what I needed.

Two

Once I was well on my way home, I dialed my cousin, Junior. He works nights at the tire plant the next town over so I knew he'd be home.

Junior answered on the third ring. "Yeah?"

"Whatcha doin'?" I drew the words out sweetly.

"Sleepin'. What d'ya think I was doin'?" he asked irritably.

Crap, he was sleeping! "I'm sorry Junior. I was hoping you'd be up."

"No prob, I need to get up anyway. What can I do ya for?"

"I need a ride to the airport." Cringing nervously, I crossed my fingers.

"Now?"

"No, I'm on my way home from a job interview. I need to pack real fast, then I'll need a ride up to Will Rogers," I explained.

The line went quiet just long enough to feed my nervousness.

A sigh of relief escaped me as he said, "I guess I kin help ya out, but I gotta ask. Why not have your daddy take ya?"

I rolled my eyes. "I don't think he'll be real keen on me going away again so soon. He's been lecturing me about how dangerous the world is." I deepened my voice in a pathetic attempt to mimic my dad, then said, "Jessie, you just need to find a nice local boy to take care of you. Get married, settle down in Tish, and have some babies. All of our friends have grandchildren already."

"Yeah, I heard somethin' 'bout that. Rumor has it you're engaged to one of them Caldwell boys," Junior said, with laughter in his voice.

"Really?" My parents were driving me crazy trying to marry me off. If they had stooped to the Caldwell's, then they were getting desperate. "Which one?"

"Don't know. They're all losers, drunkards, and wife beaters. I hear the youngest one grows weed in the back pasture." He chuckled, "Guess that makes him an entrepreneur, and pick o'the litter."

I nervously gnawed my bottom lip. "So, you'll help me?"

"Sure." His words were slow as he considered his options. "Your kids would probably end up with nine toes and half a brain or something weird like that. Anyway, it's Friday and I got the night off. Maybe, I'll round up some guys to check out the city scene. It's been awhile since we did that."

I smiled with relief. "Thanks Cuz! Meet me at my parents' house in two hours."

"Gotcha boss." He laughed.

It wasn't long before I turned onto the dirt road that filled my childhood memories. I smiled at the house that hadn't changed since I was a kid and eased to a stop next to the barn. Excitement spilled out of me as I hopped out of the cab. Pushing past the dogs, I rushed up to the house and through the kitchen door.

Stepping inside, I cringed. The house smelled of fresh baked cookies. With a frown, I glanced down at my waistband. If I stayed here much longer I was going to weigh a thousand pounds!

I had a lot to do before Junior picked me up, and not much time. Grabbing a cookie, I took a moment to read the note propped up against the cookie plate.

'Jessie, Your father and I went into town. Don't ruin your appetite. Dinner is at six. Love, mom.'

Grabbing a couple of cookies, I headed upstairs to pack. I had just finished stuffing a large carry-on full of bathing suits, shorts, tank tops, my favorite hoodie, pajamas, running shoes, socks, and my favorite red cowboy boots when I heard the dogs barking outside. A cursory examination of my packing job told me there was just enough room left for some accessories, makeup, and hygiene products. I finished filling up my suitcase, double checking to be sure that I had everything, then dug out my passport and phone charger. Sliding them into my purse, I hurried downstairs.

17

Once I reached the foyer, I peeked through the window to see what the dogs were so excited about. It was Junior, right on time. Leaving my suitcase by the door, I headed into the kitchen. There was still one more thing to do before I left.

A moment later Junior called out as he let himself in. "Hello the house."

"I'm in the kitchen," I yelled back.

He slowly strode into the kitchen just as I glanced up. His still damp, brown hair rested against the nape of his neck while the scent of his favorite cologne hung about his body. I could tell he planned to hit the club because he was wearing dark blue jeans, with the big belt buckle that said '*Jr*', his good boots, a blue and grey pearl snap shirt, and a straw cowboy hat, otherwise known as his 'goin' out' hat.

Smiling up at him, I said, "Thanks for coming to get me. I'm almost ready."

He grabbed a chocolate chip cookie off of the counter as he watched me precisely organize the note, that I had just finished writing, against the cookie plate. A flash of irritation crossed my face when Junior picked up the note and read it aloud.

"*Momma and daddy, I am going to Thailand with Barbie. I will be back in a couple of weeks. Love, Jessie.*"

Junior shook his head at me. "A note, really?"

Taking the note out of his hands, I shrugged and said. "You know that's our thing. Some families call or text, we leave notes."

He cocked his head at me. I knew that look. That look had called me on my B.S. my whole life. Well, I wasn't going to let him make me feel bad, not this time. We stood in silence, staring at each other over the cookie plate. Those chocolate chip eyes set stared up from the plate, begging me to eat them, until I couldn't resist any longer.

Grabbing a cookie, I sighed. "I've tried to talk them. They just double team me with the *Just stay here and get married and be like us* speech. Then, they pile on the guilt. You know about the guilt." I growled my frustration. "It's just easier this way."

He watched me, frowning his disagreement, as I carefully reorganized the note beside the cookie plate. Once it was arranged to my satisfaction, he picked up another cookie. "I hate to say this cuz, but you do know that you're an adult, don't you?"

I stared longingly at the cookie plate, then down at my waistline. I had already had how many cookies: three, four, twelve? I had lost count. I thought about the long plane ride ahead of me, my parents, and the inevitable phone calls designed to guilt me into returning home. Already cracking under the imagined pressure, I grabbed another cookie.

"I know. But, someone forgot to tell my folks," I answered dismally.

Hefting my suitcase, Junior gave me a serious look. "Jess, one of these days you're gonna have to grow up."

I rolled my eyes at him. "I tried that once. It wasn't any fun."

19

Shaking his head, Junior headed out the front door with me just a step behind him. I hopped up into the brown and tan F150 King Cab parked in front of the house while he tossed my suitcase into the bed of the truck. I was buckling my seatbelt when he climbed into the driver's seat, turned over the engine, and pointed the shiny new truck down the dirt drive.

"I haven't seen this truck before." I said, as I curiously checked out the cab. "I like it."

"Thanks, I bought her a couple of days ago. I've been saving up. This here's my dream truck." He stroked the dash lovingly. "She's made in America, fully loaded with everything a man could need and more. Better than a woman, and more loyal too," he said, with pride.

"I heard Ford outsources their manufacturing. Are you sure the entire truck was made in America, and not Japan or China?" I asked.

Junior narrowed his eyes in distaste. "Do you wanna walk to the airport?"

I pursed my lips. "Nope."

We drove in silence for about a mile before Junior spoke again. "We're gonna stop and pick up a couple of guys before we hit the highway. But, don't you worry now; I'll have you at the airport in plenty of time to feel bad about sneaking off on your folks like this."

"Thanks." I rolled my eyes.

About five miles down the road, Junior pulled up to the pump at the Gas 'N' Go.

"Be a good girl and run in and get me a pack of chaw and a coke while I fill up." Junior dug a folded bill from his front pocket.

"Sure. What kind of coke do you want?" I asked, taking the twenty from him.

"Pepsi."

While waiting in line at the cash register, I noticed a familiar form talking to Jr. I hurried with my purchase, hoping to catch him before he left. The checker, Leslie, wanted to gossip about my impending marriage. It took me longer than it should have to convince her that I was not marrying any of the Caldwell boys. By the time I got back to the truck, the guy I had been trying to catch for weeks was gone and Junior was ready to go.

"What did he want?" I asked suspiciously.

"Who?" Junior asked.

"The rhino on steroids you were just talking to," I responded irritably.

"Larry?" he asked with a confused look.

"Sure, Larry." I shrugged my shoulders. His name was Larry? I would have guessed it was Big John, The Rock, or something like that. "You know him?" I was surprised.

"He's renting a room over at Aunt Edna's," he answered.

"What did he want?" I asked again.

"Nothin' really."

21

"Did he ask about me?" I pushed.

"You got a new crush?" he asked with a grin.

"No." I paused. "You're gonna laugh."

"Probably," he agreed.

Rolling my eyes, I said, "I think he's been following me." The words even sounded silly to me as they came out of my mouth.

A loud chuckle erupted from Junior's gut. Trying not to grin, he asked me, "Why would Larry follow you? He don't seem like the thrill seeking kind."

"Very funny." I rolled my eyes again, "I don't know why he's following me. I was hoping he'd said something to you."

His face became serious as he asked, "What makes you think he's following you?"

I shook my head. "It's just…a feeling. Everywhere I go, he's there. It just doesn't feel like a coincidence."

"Have you asked him if he's following you?" he asked.

"No." I shook my head. "I don't actually know him. He keeps his distance."

"Cuz, all that stuff in Seattle left you a little paranoid. Larry's just in town doin' some work out by the river."

"So, he hasn't said anything about me?" I asked.

Junior was quiet a minute before answering, "Not any more than anyone else around here."

I rolled my eyes.

"You gotta admit, you're fodder for the gossip machine. Wait, he did ask about your parents the other day."

"He did?" Why would Larry the stalker ask about my parents?

"Yeah." Junior chuckled. "Your mom tried to bribe him into coming over for dinner. She wouldn't take no for an answer. She told my mom you'd make beautiful babies."

I groaned.

Junior nodded in commiseration. "He wanted to know how to get her to leave him alone. Said he was afraid your boyfriend would find out. I explained that you weren't seeing anyone, even if you were I'd put my money on Larry, but none of it mattered. So, I offered to talk to your folks for him."

"You talked to my parents about Larry the stalker?" I asked incredulously.

"Tweren't nothin'. I just explained how he was just passing through. That seemed to take care of the problem. Everybody knows your daddy wants you to marry local," he grinned, "settle down in town and have a litter."

"Great, they've stooped to setting me up with unknown drifters." I sighed, not knowing how much more of their 'help' I could take.

Junior stopped the truck in front of a familiar house. With a glance at the time, he laid on the horn, disturbing the quiet peace of the area. After anxiously watching the clock for what seemed like an eternity, but was in actuality just a few minutes, the front door finally opened. Bubba casually sauntered out to the truck, dressed similarly to Junior. This was no surprise to me. Bubba and Junior are cousins, all but twins, and practically inseparable.

Bubba climbed into the backseat and casually looked me over before speaking. "I shoulda' know'd it was you when Junior said he had to drop someone at the airport. Where you headed this time, little cousin?"

"Fuck-It Island," I answered, as a huge grin spread across my face.

He gave me a startled look. "No shit?"

"No shit," I confirmed.

Bubba asked Junior, "Didja know there was such a place?"

"Nope. Not sure there is," he replied shaking his head.

"It's in Thailand," I volunteered.

"Who you goin' with?" Bubba asked.

"Barbie, my cousin from my mom's side." I gave him a knowing look. "You remember Barbie, don't you?"

A goofy smile spread across Bubba's face as the two men nodded. "Oh yeah, we remember Barbie alright. That girl was somethin' else. She used to come visit for a couple of weeks every summer. Us boys looked forward to her visits all year long. 'Twas like Christmas." He paused before saying, "Christmas in July."

Junior spoke up. "She was the first girl I ever um…well you know."

"Oh, I know all right." I grinned at him. "She told me all about it."

Junior's face turned crimson. "She did?"

"In detail." I made a face. "It was weeks before I could go into that barn without the mental picture of you two going at it in the hay loft. It grossed me out so much that I had to trade out my chores with Greg."

Bubba laughed. "That Barbie musta knocked boots with every guy in a fifteen mile radius. What's she up to these days?"

I shrugged. "The same old stuff. She just got divorced, again, and she wants to go on vacation to celebrate."

Both of them having been through a divorce, Junior twice, my cousins wore identical expressions of understanding. They were quiet as we pulled up to a house that I wasn't familiar with. It was a small, older, red brick house with a carport instead of a garage. The house was bare of curtains and other signs of occupancy. If there hadn't been a car under the carport, in the process of being rebuilt, I would have thought it was empty. However, the car, and the tools scattered around it, suggested that the home was not as abandoned as it had first appeared.

Just as Junior reached for the horn, out stepped Mike Baine. My eyes widened. I couldn't believe what I was seeing. I turned to Junior with an incredulous look on my face. Junior was pointedly looking out of his window. I turned to Bubba. He was studying his boots. Frustrated, I narrowed my eyes and let out a long sigh. Neither man met my gaze. I couldn't help but glance out the window as Mike strutted towards the truck.

Mike Baine has boyish good looks and a quick sexy smile that used to melt me like butter. Any girl around could tell you he's incredibly hot, in a redneck kind of way. He stands about four inches taller than me, slender yet muscular, with blonde hair, blue eyes, a slight dimple in his left cheek, and an ever-present mischievous twinkle in his eye.

Mike and I know each other well. Very well. He was my first love, and my first heartbreak. To be honest, he was my second and fifth heartbreaks, too. Like I said, we have history. Our most recent history was still all too fresh for me. As he reached the truck, our eyes met. Just like that, I was reliving our last meeting.

Mike had broken his leg. Some people would say that it was my fault, but that's another story. Anyway, I felt bad for him, stuck at home by himself with a bum leg. So, I left work early one Tuesday afternoon and drove down from the city to bring him some homemade chicken soup my momma had made, and a kiss. Trying not to disturb him, I quietly let myself into his small house, located in what passes for downtown Tishomingo. Hearing a noise, I eased into his bedroom with a grin on my face. Imagine my surprise to find him in bed with my despised third cousin, Traci Lee. I was speechless at the sight of her perched over Mike in nothing but a pair of cowboy boots, and a smile.

After an eternity where I stood in the doorway letting my brain register what I was seeing, I threw the hot soup at the two of them, pot and all. I watched it bounce off of his cheating ass before storming out of the house. Mike jumped up and chased me out to the car clad in just his birthday suit, cast, and chicken noodle soup. He reached the front door just in time for me to grab my gun from the glove compartment of my car. I was so upset that I hit everything but him as he hobbled back into the house for cover. On a slow gossip day, it was still the talk of the town. I hadn't seen or talked to Mike since.

Mike hopped up into the truck, next to Bubba, and flashed me a big grin, intruding on my trip down memory lane. "Hey woman, miss me?" he asked.

He was wearing his old work boots, faded blue jeans with a Skoal ring in the left back pocket, a light grey t-shirt that stretched tight across his muscles, and a ratty mustard yellow baseball cap. I hated to admit it, but he looked good.

"Not recently. It's too bad I don't have my gun on me," I said sweetly.

"What, you're not still mad. Are you?" He gave me a disbelieving look.

Bubba snorted, and said, "Mike, you of all people ought to know that our Jessie can hold a grudge like no one ya ever met."

Mike shook his head. "Hey, I dropped the charges and told you I was sorry. I even sent flowers to your parents when I heard you'd been murdered. It was a big spring bouquet. Did they tell you?"

I nodded, continuing to stare out the window.

"I was gonna stop by when I heard you were alive and back in town. But, I was sort of seeing this girl who was a little jealous of you, because of our history. We're through now. So, I'm available." He winked.

I glared at Junior, who was pretending to find a radio station.

Bubba spoke, "Come on Jess, you can't stay mad at Mike forever. It's been what a year, since the breakup?"

"More like six months." I corrected him, moving my glare from Junior to Bubba.

"Well, that's almost a year. Anyway, Mike's our friend. Ya gotta think about us, too. We all know he's a man whore, but we accept him anyway 'cause he cain't help the way he is." Leaning forward and lowering his voice to a conspiratorial whisper, he said, "Don't tell no one. Mike here's got a drinkin' problem."

Seeing the horrified look on Mike's face, I couldn't help but smile.

Oblivious to Mike's reaction, Bubba continued with his explanation. "That's why he done what he did. He was hurtin' after you broke his leg, and got real drunk tryin' to feel better. Then, that girl just showed up out of the blue." He shook his head. "It weren't his fault. I mean NO ONE would tap that unless they was drunk. We're all afraid we'll catch somethin'. Mike did. The doc had to put him on these meds for a real long time. His wanger coulda fell off! Now, ain't that punishment enough?"

Mike glared at Bubba. "Thanks man. Do me a favor, don't help me anymore."

I couldn't help but laugh at the thought of Mike catching something from Traci Lee. "It has been a long time. I guess it doesn't matter anyway. I mean, it's not like you were the worst boyfriend I ever had."

Junior spoke up. "That's right. Least he didn't try to kill ya, like the last one."

There was a moment of deathlike silence in the truck, then Mike reached up and smacked Junior in the back of the head, with his hat.

Junior cringed. "I'm sorry, Jess. That came out all wrong."

I sighed heavily. "It's okay." I was forever going to be known as the girl whose fiancé tried to kill her.

Mike gave me a hopeful look. "How about it woman, friends?"

Why not? "Okay, we can be friends, but you gotta stop calling me that."

He gave me a big smile. "So, you're going out with us tonight? Don't worry, I'll keep the losers away from you."

"Sorry, you boys are gonna have to troll the bars without me. I'm headed to the airport." I looked at the clock on the dash. "It's awfully early. What are y'all gonna do 'til the bars open?"

Junior grinned his excitement. "We're goin' to the Bass Pro shop to have us a looksee around."

29

Bubba nodded in agreement. "But first, we're going by the gun shop. I need a new scope for deer season. Then, we'll have to do some shootin' at the range in back of the gun shop. After we're done shoppin', we're gonna hang out in Bricktown, get some barbeque and beers, and maybe catch that new action flick. You know, guy stuff."

"Sorry to miss boy's night out." I wrinkled my nose.

Mike flashed me a sexy smile. "When you comin' home, woman? I can pick you up from the airport."

"I don't think so Mike." The last thing my hurt pride needed was to get involved with him again. Last time that happened I rebounded to Jim, moved to Seattle, and ended up almost dead. "We can be friends, but that's it."

He grinned at me. "So, you're saying there's still a chance."

I was nervously watching the clock when Junior finally eased his truck to the curb at the drop off lane of the airport. Jumping down from the truck, I gave my cousins quick hugs while promising to meet up when I got back into town.

As I reached for my bag, Mike stepped in front of me. "Where's my hug?"

I narrowed my eyes. "Mike, we are never ever getting back together, ever."

"Hey, I didn't say nothin' about gettin' back together. But, you did say that we could be friends. Can't a friend give y'all a hug goodbye?" He held out his arms.

With a defeated sigh, I stepped into his embrace. His cologne washed over me, bringing with it memories of being close to him. His arms tightened around me. Then, his hands began to wonder outside of my comfort zone.

"Mike!" I shrieked, pushing against his chest.

Giving me a cocky grin that showed no remorse for copping a feel. He whispered, "I really am sorry," before releasing his hold.

A movement to my left caught my eye. A truck I thought I recognized was stopped at the curb three cars back. I could just barely see that the driver was getting out. I leaned forward to take a closer look.

"Larry?" I murmured to myself.

The mountainous man stepped onto the sidewalk, his eyes trained on mine.

My eyes narrowed while I mumbled, "I am not crazy. He is following me!"

My cousins headed to the truck, oblivious to my stalker. I stepped forward, determined to end this cat and mouse game. Without warning, Mike grabbed my right butt cheek. The surprise manhandle throwing me off balance, I teetered on the edge of the curb.

"Mike!" I screeched.

He grabbed me around the waist, pulling me back to the sidewalk. We stood heartbeat to heartbeat, looking into each other's eyes for a moment too long. Too long to prevent the familiar butterflies from surging in my stomach.

With an angry glare and a huff, I roughly pushed away.

"You were about to fall. I grabbed the closest thing." He grinned his sexy boyish grin down at me.

For a moment, we were the only ones on the sidewalk. I shook my head to clear the cobwebs of faded love from my veins, silently reminding myself of what being with Mike was like, past the little boy smile. The unanswered calls and texts, the missed dates, the late nights leaving me feeling about as special as a booty call. It only took a moment to remind myself of what I wasn't missing, butterflies be damned.

I stepped away, taking note of the confused look in Mike's eyes. With a small shake of my head, I turned away. To my left, Junior and Bubba stood next to the truck, laughing. Shooting them a dirty look, I looked down the sidewalk. Larry was gone and his truck was being inspected by airport security.

"You boys try to stay out of trouble." I called out as I turned towards the terminal doors.

Three

It took less than a minute for small bumps to form on my arms and legs making my skin the texture of a cucumber. The goose bumps wouldn't have bothered me as much if they had been a result of excitement threatening to bubble out of me. But, they weren't. They were spawned by the unnaturally cool air in the terminal. The same cool air that was causing me to curse my clothing choices. Unfortunately, the time displayed on my phone told me that I would be lucky to make my flight without delaying for a wardrobe change. I needed to get moving. A quick look at the ticket counters told me that the lines were painfully long, as they shifted imperceptibly forward.

I couldn't help but sigh as I turned towards the check-in counter. I had almost reached the line when the absence of a wait at the automatic ticket dispenser caught my attention. Biting my lower lip in indecision, I silently debated whether or not to try my luck with the machine in front of me, or stand in the long line.

I glanced towards the unsmiling crowd full of unhappy children, parents, and other travelers leaning against their bags while impatiently waiting their turn. It was a really long line. My gut told me that, if I got stuck in that line, I'd never make my flight. My gaze turned to rest on the machine in front of me. I've never had much luck with machines, but time was short. Stepping up to the ticket dispenser, I held my breath and crossed my fingers while typing my name into the computer. Amazingly, it worked on the third try.

"Yes!" I fist pumped my excitement as my ticket printed out! The old man waiting patiently behind me chuckled, causing me to explain, "These things never work for me."

"It's not just you darlin', they don't work for anyone. That's why the line is so short," he said, with an understanding smile.

"It's a sign. This is gonna be a good trip." I beamed back at him.

"I'm sure it will be, child," he agreed.

The old man stepped up to try his luck as I gathered up my ticket, purse, and carry-on bag. Grinning stupidly, I headed for security with a heady feeling that my life was changing for the better. There was a new spring in my step. My confidence was soaring. This trip was the fix my life needed. The good traveling karma at the automatic ticket dispenser proved it.

My positive attitude was quickly replaced by niggling doubt when I rounded the corner to find a seemingly endless mess of lines. As I beheld the frowning mass of people in front of me, my grin faded.

After a faltering instant, I forced a smile back onto my face, resolutely stepping forward into the throng of travelers. The spring in my step may have fled, but my spirits refused to buckle under this unforeseen obstacle. It won't be so bad, the lines will move quickly, I told myself while obediently taking my place at the end of an implausibly long security line.

Twenty minutes later, my smile was nowhere to be found as I re-evaluated the necessity of this trip. The line in front of me had barely moved while continuing to grow behind me. I glanced around, had that line on the other end moved? Yes, it had. That woman with the three little kids was at the end of the line when I was picking my line. I knew I should have gotten in that one. Nervously considering the time, I wondered if it was too late to switch lines.

I was still questioning my line-choosing skills when I noticed a guy several people behind me smiling and waving. Was he smiling at me? No, he must be waving at someone ahead of me. I glanced up the line. No one was waving back. However, there were several women, and one man, shamelessly checking him out. Curious, I peered back towards his end of the line. He waved again, flashing me a stellar smile. He was looking at me. Was I sure I didn't know him? Trying unsuccessfully to place him, I took another long look.

The stranger at the back of the line had the body of an athlete, gleaming brown eyes, even white teeth, and a laid-back attitude. His dark brown hair was worn just a little long and loose to complement the three day scruff on his face. He was dressed casually in leather-banded flip flops, cargo shorts, and a faded blue t-shirt advertising a sports team that I had never heard of. The only visible adornment on him was a braided-leather men's necklace with a metal dart pendant hanging from his neck. I had to admit, I've had worse looking guys stare at me, much worse.

Even though I was pretty sure the handsome stranger was waving at someone else, I gave him a flirty finger wave back, just in case. To my surprise, he smiled and mouthed something. I shrugged my shoulders. He mouthed it again. Silently cursing my lack of lip-reading skills, I shook my head. He smiled again. With disbelief, I watched while he slid past no less than twenty people to reach my side. The only people who seemed to care that he had jumped the line were a creepy looking and overly pale man in his fifties and a familiar looking mountain of a man, built like a rhino on steroids, at the far end of next line over. After giving the obviously disapproving rhino a small smile, I turned towards the alluring stranger standing before me.

"Hi," he said, with a smile that could melt chocolate on a wintry day.

"Hi." My mind had gone blank. He was absolutely gorgeous up close.

He gave me a contrite glance, somehow succeeding in making him look even more attractive. "I must apologize for being so forward, but I just had to meet you. I was trying to ask you to wait for me." He had an accent that I couldn't place. It was definitely European.

Glancing shyly up through my lashes, I managed to mumble, "Sorry, I don't read lips."

"Don't be, this is much better."

He took my hand, grinning down at me with a smile that made my heart skip a beat. Time stood still as we stood staring into each other's eyes. The moment was ruined when I realized that I was staring into this stranger's eyes like a love struck teenager as the people around us ooo'd and ahhhh'd. I searched my mind for something intelligent to say, coming up blank. I have to say something! Think Jessie, think! Panic seized me until I blurted out the one thing that I was thinking, and trying desperately not to say.

"How did you get all of those people to let you through the line?" My face flushed crimson as the words left my mouth. A hot guy moves the earth to meet me and I ask him how he did it? No wonder relationships never seem to work out for me.

A mischievous grin played on his lips. "I told them that you were my future wife. I just had to meet you before you got through security and disappeared out of my life forever."

"Oh." I didn't know what to say, so I asked, "Did that really work?" As I spoke, I glanced back down the line. I wasn't sure that it would have worked for me, not today.

Jenn Brink

"I'm here, aren't I? Where are you headed?" He was attempting to examine the boarding pass that sagged loosely in my hand.

Clutching my pass a little tighter, I shot him a nervous look. "New York, I'm meeting my cousin."

A warmly disarming smile interrupted my thoughts. The man in front of me eagerly said, "Me too!"

"You're meeting my cousin in New York?" I flirted.

"Only if you're going to be there," he flirted back.

We continued to flirt outrageously as the line steadily moved toward the TSA. Minutes later, I found myself approaching the front of the throng.

"Shit! I almost forgot!" I squealed in panic.

He watched, with a confused look on his face, as I quickly took off the necklace, bracelet, and earrings that I had forgotten to remove after my interview. Hastily I shoved them into my purse. It was almost my turn. Frantically, I pulled at my belt. It was stuck in the back loop of my shorts. I reached around to get it. Between the line moving and my full hands, it just wouldn't come loose. Inwardly I groaned, knowing that I looked like a dog chasing its tail.

"Please, allow me." The hot guy beside me reached out taking my purse and suitcase while I struggled to free the belt from my shorts.

After an embarrassing struggle the belt finally came free from the loop, snapping back to hit me in the arm. "Ow!" I exclaimed, shoving the offending accessory into my purse. Rubbing my arm I retrieved my things from the handsome stranger standing beside me with an expression of undisguised amusement on his face. "Thank you," I stammered in embarrassment.

He was giving me a tolerant look. The kind of look a person would bestow on the crazy old man that walks backwards down Main Street, talking to himself and yelling threatening slurs at passing cars.

"Now, you *must* explain, or I shall think you mad," he said, with a hint of amusement in his voice.

I sighed, hating to explain myself. Knowing it would make me sound like a nut, I tried anyway. "I forgot, or I would already have had them in my suitcase." He gave me a confused look, unknowingly spurring me into an unintelligible babble. "I always wear as little as possible when I fly. It's such a hassle to get undressed and then redress as you walk down the security line and I always get pulled aside by the TSA's, always." I threw my hands up while scowling at the waiting TSA. "I swear it's personal. I'm on a list or something!"

He gave me a startled look. "I wouldn't think that someone like you would get the attention of security."

"Thank you!" I agreed vehemently. "I don't think I look like a terrorist either, but apparently the TSA's do." I rolled my eyes toward the security agent in front of us.

It was my turn to go through the line. I took a deep breath telling myself that things were going well for me. This time they would let me walk through without issue, without further embarrassment. Holding my breath, I stepped up to the little metal box, smiling innocently at the waiting TSA.

This trip was no exception. There I was: barefoot, in my cutoff jeans, tank top with the built in bra, no belt, and no jewelry. I couldn't help but feel like a criminal, with my hands over my head and feet spread apart, then the TSA singled me out for a pat down. Stepping to the side, I sighed in defeat.

A greasy haired, pimply faced boy, who looked like he should be in a high school math class instead of harassing travelers as a TSA, gave me a perverted smile while motioning me to stand next to him. "Come over here for your pat down," he leered.

Now, I've been flying since I was a little girl. I have come to accept a certain amount of discomfort when going through airport security. But, I am not about to let myself get felt up by some creepy, pimple faced pervert, who looks like he spends his Friday nights playing World of Warcraft online in his parent's basement. This is where I draw the line.

A matronly looking woman with a badge that said Irene pinned to her right breast gave the kid a disgusted look, and said, "I'll take care of her, Ian."

Ian's eyes slowly swept up, then down my body, finally resting on my breasts. "Nah, I got this." He said, licking his lips.

Shaking my head, I shuddered my revulsion. "I don't think so."

Irene looked from me to Ian. "Go monitor the personal belongings, Ian. It's time for Chantal's break."

Ian looked like he was going to argue. One look from Irene and he thought better of it. He was frowning and mumbling under his breath as he skulked away. I sighed with relief while silently enduring the now routine airport pat down from a woman who looked like my Great Aunt Eva. I couldn't help but think about who I'd like to be feeling me up right now. Great Aunt Eva didn't make the list.

What had my life become? Since this morning, I'd been caught having a mini breakdown in a public restroom, stalked by a rhino named Larry, groped by my ex, chatted up by a hottie, leered at by a pimply perv, and molested by an old lady in front of hundreds of people. Some days it just doesn't pay to get out of bed.

Retrieving my belongings from the conveyor belt, I paused to scan the area for the hottie. He was nowhere to be seen, of course. I guess watching an old lady feel me up didn't do it for him. Heading for my gate, I shrugged him off. It wasn't like it mattered. He had just been a much needed boost to my self-esteem. With just five minutes before my plane was scheduled to depart, I forgot all about the handsome stranger. My gate was all the way at the end of the terminal. Rushing down the ramp as they closed the door, I realized that against all odds, I had made it.

"Karma, baby!" I shouted, just before tripping over my own feet and barreling head over heels into the cockpit. "Karma's a bitch," I mumbled, struggling to stand without further damaging the plane.

41

Jenn Brink

Four

I was in a puddle jumper heading to the Dallas-Fort Worth airport to catch my connecting flight to New York. Everywhere I turned, there was an endless sea of bored looking travelers, mindlessly staring out the grimy windows. The plane was packed.

I don't normally get motion sickness, but I was feeling it today. Maybe it was all those cookies. The stale recycled air moving through the cabin wasn't helping. We hit an air bump, then another.

Fighting back a wave of nausea, I put my hand to my mouth. I desperately needed a breath of fresh air. As the turbulence steadily increased, my queasiness intensified. Closing my eyes, I took a thin breath in an attempt to calm my nausea. In my mind, I pictured Superman violently shaking the plane from side to side.

"I can't take much more of this" I groaned, clutching tight to the armrest.

My seatmate pointedly ignored me. A moment later a passenger in the row behind me stopped the flight attendant as she stumbled past his row.

"Excuse me miss. How much longer until we land?" he asked.

She gave him a sympathetic look. "Not much longer. We're beginning the descent now."

As she finished her sentence the plane experienced another rough shake causing the flight attendant to lose her balance and fall into the unsuspecting lap of an old man seated next to her. Passengers groaned and a baby cried somewhere near the back of the plane. We leveled out. The passengers breathed a collective sigh of relief. The plane shook again causing my stomach to tighten, threatening expulsion once more.

"There's the ground. It's almost over!" I elated to my unresponsive seatmate.

I almost had the sickness under control when the plane shook again, causing the bile to turn on me. Biting my lip and trying to think of something else, anything else, I fought the sickness. Oh no! I was losing the battle. I focused my attention on locating a barf bag. After a frantic search, it became obvious that my barf bag was missing. The plane shook again, giving me a good idea of what had happened to it.

As the plane jostled back and forth, I couldn't help but picture a tiny airplane bouncing and sliding, back and forth, over a hundred overinflated balloons. That didn't help my stomach any. My skin paled further with the effort of holding the contents of my stomach in.

In the midst of silently cursing the pilot, I convinced myself he was making the plane shake on purpose, or was it God, punishing me for running out on my parents like an errant child?

"Junior was right, I should have just told them. Why couldn't I just tell them?" I cried.

Startled at my outburst, my seatmate looked at me as if I had a contagious disease. Our gazes met just as our seats began to rattle with renewed force. Without further warning, the bile soared up and out of my mouth, causing me to heave partially digested food right onto my seatmate's lap.

His eyes widened with shock and disbelief. After the moment of shock wore off, he looked down at his oozing lap in silent surprise. Embarrassment surged across my face. Avoiding his gaze, I stared down at the chunks of chocolate mixed with green and yellow goop pooling into the crevices of his pants, then up at the lit-up fasten seat belt sign.

"I am so sorry," I somehow managed to choke out with both hands covering my mouth.

Embarrassment shaded my features. I couldn't just sit here, not after that. But, I knew there was no getting up. We were in the descent and the fasten seat belt sign was on. I could only hope the landing would be completed soon. Glancing guiltily at my seatmate, I attempted to wipe the gook off of his pants with the Skymall I found tucked into the back of my seat. All while taking short shallow breaths.

44

Half a moment later, the big man sitting next to me made a loud choking sound, pulled a handful of barf bags from under him, clumsily opened one up, leaned forward, and emptied the contents of his stomach. No wonder I couldn't find any of the paper bags. My pale-under-his-beard seatmate, then turned to the teenaged girl in the seat next to him and mumbled a self-conscious apology. Her shocked eyes moved from the slimy gook dripping from his scraggly beard to the full paper bag clutched in the big man's hand.

As the big man prepared another bag, the trendily dressed teen next to him spied a spatter of goo on her pants. The slow dawning of understanding spread across the young girl's face. Desperation shrouded her features. With a *"Yelp!"* she attempted to jump out of her seat, just to be pulled back by the seatbelt she had obediently fastened half an hour ago. Tears began to pour down the teen's face. Still she fumbled with the restraint, trying desperately to free herself from the nightmare. Minutes later, she finally got the strap undone. With a hysterical shriek, she launched herself into the aisle just as the flight attendant approached to see what the commotion was about.

One sniff at our row and the flight attendant turned a greenish yellow color. With a sad shake of her head, she gave the teenager a sympathetic look. "I am really sorry." I think she meant it. "You're going to have to sit back down. The plane is in its downward descent."

"I can't. I need to go to the bathroom." The girl gagged through her tears.

45

"I'm afraid you're going to have to wait." The flight attendant told her in a no-nonsense voice. "Go back to your seat and fasten your seatbelt, now."

A horrified look passed over the young girl's delicate features. Her saucer shaped eyes met the flight attendant's just as bile spewed from her mouth coating the older woman in smelly goo, from head to foot. The flight attendant looked down at the thin smelly chunks of partially digested food and liquid dripping from of her clothes with undisguised revulsion.

With an appalled expression, the teenager slowly backed away, but there was nowhere to hide. The overly full plane was still in the air, doors locked. Giving the young girl a harsh look, the flight attendant pointed her towards the seat she had recently vacated, insisting that she fasten her safely belt.

Now, the entire plane was aware that there was a problem in aisle thirteen. Thanks to the recycled air, it was all you could smell. We couldn't escape it. Watching the big man fill up a second bag, made me want to be anywhere else. I turned my head to the side to take a shallow breath, trying not to move or breathe any more than necessary. The putrid smell was overpowering.

After what seemed like an eternity, the doors opened letting us out of the metal puke box and into the terminal. Avoiding each other's gazes, we rushed en mass to the exit, devoid of the usual polite protocol as we hurried to escape the odor of sickness.

After scrubbing myself in the bathroom sink, I pulled out a clean pair of shorts and a red t-shirt from my suitcase. Clothes in tow, I headed for the privacy of a stall. It wasn't long before I was faced with a dilemma. There were no empty stalls and the line was not short. I could get in line, in my vomit soaked clothes, or change at the sink and hope no one called security.

There is no modesty when you're wearing puke in public. Backing into a corner, I quickly stripped off my soiled clothes, then proceeded to redress. A cursory glance up and down told me that I had washed off the traces of regurgitated cookies and whatever my seatmate had ingested over the past twelve hours. Giving myself the sniff test, I decided it would have do. Either the smell was gone, or I had become immune.

What next? I frowned down at my small pile of dirty clothes on the floor, reeking of bile. If I put the clothes in my carry-on everything would smell. I struggled with the dilemma for a moment. I couldn't do it. I had smelled enough vomit to last me a lifetime. Grimacing, I shoved the pile of clothes into the trash can next to the sink, then ran my tongue across my teeth.

"Eww!" My mouth tasted nasty.

A quick dig through my suitcase produced my toothbrush and a travel tube of toothpaste. I really wished that I had some mouthwash, but my bottle had been too big to get through security. Once my mouth finally felt clean, I carefully put my toothbrush and toothpaste back into my suitcase, then squirted on some perfume to hide any lingering odor.

Feeling better, I walked out the door wondering how I could even think about food after that. You would think my appetite would be gone forever. No, I was hungry, really hungry. With a shrug, I decided it was probably because I had just emptied out the meager contents of my stomach on the plane.

"At least I won't have to worry about all those cookies making me fat anymore," I said to no one, as I stepped back onto the Terminal, earning me more than a few odd looks.

Five

Sitting at a bar with a margarita while enduring my layover, I couldn't decide if this trip was destined to be incredible or terrible. On the one hand, the ticketing machine had worked. And, I got to flirt with a super cute guy while waiting to get through security. On the other hand, I had been leered at by a pimply perv, not just wanded but felt up by an old woman, locked into a flying puke coffin, forced to do the walk of shame across a busy airport terminal with bile chunks stuck to me, and publicly bathed in a sink.

After comparing the good with the bad, it was clear that this was the trip from hell. Frowning down at my half eaten quesadilla, I shuddered at what the rest of the trip might have in store for me. The trip had just started! My parents were right, I should have stayed home.

My phone started singing. I didn't have to look at the screen to know who it was. That was my daddy's ringtone. I bit my lip while debating whether or not to answer it. The music stopped, allowing me to breathe a sigh of relief until I heard it again, a moment later.

"Shit," I mumbled under my breath.

The guy sitting on the stool next to me gave me a creepy once-over. "What's the matter sweet thang? You runnin' away from someone?"

"Something like that," I replied before putting the phone to my ear. "Hi daddy," I said, forcing myself to smile.

"Girl, where are you?" He didn't sound happy.

I gave a small sigh in to the phone, then said, "I'm in DFW waiting on a layover. My plane to New York boards in about fifteen minutes."

"DFW? What are you doing in Texas, girl?" His tone was tense.

"Daddy," I frowned. "You know what I'm doing here. I left a note."

"Girl, you're s'posed to be at home where your mamma and I can keep an eye on you." I could almost see him shaking his head. "If you run off like this you're gonna make your ol' daddy worry."

"Daddy," I protested.

Ignoring my protest, he continued his rant, "You know goin' off with that Barbie is a bad idea." I could picture him shaking his head at me, like he always does when I do something stupid. "You girls always get in a heap of trouble when you get together."

I rolled my eyes. "Daddy, we're going to the beach. What could possibly happen? Besides, I don't need anyone to keep an eye on me. I'm a grown woman," I said into the phone.

I knew it was a bad idea as the words left my mouth. But, it was too late to take them back. Those seemingly innocent words had started up an old argument, one that I had memorized years before I had graduated from high school. The whole conversation centered around me getting married, and settling down, close to home, under the ever watchful eyes of my parents. It wasn't long before I found my attention wondering.

I sighed my frustration. "Daddy, I'm thirty years old. When are you going to start treating me like an adult?"

"When you start acting like one," he retorted.

"I am acting like one," I defended, with a roll of my eyes.

The bartender gave me a sympathetic look, offering me another margarita. I was tempted, but shook my head, waving him off.

He shrugged, then pointed at the television above the bar, asking, "Did you hear about that?"

I shook my head, only half listening to the one way conversation on the other end of the line.

"Some famous guy, I've never heard of, paid a million dollars for this necklace." He motioned to the television screen. "When he got the box, it was empty. They're calling it an international issue." He shook his head. "We've been at war for over a decade, I just lost my health insurance because of Bamacare, I'm working three jobs just to make ends meet, our schools are broke, and this what is our government is worried about? Some Russian guy ripping off Mr. Deep-pockets. No one cares about the little people these days..."

I looked at the clock on my phone. Daddy was listing off available locals. I know it isn't because he really likes these guys or even thinks they are the best husband material out there. In my daddy's eyes, each of my potential suitors had one important thing going for him, local ties. Daddy figured any issues they had he could fix with a job on the farm, a stern talking to, and Pastor Dave's help. I wasn't so sure.

"Uh huh," I muttered into the phone.

With a quick roll of my eyes, I motioned for the check. I hadn't heard a word of what daddy was saying. He was bound to notice that I wasn't listening soon.

"Girl, are you there?"

"Uh huh," I muttered again.

"This is what I'm talking about girl, you've got to settle down and focus. Stop all this running around the countryside nonsense. I'll be there in a couple of hours. Don't talk to any strangers," he insisted.

"No daddy. I'm meeting Barbie in New York, then we're going to the beach. I'll be back in two weeks," I said firmly, forgetting that a moment ago I had all but talked myself into going home.

The bartender was still complaining about the news and economy when he brought my check. Another conversation that I preferred not to get involved in. I nodded my thanks as he took my bank card.

I could hear my daddy take a breath. "You've been in enough trouble lately, girl. You don't need to be gallivanting off with anyone, especially not that Barbie. She's a wild one, reckless, and a bad influence ever since you was babies. What you need to do is come home right now, get yourself a job, and a nice local man to take care of you. Then, you can settle down and have some kids. That'll keep you out of trouble for a few years."

The bartender brought my bank card back while I wearily feigned listening to the old argument. I signed the slip, mouthed 'Thank you', then turned my attention back to the phone.

"I'm sorry daddy, but I don't want to settle down with some nice local boy and have a bunch of kids. I want to go with Barbie to the beach."

There was a pause on the other end of the line. "This is about that fellow, isn't it?"

"No daddy. It's about me wanting to go to Thailand and lie on the beach. I need to catch my plane. I'll see you in two weeks, love you." I hung up quickly before he could say anything else.

On my way to the gate, my phone rang again. Fishing the phone out of my pocket with one hand while dragging my carry-on behind me with the other, I somehow managed to get the device loose without losing my footing or making a complete spectacle of myself; not without earning a few annoyed looks from my fellow travelers. I answered the call whilst dodging the obstacles of people and baggage meandering through the terminal all around me.

"Hey momma," I said into the phone.

"Jessica, what are you doing?" She sounded frantic.

"Momma…"

"You shouldn't have left. Your father is having fits." She was going for the guilt.

I rolled my eyes. "Momma, I can't live the rest of my life in Tish just because of one bad experience. I'm an adult. If I want to jump on a plane and go on vacation I should be able to."

"How are you going on vacation? You don't have a job or any money," she pointed out.

"It's Barbie's idea. She's paying for it because she wants me to go with her. She knows I've been depressed sitting at home," I explained.

I knew she would be shaking her head. "Jessica, this sounds like a great way to take your mind off of that boy you met in Seattle, but you can't go. You have a date tonight. Trust me, the best way to get over someone isn't by going on vacation, it's with another man."

I frowned. "I am not going because of Eric. I told you, he was just a friend helping me out."

"Uh, huh…" She wasn't convinced. "A friend who went out of his way to bring you home in his private jet? You can't lie to me Jessica. I saw how you two were looking at each other. Your father almost went for his gun when he saw that boy look at you that way."

"Mother!" This was getting annoying. "Believe it or not, I'm fine. I'm not going because of some guy I haven't heard from in weeks. And, I'm not going so I can run away from my problems. I'm going because it sounds like fun and it's not hotter than hell there."

"Well, what am I supposed to tell your date?" Her voice revealed her agitation.

"Hold on, did you say that I have a date, tonight?" I wrinkled my brow. "With who?"

"I invited that nice Caldwell boy over for dinner. He came by the other day to help your father fix the tractor. He was so nice to ask how you were doing since you got back home. I couldn't help but notice that he's little sweet on you. God knows you're not getting any younger."

I sighed before asking, "Which one?"

"Ray, he's the oldest. If he doesn't work out we can move down to one of the younger ones. Anyway, I'm making fried chicken, mashed potatoes with gravy, corn on the cob, and homemade ice-cream for dessert." She thought she could tempt me with food? Had she ever looked at Ray Caldwell?

I groaned my displeasure. "I'm sorry momma, but I'm not rushing home to have dinner with the catch of the day. Besides, Ray Caldwell is a loser. He's pushing forty, short, balding, spends all of his money on comic books and porn, and lives with his parents."

"He has a job."

"He works at the Gas 'N Go."

"Would one of the other Caldwell boys be better?" Instead of being discouraged, her tone was helpful.

I closed my eyes. This wasn't happening. "No momma! They are all disgusting. Jerome is a pervert and he pees himself. George just got arrested for assaulting his girlfriend, and Donald is a pothead!" I groaned, "I gotta go. I have a plane to catch. See you in two weeks."

"But, what about your date?" She sounded hurt.

"Momma, I don't have a date. You and daddy have a date." I was irritated. "I don't need a man right now. What I need is a life! So please, do me a favor. Stop setting me up with whichever local loser happens to stumble too close to your door."

"Don't you think you're being a little harsh?" she asked, in her superior mother's voice.

"Harsh? Last week you set me up with a homeless drifter you met outside of Movieland. I heard dad promise him a job if he married me. On Sunday, I heard you trying to set me up with Jerry. Jerry shares the same taste in guys as me, everyone knows that! Then there was the twenty year old high school dropout you found wondering around the Gas-n-go, the forty year old and divorced three times, with four kids, banker, and stalker Larry. You even tried to set me up with a third cousin!"

"Carl's not really your cousin. Everyone knows Aunt Dot was sleeping with Walter about the time she got pregnant with Carl. And, Carl looks just like Walter did twenty years ago."

"Poor Carl," I muttered, rolling my eyes.

"Jessica, there are only so many available men to choose from. You're going to have to lower your standards, just a little bit, or you'll end up an old maid. I mean, you're already thirty. Sarah Goodman's daughter is two years younger than you and has four kids. If you wait too long, you'll be lucky to pop out one before your ovaries shrivel up and die."

"Mother!" I groaned.

"What about your father? Your leaving has really upset him." She pleaded. "You know he has a heart condition."

I rolled my eyes. "Daddy does not have a heart condition. Heart-burn is not a heart condition! Just take him out to Randy's Bar, buy him a beer, and let him play some pool. He'll get over it." I shook my head. "I've gotta go."

Holding the silent phone, I couldn't help but wonder why they felt the need to marry me off and make me like them. Why couldn't they accept me for who I am? And, why did everyone assume that I was stuck on Eric? I shook my head as I slid the phone back into my pocket. Just as I reached my gate, the phone rang again. This time it was my brother, Greg.

Greg is two years older than me and has always thought that he could tell me what to do. Growing up he was the golden child; attractive, fun, straight A's kindergarten through high school graduation, excelled at sports, and got a full scholarship to Yale. While Greg was busy being Mr. Perfect, I was cutting gum out of my hair, skipping school to go swim in the river, losing my lunch money, skinning my knees, and turning in C plus work because I had better things to do than homework.

These days, Greg is living the dream as a successful FBI agent with a two bedroom bachelor apartment in downtown Boston and a solid investment portfolio. What did my carefree attitude get me? A basic liberal arts degree from small town State U that won't even get me a job serving coffee to someone that makes as much as Greg. I sighed with irritation while reaching into my pocket to shut off my phone. I was going to have to do it soon anyway, and I'd had enough of being treated like a kid for today.

Arriving at my gate, I discovered that my flight was delayed. The plane hadn't landed yet. Great! Now, instead of just getting to New York late, I'd be arriving sometime after midnight. I sighed my displeasure, today was turning into a really long day and I had an early flight to catch in the morning. I bit my lower lip. Since I'd boarded the plane in Oklahoma, my trip had gone from good to awful to unbelievable. I just hoped that it wasn't a sign of things to come.

Since I had nothing else to do, I checked out my fellow travelers. It was the usual assortment of businessmen, parents with babies, old people, lovey dovey couples, and casual travelers. No one very interesting, at first glance.

Then, I saw someone I knew. I couldn't believe it, or could I? I probably wouldn't have noticed him, but he stood at least a head taller than everyone else and looked like he could bench press a small

58

car. Junior had laughed at the idea that he was following me. If he wasn't following me, then why was he everywhere I went?

I shook my head, "Maybe Junior was right. I am paranoid. There is no reason for this guy, or anyone else, to be following me," I assured myself.

He had never spoken to me. He wasn't looking my way and didn't appear to even notice me. Right now, he was noticing the blonde in the hoochie mama skirt and boob shirt standing next to him. She was noticing him right back. Come to think of it, that woman, reading *Cat In The Hat* book to the three kids in the corner, was in the security line with me, as well. Maybe, she was stalking me too. More likely, we were all headed to New York out of OKC. I mentally rolled my eyes shaking my head at my paranoia.

"I really should stop watching those crime TV dramas," I said to no one.

I needed to get on the plane before I convinced myself the whole airport was out to get me. A quick glance at my phone told me the plane was now ten minutes late. You could see people starting to pace, enough of them had approached the flight attendant at the boarding area that she had left her post. It looked like it was going to be one of those flights.

I sighed thinking that I had another forty plus hours of flying to do and hoping that today wasn't any kind of indicator of what was to come. A little voice in the back of my head wondered if maybe my parents were right. I should just turn around and head home. I took a deep breath, calming myself.

"No, I'd rather sit through another horrible flight and who knows what else than go back home to be fixed up with whatever bottom dwellers my parents could dig up for me," I said to the old man sitting next to me.

He didn't even look my way. Maybe he had his hearing aid turned off. If I was him, I'd turn my hearing aid off so that I wouldn't have to talk to strange people who talk to themselves.

My thoughts were interrupted by a loud, annoying voice. A quick glance around the waiting area revealed the source to be one of the other passengers. She was trying to entertain herself by talking to anyone who got too close. I looked her over. She was probably in her early twenties, but her skin was already aged from the tanning bed, making her look much older. The heavy fake tan and her mid-eighties outfit made her stand out in the airport like an American football player in China.

She was sporting purple flats that almost matched her multicolored tights, a pretty uncomfortable looking camel toe, an oversized off the shoulder pink t-shirt with the sleeves and waist cut into uneven strips, and an unflattering belly roll hanging over the waistband of her tights. Her faded red hair was worn late eighties Madonna style with a landing strip of brown roots at her scalp. The ensemble was completed by white feather earrings hanging the length of her hair, dozens of mismatched bracelets, thick black eyeliner, and heavily applied mascara over bright green, blue, and gold eye shadow. The effect was stunning, in all the wrong ways.

Looking a little lost, she paused in front of Larry, just as the woman he had been talking with scurried off to the bathroom. I couldn't help but smile at the panic crossing his face as Cyndi Lauper sized him up with a friendly smile. While I reveled in Larry's discomfort, his eyes searched out mine in a silent plea for help. So, he had noticed me. I wasn't paranoid after all!

With a small shake of my head and a smile, I told him he was on his own. Surprise registered in Larry's eyes just before he firmly stepped away from the girl. Watching him try to distance himself from the eighties queen, a twinge of guilt hit me. I shook it off.

"It's not like we're friends. He's stalking me," I said to the now empty chair beside me.

I was still speculating my possible paranoia while the girl continued to search the waiting area for a willing conversationalist. I had to admire her tenacity as she attempted to engage passenger after passenger. A business traveler gave her a startled look before politely excusing himself to dig through his briefcase. Next, she attempted to join a conversation with a mother and her teenaged daughter. After a polite amount of time passed, they too excused themselves. Passengers throughout the waiting area were quickly finding things to do as she looked around for a sympathetic ear. I almost felt sorry for her, almost.

Oh crap! She was heading my way! Karma was getting even with me. I hurriedly pulled out my phone. Turning it back on just as the eighties reject reached me, I felt the beginning of a vibration coming from the device in my hand.

In a panic I yelled, "Hello!"

"What the hell are you doing?!" The voice on the other line yelled back, causing me to reconsider my decision to answer the call.

Wincing, I held the device away from my ear. Once I was sure he was done, I moved it back to my face. "I'm waiting on my plane to show up so I can board. What is your problem?"

"What is *my* problem?" he growled into the line. "My problem, little sister, is that you are supposed to be in Tish with mom and dad. Instead, you're at the airport, heading who knows where, which has mom and dad calling and interrupting my date so many times that she just left."

Did he honestly call me to complain that his date had walked out on him? "Greg, I am struck by your concern for me. And, I feel simply terrible that my actions have prevented you from getting laid with yet another bimbo whose name you probably don't remember. Fortunately for you, the night is still young. So, I'm going to recommend that you walk down to the nearest bar and hold your credit cards up way over your head. It might take a half a second to replace your bed warmer, but it'll be okay." I noticed the other passengers swarming my gate. "Thanks for the concerned call. I've gotta go. My ride is boarding."

"Jess," Greg begged, "Would you please just go home? It's only been three weeks. Mom and dad are still upset about Seattle. They just need more time."

"Greg," I took a deep breath. "You don't understand. They're suffocating me! I can't do anything without getting at least three phone calls. The other day I stopped to pick up some ice-cream at the Gas-N-Go, after one of the most embarrassing job interviews that I ever hope to have to sit through. They called the police looking for me. Uncle Bill came into the store, lectured me in front of everyone, followed me out, and escorted me home with his flashers and sirens wailing. All because I forgot my cellphone, and I didn't go straight home! And, they keep setting me up with every unmarried loser they find wandering the town."

"It can't be that bad," he said, without sympathy.

"No, it's worse. There is nothing to do and nowhere to do it at. All of my friends from high school have either moved away or had a houseful of kids. I'm going crazy out there in the sticks. I just can't take it anymore!" I paused before saying, "Barbie asked me to go with her on her vacation. This is my chance to escape, and I'm going."

"Wait a minute, you're with Barbie?" There was real concern in his voice now.

"Not yet. We're meeting on the way," I explained.

"On the way to where?" he asked suspiciously.

Smiling, I said, "Fuck-It Island." I just couldn't say it without smiling.

"Where?" He sounded confused.

"Fuck-It Island, it's in Thailand," I explained.

"No, no, no!" he insisted. "You and Barbie are not going to Thailand."

I rolled my eyes. "Yes, we are. We're going to go lie on the beach on Fuck-It Island, eat Fuck-It food, drink Fuck-It punch, and forget about my shitty life," I said irritably.

"It's Phuket Island, the H is silent," he corrected me.

"It doesn't matter how you pronounce it, we're still going," I responded.

"No, you're not." I could hear the agitation in his voice. "The only place you're going is home to Tish. The State Department does not endorse travel to Thailand right now. There are terrorism risks, political unrest, social predators, and it is way too easy to get arrested for little things. If something happened, it could be weeks before we found out. And, something always happens when you and Barbie get together. Hell, shit happens to you when you're by yourself!"

I rolled my eyes again. "Greg, we're going to a beach resort full of tourists. If it was such a problem, then we wouldn't be able to get onto a plane and fly into the country now would we? So, stop being so overprotective, and go find a bimbo to replace the one you lost. I can take care of myself."

"Like you took care of yourself in Seattle?" he growled.

"Hey!" I glared into the phone. "You introduced me to Jim."

"I may have introduced you, but I didn't tell you to date or move in with Jim. I sure as hell didn't tell you to go looking for him when he came up missing. I believe I told you to go home. You being involved in that mess was your own doing. You always jump into messes. You never stop to think." He paused. "Jessie, please, just this once, go home."

"It's too late," I lied. "I'm already on the plane to Thailand."

"I'm sure you have a layover somewhere. As soon as the plane stops, get on a plane heading home," he insisted.

I sighed. "Greg, I'm not going home until after I've finished my vacation. Barbie and I are going to lie on the beach, celebrate her divorce, and drink my problems away. Get over it." I hung up the phone, quickly switching it off again. Tucking the device into my purse, I silently vowed to leave it turned off until I returned to the states.

By the time I had finished my conversation with Greg, the boarding area was empty. I quickly showed the attendant my boarding pass and stepped through the gate. Like the last one, this plane was full. With my mind on the conversation with Greg, I stumbled through the narrow aisle looking for my seat. I was still grumbling to myself when I tripped over someone's under the seat baggage.

"Shit!" I grumbled loudly as my balance shifted to the left. My hands grasped widely into the air before locking onto the head of a hugely pregnant woman seated next to the aisle.

"Hey, watch it!" She hastily pushed me away, causing me to lurch forward into the aisle and the guy in front of me.

"I am so sorry," I apologized, picking myself off of the man.

He turned to face me, flashing a disarming smile. "Don't worry about it. I liked it." He winked.

My jaw fell open as my brain worked overtime to catch up to what my eyes were seeing. It was the hot guy from the security line. I had completely forgotten that he was going to New York. Feeling a stupid look settle across my face, my cheeks caught fire. Floundering for something to say, I gave him a weak smile.

He handed me a piece of paper. "Looks like your home."

"Uh," I mumbled incoherently.

He was holding my boarding pass. I must have dropped it in the confusion. Awkwardly, I searched my brain for a way to explain away our meeting without sounding like a crazy person. Somehow, *'Sorry, I'm a hopeless klutz'* just wouldn't cut it. Instead, I just gave him a blank look causing him to motion towards the seat in front of me. The numbers matched the assignment on my boarding pass. I nodded dumbly. A quick glance at the seat in front of me caused my face to fall.

"Great," I quietly muttered under my breath.

The hot guy in front of me gave me a quizzical look as his gaze followed mine. "It looks like you won the seatmate lottery." He grinned down at me.

I rolled my eyes and whispered more to myself than anyone, "Lucky me."

His laughter stung as he continued down the aisle to his seat. I stared longingly after him. It's official Jessie. You are not having a bad day, you are having a bad life. I stood in the aisle a moment longer, contemplating my seatmates. In the window seat sat the eighties reject from the terminal. A hugely obese middle aged woman, who looked like she was sleeping off a Valium, was in the aisle seat. Sighing at the thought that I would have to sit between them all the way to New York, I double checked my seating assignment. It was the right seat. Biting my lower lip, I looked up and down the aisle at the rest of the plane. It was packed.

Sighing again, I couldn't help muttering to myself, "Great, that's just great."

I looked closer at the woman in the aisle seat. Was she dead? I leaned closer to get a better look. No, she was drooling, dead people don't drool. I told myself that it wouldn't be so bad. She was probably going to sleep the whole trip. At least she wasn't snoring, and she almost fit into her seat. Fortunately for me, I just threw up two days' worth of food. I must have lost three or four pounds. Right? I glanced across the row at my other seatmate. Hopefully, Cyndi Lauper would sleep too. She returned my look with an eager smile, scooting over to make room for me. I frowned, she didn't look sleepy. She looked like she'd just sucked down a couple of pots of coffee mixed with Red Bull.

After stowing my bag in the overhead compartment and carefully edging past the woman in the aisle seat, I sat down. The captain announced our take off while the flight attendants made sure that we were buckled. So far so good. Then, my brightly colored seatmate turned her iPod up so loud that it hurt my ears. My eye twitched. How could she stand the noise? I glanced her way. Maybe she's deaf. She saw me looking at her and took one of the ear buds out of her ear without turning the volume down, causing me to flinch.

"Hi, I'm Dana," she practically yelled.

"Jessie," I answered, wincing at the volume assaulting my ears. "Would you mind turning that down?" I motioned to the IPod in her lap.

"Oh sorry, I just love Five Finger Death Punch. Don't you?" She imperceptibly adjusted the volume on her IPod. "Where are you headed?"

"New York City." I sighed, resigned to the deafening music.

"I know right, that's our next stop. I'm totally going to Albany to visit my best girlfriend from high school. We were inseparable our whole lives. After graduation, we like went to different colleges. She goes to Saint Rose, right. Well, she's real busy with school and stuff. But, she's going to spend a couple of days with me 'cause we're such great friends, right. I'm like so excited to see her! Anyway, I go to San Francisco State. It's so awesome, but I'm taking a break, right. I mean you like have to travel when you're young, right? Traveling is so awesome. Like, I just left my Aunt Betty's in Fort Worth. I was there for a whole week. It was so much fun, right." She continued to yell over her iPod without taking a breath or pausing between sentences.

"Uh…huh." I desperately dug through my purse for my headphones, earplugs, an Ibuprofen… All the while, wishing that I had Eric's stun gun with me.

After almost a whole ten seconds of muteness she started talking again. "You're going to New York City, right? That is so awesome, you know."

"Uh…huh." My digging had turned frantic. When was the last time I cleaned out my purse? I wasn't even sure all this crap was mine. Maybe a squirrel was using it as a nest. The music was giving me a headache. My seatmate was having a complete conversation with herself. And, the kid behind me had started whining for a fruit snack, kicking my seatback to make his point.

"Where are those earplugs?! Please, don't tell me I took them out of my purse," I moaned.

She continued to talk, even though I was obviously not listening, "…Like, New York is the most awesome city, ever! I've never been there, but it's totally on my list, you know." She paused giving me a perplexed look. "What state is that in?"

I stopped searching for my headphones to look her in the face. Was she joking? "What?"

She spoke slower, as if she were speaking to a simpleton, "What state is New York City in?"

Jenn Brink

I blinked my confusion. Was this a trick question? "New York," I answered slowly.

She looked at me blankly.

I tried again, this time speaking slower and more even. "New York City is in the state of New York." Could this girl really be that dumb?

"Oh, I know, right." She still looked confused.

"This isn't happening to me," I said, but no one was listening.

The girl to my left returned to her monologue despite the obvious fact that I wasn't paying any attention to her words. At least the kid behind me had stopped using my seat to practice his punting skills.

I had just closed my eyes, practicing my relaxation techniques, when something hit my shoulder. Suspicious of what I would find, I slowly opened one eye. My suspicions were correct. It was the woman in the seat to my right. Her head was now resting heavily against my right shoulder as she began to snore loudly. I watched in horror as a stream of drool slid slowly down the side of her face, towards my shoulder. Frantically, I attempted to push her head the other direction. The head flopped back and forth, ultimately landing with a thud on my shoulder, splashing drool all over me. I grimaced in disgust as she began to snore again.

This was too much. I gave her shoulder a harsh shove, causing her body to tilt heavily away from me, taking the head with it. Once her upper body was leaning to the right her lower body started spilling

70

into my seat forcing me into a cramped position. I contemplated shooting myself as the girl in the window seat began to sing loudly over the even louder music coming from her IPod. With a frown, I realized that I hadn't brought my gun. Suddenly, I knew the real reason behind the airports gun rules.

Depression assaulted my senses as the reality of my four hour flight hit me. I was in airplane hell, for the second time that day. I was considering spending the rest of the flight in the toilet when the flight attendant stopped at our row.

"Excuse me ma'am." He was speaking to Dana. "The gentleman would like to know if you would mind trading seats with him so that he and his wife can sit together." He gestured from me to someone a few rows back.

I tried to turn in my seat to look. I couldn't get myself lifted up high enough to see over the seatbacks.

"Sure." Dana gave me a questioning look. "I didn't know you were married."

"Oh, yeah." I looked at my empty ring finger. "I lost my ring just this morning. It fell down the garbage disposal while I was doing the dishes," I lied.

"That's terrible!" she exclaimed as she slid past me.

Six

Peace at last! Gratefully, I eased into the abandoned window seat, wiped the drool from my shoulder, and breathed a sigh of relief. The woman in the aisle seat had fallen half into the walkway. I watched as two flight attendants attempted to shove her back into her seat while she snored, blissfully unaware.

By the time my 'husband' arrived they had somehow managed to get most of the woman stuffed back into her seat. He slid into the spot that I had vacated, smiled charmingly, and held out his hand. "Random Chance at your service." It was the same hot guy that I had met at security and almost knocked down while boarding.

Taking his hand, I gave him a quizzical smile. "Forever grateful."

"Random Chance is my name." He laughed

I pursed my lips looking around for the flight attendant. I did not feel up to dealing with a crazy person right now or worse, some guy with bad pick-up lines.

"I can prove it," he said, pulling out his wallet.

I watched with undisguised interest while he removed a picture ID from its clear plastic cover and handed it to me. Okay, his name really was Random Chance. It was right there next to his picture. Who has a good license photo? I thought it was illegal to look good in a government ID. His license said that he lived in New York City. He must be headed home. Hmmm…according to his license he was three years older than me, five-foot-ten and three quarters, and weighed one hundred and eighty pounds. I looked at the man sitting beside me. I would have guessed him at twenty eight. He reached for the plastic card before I got a good look at his address.

Giving him a sheepish grin, I said, "I'm sorry. It's been a weird day."

"Don't be, I get that all the time." He laughed. "I hope you didn't mind my telling the flight attendant that we were married, but you looked so unhappy over here. I just had to save you from a long and tedious plane ride. More important, I never got your name." He winked.

"Oh!" I hesitated, what the hell! He was easy on the eyes, didn't have a screaming IPod growing out of his head, and appeared to be able to make intelligent conversation. I smiled, and said, "Thanks for the rescue. There are no words for how horrible my trip has been, so far." I held out my hand, and smiled. "I'm Jessie."

"Well, it's a good thing that I came along to save the day, Jessie." His smile widened, as he said my name.

Smiling my thanks, I felt my cheeks warm in an all too familiar blush. Maybe this trip wouldn't be so bad after all.

By the time we landed at LaGuardia it was nearing eleven o'clock. Although it was only nine pm at home, it had been an emotionally exhausting day. I was looking forward to snuggling into the imported silk sheets and down comforter that I knew waited for me in Barbie's guestroom. Wearily, I lugged my carry-on across the terminal, out of the airport, and across the sidewalk to the nearest cab. As the cabbie stowed my bag in the trunk, I slid into the backseat; not even bothering to stifle my yawn. Just as my eyes began to close, the passenger door opened.

"I'm sorry. I didn't realize this cab was taken."

Funny, he didn't look sorry. Maybe it was the grin stretching across his face that made it hard to believe.

"That's okay. I don't mind sharing, if you don't." I gave him a sleepy smile.

Random grinned down at me. "I was hoping you would say that. Wait here while I put my bag in the trunk."

"Wait here? Where does he think I'm going?" I asked the empty seat beside me.

It didn't take him long to settle his bag next to mine, then we were on our way. He was also traveling light, with just one small carry-on case. The streets of New York glided past while I fought the sandman next to one of the best looking guys I had ever seen, up close.

Random slid a little closer, smiling at some secret joke. He had an amazing smile. I felt myself smile back.

Random cocked his head to the side. "What do you say we take a detour? I know a great place. Let me buy you a drink?"

"I shouldn't." I bit my lip in thought. "It's late, I'm tired, and my cousin is expecting me."

He looked down at his watch. "It's not that late. Besides, we've been sitting on a plane all day. You need to move around some before you go to bed."

"Really? So, you're a doctor?" I asked.

"No, I'm in acquisitions. Right now, I'm attempting to acquire you." He grinned unapologetically.

I rolled my eyes at the line, but inside I was smiling. It felt good to be pursued. I hesitated, internally debating the idea of going out with the handsome stranger beside me. Suddenly, my inner voice jumped into the silent argument insisting that it was irresponsible; he wasn't right for me, I didn't know anything about him, and couldn't I tell he was after more than just a drink?

"I don't think so. I really do have to get up early tomorrow," I mumbled giving in to reason and responsibility.

Disappointment lined his features as he pleaded, "Just one little drink? I promise to get you a cab as soon as you're ready, no strings."

Indecision played through my mind as I debated his offer. He was right, we had been flying all day. Anyway, I kind of owed him.

He had saved me from sitting next to the eighties reject with her annoying IPod. Also, I could tell that he liked me, a lot. The attention was great for my still rebounding self-esteem. Despite the little voice in the back of my head, I liked Random. What wasn't to like? He was good looking, intelligent, and funny, with a super sexy accent. So, why was I hesitating?

A picture of Eric popped into my mind, causing me to frown. Were my friends and family right? Was Eric the reason for this romantic funk I'd been in? Was he the reason that none of the men I'd met had sparked my interest? Okay, maybe my interest had been sparked a little, but no one had come close to measuring up to Eric. Sadly, I shook my head. They always come out of the woodwork when you're not interested. Interested or not, I needed to get Eric out of my head so that I could move on with my life.

"What is wrong with me?" I whispered to myself.

"Nothing from where I stand." Random was gazing admiringly at me.

I gave him a weak smile. "Thanks, but I…"

Wait a minute. Was I really going to blow Random off because of a little over a week with some guy? Some guy I hadn't heard from in three weeks. It wasn't like he didn't have my number. Of course, I hadn't called him either, but that was different. He was the one who had said that he didn't want a relationship. I really couldn't call him, could I? I mean, I didn't want to seem desperate.

"But, what?" Random's voice interrupted my thoughts. "You have a boyfriend? Husband?"

"No." I shook my head.

He looked confused. "You have a girlfriend?"

"What? No! I just ummm..." Think fast Jessie! "I'm just in town for the night. I fly out again in the morning, early."

"Well then." He leaned in close. "We'll just have to make the most of tonight, won't we?"

That's it Jessie! No more moping or taking the responsible path. It's time to get over Eric, and all of those other poor choices in men. My inner voice was tired of my whining. I couldn't blame her, I was too. I hesitated a moment before taking a deep breath and pushing Eric out of my thoughts.

With a deep breath, I looked Random in the eye, and said, "What did you have in mind?"

He grinned, making me feel as if I'd made the right decision. "I don't want to scare you off so how about that drink? I know this great place over on Fifth Avenue called The Rooftop Bar."

"What a coincidence," I smiled, "That's where I'm headed."

He treated me with a dazzling smile. "If you're hungry they make great appetizers. My dinner was a handful of peanut packages. Say the word, and it's a late dinner."

Leaning my head back onto the seat, my body reminded me that I really was very tired. "That sounds nice." A big yawn interrupted me. "But, I really can't stay long. It's been a long day, and I do have an early flight tomorrow."

He pursed his lips, and said, "That's funny, we talked all the way here. You never mentioned that you were just passing through."

"You were too busy doing your impersonations for me, and then how many games of hangman and tic-tac-toe did we play? I've never been so entertained on a flight before." I forced a smile.

He gave me a pretend bow. "I'm happy to be of service. Would you like to see another magic trick? They won't let me do the fire ones on the plane."

"Fire?" That sounded like a bad idea waiting to come to fruition. I shook my head. "Please, no more magic tricks!"

He laughed with me before asking, "So, where are you off to tomorrow?"

"Phuket Island." Not wanting to look like a fool in front of Random, I made sure to pronounce it correctly as I choked back a yawn.

Surprise registered on his face, then he said, "That is one of my favorite places."

"You're not just saying that to impress me are you?" I asked suspiciously.

"No, but I'll take what I can get." He winked. "My grandfather retired there. He owns some property on the island. Perhaps, I'll see you there. So far, *chance* has been on my side."

Laughing at his joke, I decided I must be even more tired than I thought. It wasn't all that funny. On the way to the bar, I texted Barbie to let her know where I was going and that I would be late getting in. I didn't want her to wait up or worry, especially after making such a fuss about her not going anywhere.

It was a little after two in the morning when I stumbled into Barbie's Fifth Avenue apartment. After just one knock, Barbie opened the door, allowing me to fall inside. I'd had one too many Long Island Iced Teas at the bar and was seeing life through a murky layer of alcohol.

Unintentionally, I had left the bar without saying goodbye to Random. I was on my way back from the bathroom when I could swear I saw Eric getting into the elevator. Of course, I had to follow. By the time I reached the ground floor, he was gone. I was drunkenly trying to find my way back up to the club when Larry the stalker appeared out of nowhere.

Immediately recognizing my vulnerable state, he had me poured into a passing cab before I realized what was happening. Without a word, he hopped into the cab with me, escorted me to Barbie's front door, leaned me against it, and rang the bell. Of course, he was nowhere to be seen when Barbie opened said door. Even in my fragile state, I realized that I should have been alarmed. For some reason I wasn't. Most likely my judgment was impaired by the high blood alcohol content and sleep deprivation.

"You weren't going out after me, were you?" I slurred, shifting into a more upright position.

Barbie was standing over me, speechless, and fully dressed with her purse in her hand.

I frowned with annoyance. "I told you I was stopping for drinks with the hot guy from the plane."

"I just got in." She stared down at me. "After I got your text, I figured you wouldn't be home for a while, so I met up with some friends."

"Good." I yawned. "I'm exhausted."

"Me too." Still staring at me, she secured the door. "It's been a few years since I saw you looking this bad. Are you okay?"

Stumbling into the living room, I nodded.

Flopping onto her big overstuffed couch, she looked at me expectantly, and asked, "So?"

I gave all three of the Barbies sitting in front of me a confused look. "So, what?"

In unison, they rolled their eyes in frustration. "So, did you get any?"

Was I supposed to pick something up? I couldn't remember. "Any what?"

"Oh My God! Are you really this dense, or are you just playing with me?" she shrieked.

I covered my ears for protection from the high pitched banshees shrieking in my brain. The Barbies were loud, and there was already a steady hum inside my head. It had come with the slowly spinning room. I blinked, trying to steady the room. "I'm really that drunk, but that doesn't make me hard of hearing. What are you talking about?"

They sighed lifting their hands in exasperation as they merged together, looking like a Hindu goddess. "Sex, did you get any sex? On the plane, in the cab, at the bar, anywhere?"

"Oh, did I get any of that?" I waved them off. "We just met a few hours ago."

"I thought you said he was hot." The goddess pouted.

"He was, but I'm not going to have sex with a guy after just knowing him a few hours. I mean, who does that?" I paused realizing who I was speaking too. "Oh, shit! I didn't mean…what I meant to say was other than you three and Greg, are there other people who do that?" The Barbies looked irritated. I'd read somewhere you shouldn't anger a Hindu goddess. "Well, I guess there would have to be, or who would you do it with?" I closed my eyes to the still whirling room, making me even dizzier. Opening my eyes, I mumbled, "I'm just gonna shut up now."

Barbie waved my words away. I blinked. What had she done with the other Barbies? "Whatever, tell me about the hottie and the date," she insisted with a grin.

I shrugged. "There's really nothing to tell, just some guy I met on the plane. He lives in the area, we shared a cab from the airport, and he invited me out for drinks. I'll tell you all about it in the morning. It'll give us something to do during the plane ride."

"That's a good idea," she agreed. "Let's get some rest. I want to be at the airport no later than six, earlier would be better."

Rubbing my eyes, I yawned again. "So, we're getting up at what, five-thirty?"

She narrowed her eyes at me. "Earlier, I just told you I want to be *at* the airport by six, and," she leaned over to sniff me, "you smell."

I lifted my arm, sniffed, and made a face. "Eww...deodorant fail."

"It's more than that. It's...I don't know what it is, but it's not good. Your date must have had no sense of smell." She wrinkled her nose.

I thought a minute. "Oh, I was on the plane ride from hell out of OKC." I yawned again, almost falling over in the process. "The turbulence was the worst. A bunch of us got motion sick. It was horrible." I shuddered at the memory. "People were puking their guts up all over the plane. I washed up as best I could in the bathroom." I started to cry. "I had to sacrifice my clothes and shoes to the trash can. I really liked that shirt. It was a good shirt, always there for me. It never ran off, slept with other girls, or ignored my calls." Tears were streaming down my face as I spoke. "I miss my shirt."

"This would only happen to you." Barbie shook her head as she half carried me toward the guestroom.

I shook my head. "That's not true, it happened to about a hundred other people, too."

She gave me an odd look, then said, "You started it, didn't you?"

I opened my mouth to protest, but no words came out. I tried again. "I am deeply hurt that you would say such a thing."

"Oh my god, you did start it! Jess, that is so gross!" she squealed.

"I couldn't help it," I cried. "I tried to hold it in. The plane just kept jumping and shaking and rocking, and then the bile came. I couldn't get it to go away. It was horrible."

She gave me a disgusted look. "Just don't puke on me tomorrow or in my bed tonight."

"Don't worry," I laid my head on my hand. "Today was absolutely the worse day of my life. I don't ever want to be locked in a plane full of vomit again. There are no words to explain how awful it was." I shuddered through the tears.

She shook her head at me. "You, cousin, are a walking disaster. Let's get to bed."

Realizing that I had somehow made it to the guestroom, I nodded my agreement. She turned to leave. I grabbed her arm.

"Barbie," I slurred, "I know it sounds silly, but I could swear that I saw Eric tonight. He was all dressed up in Rambo black and everything."

Barbie rolled her eyes at me.

"No really!" I begged her to believe me. "Also, that guy I told you about, the one who's been following me. He followed me all the way to New York, to your apartment."

"Uh huh." She gave me a stern look. "Did you see the Wolfman's face? Are you sure it was him, or was it just some guy about the right build?"

I looked away, unable to meet her eyes. "I only saw him from behind. But it was him! I know it was!" I insisted.

"Was this before or after you drank so many Long Island Iced Teas that you couldn't see straight?"

I frowned, "After."

She gave me a knowing look, but didn't say anything as she walked across the room.

"Well, it could have been him, right?" I gave her a hopeful look.

At the door, she turned around. "Jessie, you've been seeing the Wolfman everywhere you go." She shook her head. "You know he's got better things to do than stalk you. He has a company to run." Her face softened as she looked at me. "You need to let him go."

"I know, but I really saw him this time." I gave her an earnest look.

She gave me a stern look. "You mean you saw a man from a distance who was built and wearing black, who you conveniently lost in the night before you could confirm his identity?"

I bit my lip and reluctantly answered, "Yes."

Barbie shook her head, giving me a sympathetic look. "Do you know how many men wear black in this city? Some of them even work out."

I set my chin in a defiant gesture. She was not telling me what I wanted to hear.

"Jessie." She sighed. "I'm sure in your drunk and tired state that you think you saw the Wolfman, but you must know that it's not likely. Even if you did see him, so what? It's not like he stopped at your table to say '*Hello*'. He disappeared into the night without a single word. Now, he's already told you that he's not interested in anything more than a raunchy fling. You had your fling. So, unless he's called you and said that he changed his mind, which I know he hasn't, it's over. You need to move on."

Unable to meet her eyes, I looked down at the floor. "Yeah..."

"Trust me when I tell you that there are lots of yummy men out there that would love to help you take your mind off of Mr. Unavailable. You just have to give one of them a chance." She gave me a big hug.

"I guess you're right." I sighed, hating the truth of her words.

Seven

It felt like I had barely closed my eyes when daggers of light ruthlessly assaulted my eyeballs.

"Owwwww!" I screeched my pain.

"Time to get up," Barbie cheerfully announced.

"Huh? What time is it? It's still dark outside," I grumbled while awkwardly pulling the covers over my head.

"It is four o'clock. Time to get up!" she shouted, sounding like my mother, and giving me an unappreciated flashback to high school.

"Wake me up at five-thirty. I promise to shower fast," I moaned through the fluffy pink comforter.

"No, you won't. You never shower fast."

"I will this time." I burrowed deeper into the covers.

"We can't risk missing our flight. Get up!" She poked me.

I slapped her away with a pillow. "Go away."

"No! Quit throwing my things at me." She crossed her arms. "If you don't get up in the next five seconds, I'll use Grandma O'Grady's no fail trick."

Grandma O'Grady would give you one chance to get up. If you refused, she would rip the covers off of the bed and throw a huge pitcher of ice water on you. It was the worst way that I could think of to get dragged out of bed.

I lowered the comforter until it was even with my eyes and peered at Barbie. "You wouldn't."

She had a self-satisfied smirk on her face and a dare me attitude. "You'll find out in about four more seconds."

"Fine, I'm up, see?" I groused, edging out of the king sized bed.

Forty-five minutes later we were showered, dressed, and crawling into a cab.

"I can't believe you're bringing so much stuff. Did you leave anything here?" I was helping Barbie shove her luggage into the cab while trying to figure out where we were going to sit.

"OMG, you're cranky when you're hungover." She rolled her eyes.

"Seriously, do you plan to come back, or are you taking up residence in Thailand?" I complained while trying unsuccessfully to shut the door to the cab from my seat.

"Hey, I need all of these things," she insisted.

She pushed on my door from the outside. It bounced back, and I gave her a, 'I told you so look'. She gave the door another hard shove, but it still didn't close. A grunt escaped from my throat as she threw all of her weight against the door, painfully pinning me between the now closed door and her suitcases. A moment later, I heard her make a similarly unnatural noise as the cabby closed her door with a hard shove.

"You can't possibly need all of these clothes."

"I might."

I tried in vain to see her over the suitcases. "You're going to wear all of these clothes in the seven days that we're going to be at the beach? Are you planning multiple wardrobe changes during the flight?"

"We could get bored and want to do something other than lie on the beach." I could hear her cursing under her breath as she attempted to make a little more room for herself under the pile of luggage. "You never know what might happen. We could get invited to a party. We wouldn't be able to go without the proper clothes, shoes, and accessories. And, you know how much I like parties."

"I really wish you would learn how to pack lightly. It's going to take us forever at the airport because we'll have to wait in line to check your luggage. Then, we'll have to wait for it to get unloaded." I paused before asking, "How are we supposed to move all of this stuff by ourselves? They don't have nice doormen sitting around the airport waiting to *'Help Ms. O'Grady with her baggage'*," I mimicked Barbie's doorman's European accent.

Barbie leaned back, catching my eye across the back of the seat. "Some guy will help me out. I always meet the nicest people in airports. More important, I can't believe you brought so little."

I shrugged. "I just brought what I need for a week of lying on the beach."

She pushed a suitcase forward so we could see each other while we argued. "What if we go somewhere where we need to dress nice?"

"Oh, I brought a dress." I smiled with pride at my forethought.

"A dress? Did you bring heels?"

"Um…I may have forgotten the heels," I admitted reluctantly.

She gave me a disgusted look. "Are you sure we're related?"

"No, I'm not." I shook my head.

Once we finally made it to the airport, it took another fifteen minutes for the cabbie to help us get Barbie's luggage out of his cab and onto the sidewalk. He hadn't been able to fit all of the bags in the trunk so he'd had to put some of it in both the front and back seats. Even with me holding my carry-on, there had been barely enough room for the three of us and all of the luggage in the cab.

Frowning, I watched as people passed by. Some stared in disbelief at the huge pile of bubblegum pink luggage spelling out 'BARBIE' on the sidewalk. I didn't see any nice men tripping over themselves to carry the bags. I suspected that I was her gallant help today. Where was my stalker when I needed him? With a disgruntled sigh, I helped to lug our purses, my carry-on bag, Barbie's five huge suitcases, and her oversized makeup case into the airport and down to the check in counter.

Remembering my success at the OKC airport the day before, I stared longingly at the short line behind the electronic ticket dispenser. Briefly, I thought about letting Barbie deal with her luggage alone, and going back to that much shorter line. I fantasized about the machine giving me my boarding pass and slipping effortlessly through security. I would find a Starbucks and order a yummy breakfast sandwich and hot chocolate. I could almost taste it now. I bet I would even have time to catch up on the tabloid gossip before Barbie caught up to me. A smile crept onto my face at the thought.

One glance at the blonde fashionista in front of me and reality came crashing back. I couldn't abandon Barbie, my cousin, best friend, and the person paying for my vacation.

I sighed, muttering to myself, "It really was just a fantasy. The more likely scenario was that I would stand in the short line, for much longer than necessary. When it was finally my turn, the machine would refuse to give me a ticket, forcing me to go back to the really long line at the counter. I would make it to security with only minutes to spare before takeoff. I would be forced to step aside while other people slipped effortlessly past. My dignity would be seized as a pervert in a uniform strip searched me, finding nothing but my cute

belly button ring and that tattoo I got during spring break freshman year. The time lost would result in me missing my flight. After which, I would be forced to sit in the airport on standby for the next twelve hours."

An older couple walking nearby gave me a startled look and a wide berth.

"You're doing it again." I shook my head at myself.

Turning away from her conversation with the businessman in front of her, Barbie demanded, "What are you muttering about? People are starting to stare."

"I know," I agreed while helping to drag Barbie's army of suitcases to the back of the very long line.

Fifty-five minutes later, we finally left Barbie's luggage at the baggage check. Now, it was someone else's problem.

"I'm hungry," Barbie said wistfully and unnecessarily, since her stomach was singing an opera.

"Me too, I really need some hangover food," I agreed.

"I don't think there's a Taco Crack in the airport," Barbie responded nonchalantly. "You shouldn't have drunk so much, then you wouldn't be suffering."

"I know," I whimpered. "Do you have any of that super headache stuff?"

"Never leave home without them." She rummaged through her purse, dug out a bottle, and handed me a huge pill.

"You are a lifesaver. I don't suppose you have liquid in that purse?" I asked, knowing the answer.

"Don't be a baby. Just put it in your mouth and swallow it with your spit. That's what I do."

After three tries, I finally managed to get it halfway down my throat. The uncoated pill was stuck. I gagged. It was all I could taste, and it wasn't pleasant. Trying desperately to dislodge it, I started coughing.

Barbie rolled her eyes, and said, "Suck it up before they quarantine you, and I have to go lay on the beach by myself."

Taking our place in the security line, all my hopes and dreams for something to drink were squashed. The line here was even longer than the one we had just left. Slowly we dragged our sleep deprived, hungover, food divested, and liquid deficient bodies toward the TSA with just our purses, Barbie's makeup case, and my carry-on. After the tenth time I checked my phone for the time just to see that it had only been ten minutes, Barbie snatched it away and slid it back into my purse.

Time stood still as the line crept maddeningly forward. When I dared to check the time again, it had been a half hour and we were nowhere near the front. I zoned out, asleep on my feet. With a start, I caught myself falling. Shaking my head to wake up, I frowned. The place was eerily quiet with zombified people waiting for the line to move.

"What could be taking so long?" I moaned, startling the man in front of me.

Wiping the drool from his chin, he groggily shook his head. I guess I wasn't the only one who had a late night last night.

Barbie jumped up trying to peer over the heads in front of her. "I can't see."

I smiled at the sight. "At least I'm not the only one who doesn't do well with waiting, lines, or anything that involves high amounts of patience."

Barbie rolled her eyes at me for the umpteenth time since she had woken me up. Without warning, she smiled. "Look! The line is moving!"

Cheers rang throughout the security area as people realized that the lines were starting to move. After what seemed like an eternity, we finally reached the TSA's. It was our turn to put our stuff on the conveyor belt to be x-rayed and step through the little security box for a full body scan. Barbie eased through security with a wink and a smile. Then, it was my turn.

Stepping into the x-ray box, I crossed my fingers. My spirits fell when the TSA motioned for me to step aside. I was operating on a little less than two and a half hours of sleep, my stomach was roaring like a wild animal, I'd lost my buzz from the night before, it felt like someone was attempting to drill a hole at the base of my skull, and I had a giant pill stuck in my overly dry throat. Cranky and feeling picked on, I knew better than to refuse. So, with an intentionally loud groan, I followed the instructions. I found myself counting to ten very slowly as an attempt to calm down while the TSA wanded me. It took a lot of effort, but I remained civil and obedient throughout the embarrassing inspection. The TSA then told me that he was going to have to pat me down. That was the final nail in the coffin the TSA's had been building the past two days.

"You have got to be kidding me," I growled.

"What?" He had the nerve to look surprised.

"Tell me what it is about me that screams *security threat* to the point that I always get pulled aside, and this is the second time in two days that you people want to feel me up?" My voice was slowly rising with every word.

He watched, open mouthed, as I challenged him.

I gestured to myself. "It's not like you can't practically see through my clothes." I was standing in my bare feet wearing form fitting black yoga pants that hung low on my waist and a stretchy black t-shirt.

The TSA gave me an uncomfortable look. "I'm sorry ma'am." He frowned. "I am going to have to ask you to be quiet and spread your arms and legs so I can do a more thorough body check."

"*A more thorough body check*!" My eyes widened and my voice raised an octave. "You have not only x-rayed and wanded me, but now you feel it is necessary to put your hands on my body and feel me up!?"

"No ma'am. I wasn't meaning to…it's just procedure," he stammered under my glare. "We have to be thorough…" He trailed off, his eyes searching the area, desperate for an intervention.

"Mister, the only way you could possibly get more thorough would be a cavity search." I gestured down my body. "These clothes aren't hiding much. What they did hide was revealed on your machine over there. The only thing you haven't seen is my thong and bra." I looked over my shoulder at my butt. "At least, I didn't think you could see my thong."

We both looked down at the strap of black silk peeking over the waistband at my hip.

The TSA gave me an exasperated look, then motioned me to the side with his wand. "Ma'am, would you please just follow instructions? You're holding up the line."

Raising my eyebrow at the TSA, I glanced at the line. People may be staring, but the line was definitely moving. He sighed his frustration, motioning again with his wand.

I gave him my best glare and hissed, "What do you think I could possibly be hiding in here?" I ran my hands from my breasts to my legs. "I don't even have pockets!"

"Ma'am are you refusing the screening?" He raised an eyebrow in challenge.

"No, I am not *refusing the screening*. You know that I can't *refuse the screening* because I have a plane to catch. What I am doing is protesting the unnecessary measures that you, and all of the other TSA's, use on me, every single time I fly," I snapped.

"Ma'am, I'm afraid that I'm going to have to ask you to step aside while I get my supervisor." He took a deep breath before exhaling his exasperation.

"What?!" My voice rose another octave. "I don't have time to stand around waiting for your supervisor. I've got a plane to catch."

He gave me a hard look. "I don't like your attitude. You may be a security risk."

"Now my attitude makes me a security risk? You have got to be fucking kidding me!" I exclaimed loudly.

"There is no need for foul language," he snapped with a nervous glance at the gathering crowd.

"That's easy for you to say. You're not the one who's about to miss your flight for no good reason." I bit my lip, narrowing my eyes. "Okay, what do I need to do to get through security?"

"If you'll just step aside…" He sounded like a broken record.

"I told you, I'm going to miss my flight!" I cut him off. "Do you want me to strip? Is that it? Will that convince you that I have nothing to hide, so I can go catch my flight that will be boarding any minute now?" I wasn't yelling, but I wasn't speaking softly either.

The TSA was now desperately looking around for help. "Ma'am, if you'll just step aside my supervisor will be here…"

"Fine, if that's the way you want to do things," I announced, raising both hands in mock defeat before slithering out of my shirt.

His mouth hung open as I placed the black cloth into his hand. Dumbstruck, he watched while I reached my hands around my back to unclasp the pink with black polka dots bra my shirt had revealed.

"Alright!" Someone yelled from the line.

"Take it off, baby!" A man called from the other side of security.

The TSA turned beet red as the crowd began to chant. "TSA! TSA! TSA!..."

Flustered, he roughly pushed the shirt at me. "Just put your shirt back on and go."

"Thank you." I smiled sweetly as the crowd "booed" the TSA.

Barbie was waiting for me next to the conveyor belt with our stuff. I couldn't help but frown as I approached her. She was wearing snap up blue jeans with a cute belt, sparkly sandals, a loose fitting blouse over a tank top, too many bracelets to count, two necklaces, long dangly earrings, four rings on her fingers, a watch, and a toe ring. Despite all that, Barbie had breezed through security like it wasn't there. Life, and airport security, just isn't fair.

She rolled her eyes as I approached. "Was that really necessary?"

I shrugged. "Probably not, but it made me feel better. As a bonus, I didn't get patted down."

"No." She laughed while handing me my purse. "You exposed yourself to the whole airport."

"At least I was wearing a cute bra," I said, heading to our gate.

She nodded her agreement. "That is a cute bra. Where'd you get it?"

"Vickie's, I bought it with Jim's credit card in Seattle. It was full price." I smiled at the memory.

Our plane was getting ready to board, but we were both starved. On the way to our gate, we made a quick breakfast stop at the airport Starbucks. Of course, they were sold out of the breakfast sandwiches. I had to settle for a cut rate pastry. It wasn't the breakfast that I had wanted, but I felt a lot better with something in my stomach. As we hurried away from the Starbucks, my phone began to sing. Without looking, I knew it was Greg.

I sighed before answering, knowing the call would be painful. "Hey big brother, what's new?"

"Why don't you tell me?" he asked testily.

Barbie gave me a questioning look.

I shrugged in response to her unspoken question. Turning my attention back to the phone, I asked, "Is this about going to Thailand again?"

"No." I could hear his frustration. "This is about my little sister stripping in front of security at LaGuardia."

"I didn't strip. I just took my shirt off in protest of the TSA harassing me." I rolled my eyes. "Anyway, that just happened. How did you hear about it? You're not here are you?" I looked around, but didn't see him. "You can't stop me from going to Thailand. I'm an adult and a citizen. I have rights."

"Calm down, I'm in Boston. I know because your little strip tease is all over the internet. The news, YouTube, Facebook, Twitter, it's everywhere." I could feel his irritation emanating through the line. "Apparently, several of your fellow travelers used their cell phones to videotape your little *'protest'*. Now, you're famous."

"Shit!" I exclaimed.

Silence echoed through the line. I was pretty sure Greg was working hard to keep his temper under control. I wanted to say something, but I had already said the only word that existed in my vocabulary at the moment.

"Do you understand the grief that I'm getting from the guys at work? I'm the guy whose little sister stripped at LaGuardia," he growled. "Can't you go anywhere without causing trouble?"

"It couldn't be helped." I frowned. "The TSA was being unreasonable."

"So you took your shirt off?" he growled. "I saw the clip Jess. He had to stop you from taking off the bra. I do not want to see my little sister's breasts on national television."

"You wouldn't have." I rolled my eyes. "They would have covered them up with one of those black rectangle things." I wondered who all had seen the clip: my parents, grandma, Eric?

"You're lucky you didn't get arrested for indecent exposure," he grumbled.

"How do you know that I didn't?" I quipped.

I could almost hear him counting to ten just before he said, "Jess, just do us all a favor and go home, before you get yourself into real trouble."

"Thanks for the heads up. I promise to stay out of trouble for the rest of the trip." I gave the phone my best innocent smile.

"You couldn't stay out of trouble if your life depended on it," he protested before disconnecting.

Barbie was waiting impatiently for me to fill her in. "What was that about?"

I bit my lower lip. "I was filmed stripping at security, and it's gone viral."

Her eyes widened. "Really?"

I nodded unhappily. "Greg said it's already hit social media, the news, and who knows where else."

"You, cousin, are a mess." Barbie was trying so hard not to laugh that she was turning purple. "Hey! Between running off to Seattle with a mobster and this, I'm not the family delinquent anymore. Am I?" At that she burst into uncontrolled laughter.

Oh god, she was right. My spirits sank as the laughter echoed through the terminal tempting me to break into a run. Could I outrun the sinking feeling in my gut?

Pursing my lips, I narrowed my eyes at her, "Are you really taking joy in my humiliation?"

She grinned, "What are friends for?"

A moment later the mirth was forgotten. "OMG! Jess, look over there! I think I'm in love."

"Again?" Turning to see who today's unlucky bastard was, I stopped in my tracks. "NO!" Our eyes met across the crowded room. "Barbie!" I hissed. "It's him! It's him!"

"The Wolfman?" she asked.

"No! My stalker, Larry!" I whispered looking around for a security guard. Not seeing any, I asked Barbie, "Why is there never a security guard when you need one?"

"Your stalker's name is Larry?" She shook her head as if to say, 'You can't even attract a good stalker.' "You can't call security because you think that's the guy who's been following you. You have to have proof." She whispered back. "Are you sure that's the guy?"

"Yes, I'm sure! He's been following me for two weeks."

We stood side by side watching closely as Larry calmly drank his coffee with his back to the window. He looked like a normal traveler, except he could probably bench press the plane.

"He doesn't look like much of a threat," Barbie said.

"What! Look at him! He's built like a rhino on steroids. How is that not a threat?" I demanded.

"Well, yeah he's big. I wonder if he's big everywhere?"

"Barbie!"

Barbie rolled her eyes, "What? You haven't wondered?"

I gave her my 'be serious' look. "Can we please focus? This is serious. This guy has been stalking me for the past two weeks!"

"Well, you obviously haven't taken advantage of the situation," she said, matter of factly.

"Barbie," I growled.

"What? Sure, Larry the rhino looks tough and scary, but he hasn't even looked your way. And, he did deliver you safely to my apartment last night. Are you sure he's following you? Maybe he just happens to be in the same places you are," she suggested reasonably.

"I'm sure." I glared at her.

"Why don't I go ask him if he's following you? Then, we'll know," she asked.

Before I could answer, the attendant announced the beginning of the boarding process. Barbie looked at my stalker longingly before turning toward the gate with her boarding pass held out.

I grabbed her arm, "You've got time. They called first class."

She shook me off, moving forward. "Believe it or not, I like to take the time to enjoy myself."

"What?" I asked

She shook her head at me, "You don't think I'm spending the next forty hours in coach do you?"

I looked down at my boarding pass. "We're traveling first class? I hope that means this trip is gonna get better because so far I'm thinking that maybe I should have stayed home. My luck has been worse than normal since I got on that plane in OKC."

Eight

The wheels finally grazed asphalt at the Phuket airport, after three days and four layovers, flying almost ten thousand miles across an ocean, and more time zones and countries than I cared to count. It felt good to know that I wasn't getting onto another plane for a week. I was pretty sure that if I never got onto another plane, it would be one day too soon.

Barbie and I reached the designated baggage pick-up site for our flight just as the luggage started coming out. Barbie stood at the front of the group of passengers, eagerly anticipating the arrival of her things. With thinly concealed impatience, she jealously watched the other passengers pick up their suitcases and leave the baggage carousel. It didn't take long for her to tire of waiting and begin tapping her foot in irritation.

The minutes ticked by. Barbie's smile had long ago worked its way into a scowl. My left eye had begun to twitch in time to the echo of her stiletto on the tiled floors. We still weren't seeing the matching bubblegum pink bags spelling out 'B A R B I E'. She had brought five huge bags and a makeup case. Each bag bulged at the seams and looked like they came with the pink dream house we had played with so many years ago.

"Are you sure this is the carousel?" I asked Barbie.

"Yes." She pointed to an affluent looking older couple as they walked past us. "We were on the plane with that guy and his wife. They just picked up their luggage from here." Continuing to search for familiar faces, Barbie pointed to a balding man with a flat face. It looked like someone had hit him one too many times with a brick. "And, that man...his name is Radford, Rupert, Ralph...whatever, he was on our flight too. We just saw him pick up his bags from here."

I turned my gaze to her. "I don't remember him. When did you talk to him long enough to exchange names?"

"It was somewhere over the Atlantic. You were sleeping when he invited me to check out the lower deck." She shrugged noncommittally.

My eyes widened and my mouth fell open. "You had sex with him? You don't even know his name!"

"You're just jealous because I do what I want while you force yourself to live by some restrictive moral code." She waved me away in irritation.

"I'm not jealous. I'm disgusted." I glanced at Ralph or whatever his name was. "He's not even good looking."

Her gaze followed my glance. "I know, but I was bored. It was a really long flight. Anyway, I've always wanted to become a member of the mile high club."

I gave her an appalled look before slowly shaking my head.

"What?" she demanded.

"Let's just find your luggage and get out of here before you get bored and decide to hump one of the baggage handlers," I grumbled

In silence, we waited by the baggage carousel until all of the suitcases had been claimed. When the last piece of luggage had been picked up, I looked around the empty chamber. There was still no sign of Barbie's luggage.

"Shit! They lost my luggage!" Barbie had finally come to the same conclusion that I had drawn minutes earlier.

She strode purposefully up to an employee, waving her angry hands like a matador waving on a bull. Secretly, I hoped that they wouldn't find Barbie's luggage, today. I didn't want to have to lug it out of the airport, to the hotel, and up to our room. If I got really lucky it wouldn't catch up to her until she got home to New York.

A high pitched sound was coming from across the Terminal. I turned to investigate, fearing Barbie had just killed a man with her bare hands. Relief found me as I rounded the corner. There were no dead bodies in sight. Barbie was loudly speaking in an unnaturally high pitched voice. Her hands waving wildly while an airport employee nodded encouragingly, a sure sign that he didn't understand a word she was saying.

"I am sorry," the man said once more in his stilted English.

He reassuringly bobbed his head as Barbie angrily wrote down her information. When she had finished writing he made a big show of taking the paper over to another employee. For Barbie's sake, I hoped someone there could read her angrily scribbled English.

Stepping away from the counter Barbie continued to mutter under her breath, "My luggage, they lost my luggage!"

"Don't worry about it. You still have your makeup and hair supplies. I've got an extra swimsuit. I'm sure the airport will have your luggage delivered to the resort by tomorrow." I smiled encouragingly.

"Sure, that's easy for you to say. They didn't lose your luggage!"

Oh no, she was showing signs of panic. "Just stay calm and distract her from the issue," I told myself.

"What?!"

"Did I say that out loud?" I asked.

"Yes," she growled, shooting me daggers.

I rolled my eyes melodramatically.

"You don't care," she pouted. "You just don't understand. You would if they had lost your luggage."

"I packed light and kept it with me." I reminded her as we headed toward the doors.

Barbie was still grumbling when we stumbled outside, into the sunlight. As the light punctured our skulls, Barbie and I groaned. We were dehydrated, travel weary, and hungover from too much airplane booze and not enough water.

"Who turned on all the lights?" Barbie whined, fumbling in her purse for her sunglasses.

"It's the sun. You know that bright shining thing that makes the beach so damn sparkly and attractive," I grumbled, shoving my sunglasses over my eyes.

"Right. There's our shuttle." She led the way to a large yellow van with the resort name painted on the side.

"How far are we from the hotel?" I asked the driver, as I slid into the empty seat behind him.

"Phuket Island is not large. It is only thirty miles from the farthest tips and thirteen miles wide." His English was good although pronounced with a heavy Thai accent. "The resort lies in the middle of the island, not far."

The shuttle took us through colorful streets full of pedestrians, automobiles, bicyclists, motorcycles, and scooters. Enjoying the ride, we marveled at how the city mixed modern high rises with antiquated structures, somehow managing to keep an Asian mien. Barbie pointed out a large elephant sculpture as we passed by a city park. A few moments later, we watched a group of monks solemnly shuffle past a larger than life concrete goddess waving her multiple arms.

Too quickly, the driver left the city to travel through a small plains area, surrounded by mountains, exotic undergrowth flowers, and trees. The van sped from small town to even smaller town allowing Barbie and I to marvel at the many temples and sculptures evidencing the ancient religions and customs of the area. We became so entranced in the beauty surrounding us that we forgot about the lost luggage and our hangovers. Forgot, until the driver turned onto a private road hidden in a thick forested area.

"I'm going to be sick," Barbie moaned, clutching her stomach.

I had to admit the driver's reckless careening up the mountainside was disconcerting, and not a good fit with my alcohol soaked insides. Swallowing down the threatening bile, I distracted myself with the view. It was majestic, like a travel brochure to an ancient forgotten land.

Abruptly, the shuttle stopped in front of a modern, yet stunningly beautiful, building. The walls were made primarily of glass, complemented by dark wood, mixed with rock accents, and topped with the angled roofs associated with Asian architecture. The beautifully simple structure was surrounded by native greenery and regional flowers, giving it the appearance of being a part of the mountain.

"Not a minute too soon," Barbie announced vaulting from the vehicle.

By the time I joined Barbie and the rest of the recently arrived vacationers, the driver was explaining how the resort was newly

108

remodeled and built on the hillside overlooking Kamala beach and the Andaman Sea. We stood in front of the magnificent structure, gawking at the unworldly beauty encompassing it, while a small army of attendants converged on the shuttle to transport our luggage up the steps and through the ornate double doors. Everywhere we looked were small sculptures of elephants, beautiful artwork, expensive looking vases, and many-armed women. We stood marveling at the opulence surrounding us as we waited our turn to check in.

I turned to Barbie. "If this is the lobby, what do you think our rooms look like?"

"For what it's costing me, they had better be just as exquisite." She paused. "But, more so."

I had barely finished gawking at the lobby before the bellboy arrived to lead us to our rooms. Barbie had reserved a two bedroom terrace suite that was a cut above anyplace that I'd ever lived and most places that I'd visited. We stood side by side in the living room gazing out the floor to ceiling windows that made up the exterior wall of our suite. It was breathtaking how the white sandy beaches and cerulean blue sea below us reflected the perfect skies above.

This was what I imagined heaven must be like. I couldn't help but smile, stepping through the floor length glass doors into our own Zen garden. The private patio was decorated with trees, bushes, and flowers along with a couple of lounge chairs and a small table. Looking out, we could just see similar patios staggered through the ever present florae.

With wide eyes I turned to Barbie. "All I can say is WOW! I love this place. I may never leave! Thank you for badgering me into coming." I hugged her. "I'm sorry for being so difficult the past few days, make that weeks. Things have been hard lately, but I promise to do better." I sighed. "This view alone makes up for the horrible trip out here."

"Yes, it does and you're welcome." Barbie smirked at me as we called a truce to our petty arguing. "So, what do you want to do first?"

"What are our options?" I asked, leaning over the railing to survey our surroundings.

"Let's see…we can go scuba diving, parasailing, cruising on the resort yacht, jet skiing, swimming, shopping in one of the nearby towns, or we could go on an elephant safari." She was reading off of a brochure that she had found in the lobby.

"How about we go get a sandwich and something to drink. Then, we can head down to that beach to lie under the warm sun and check out the eye candy?" I suggested. "I haven't really slept in days. I think I need to be rested to enjoy all of that other stuff."

"I like it," Barbie agreed.

Fifteen minutes later, I was standing in my room staring into a full-length mirror in dismay while poking at my abdomen. I had a jelly belly. When did that happen? Three weeks ago, I'd had both abs and buns of steel. Keeping the mirror in view, I turned to look over my shoulder at my backside.

As I was bending to get a better look, Barbie walked in. She was wearing my extra swimsuit. I couldn't help but notice that there wasn't any part of her body that needed tightening. I took another look at her and my frown deepened. She definitely did not have a belly roll.

She glanced at my frown, then asked, "What's the matter?"

"This!" I exclaimed, pushing out my lower lip while I irritably poked at the offending belly roll.

Cocking her head to the side, she asked, "What happened? I thought you were running, using the punching bag, and doing yoga."

"Oklahoma happened." I rolled my eyes. "It's just too damn hot to go for a run, and there is no punching bag at my parents' place. I kept up with the yoga, until I dislocated my shoulder."

"When did you dislocate your shoulder?" Barbie asked.

"A couple of weeks ago, during yoga," I mumbled.

Barbie gave me a judging look, and asked, "During yoga?"

Shrugging my shoulders, I said, "During yoga." Playing with my belly roll, I added, "Mom's been baking and cooking for me too."

Barbie gave me a stern look. "Stand up straight, and stop playing with it."

Giving myself a dirty look in the mirror, I did as I was told.

"Jess, it's not that bad." She laughed. "It's barely noticeable when you're not slouching and poking at it. With a little exercise and a low cal diet, it'll be gone in a couple of days."

I looked in the mirror hopefully. "You think so? I mean you're not just saying that to make me feel better are you?"

She shook her head. "You know I don't just say things to make people feel better. That's why everyone thinks I'm a bitch."

"That's true," I agreed. "Okay, starting in the morning, I'm back on my exercise routine. No excuses. I'll run a couple of miles on the beach every morning." I patted the belly roll, and said, "This will be gone in no time."

"That's the spirit. There's a really nice gym here at the resort we can use," Barbie added.

"You're going to exercise with me?" I asked in surprise.

"Of course. Without a regular gym routine, I'll look a lot worse than you in no time at all. I can't let that happen." She winked, then said, "I'm husband hunting."

I looked down at the waves lapping the sand below us. "We'll start with a run on the beach in the morning."

"What time are you planning on going running?" she asked.

"Early, before the beach fills up," I answered. "How does sunrise sound?"

"Ghastly." She frowned at the idea. "Count me out. I'll hit the gym with you mid-morning." She paused in thought. "I like to go around ten when I'm at home. I'd like to keep to my routine while I'm here, otherwise I'll be out of the habit when I get back."

"Sounds good to me." I nodded in agreement, knowing I would enjoy my morning run more alone.

"Now, let's get down to that beach. I'm ready for some R and R." Barbie grabbed my sunscreen off of the table and headed towards the door.

A half hour later our bikini clad bodies had been coated in sunscreen and dipped in the ocean. We were lying on the beach waiting for a well tipped attendant to bring us sandwiches and Phuket Punch. I wasn't sure what was in it, but Barbie was excited to try it. That alone told me it was probably close to one hundred proof.

"I love Fuck-It Island," I said, as we lounged in beach chairs watching a group of sun-kissed hotties play volleyball in nothing but their shorts and muscles.

"Me too," agreed Barbie as she eyed a group of golden skinned, heavily inked, brawny guys sauntering down the beach in front of us.

"Come on, let's go make some friends," she said, standing up with a take no prisoners look on her face.

"You go. I'm gonna take a nap," I told her closing my eyes.

"You can sleep when you're dead," she declared. "Right now, I need a wingman."

I opened one eye to give her a suspicious look. "What do you need a wingman for?"

She stared down the beach towards the group of golden skinned man-candy. "See the brunette on the left?"

My eyes followed her gaze. The brunette on the left was tall, with broad shoulders that had been artfully inked, hard muscles, long dark hair, a perfect golden tan, and tight European swim trunks that seductively hugged his pelvis. He looked like a bad idea. I was still getting over the last bad idea that crossed my path.

I leaned back into my chair, pointedly closing my eyes before responding. "He's pretty, but not any better looking than half the men on this beach."

"Liar. He's more than pretty. He's got great eyes, and a killer smile. You're just afraid to get out of that chair and meet someone." She cocked her head to the side, daring me to argue.

"I couldn't see his eyes, but I don't doubt he's a killer," I said dismissively.

"Be nice. You're looking at my future ex-husband," she said excitedly.

I rolled onto my stomach. "Why don't you take a marriage break? You might enjoy being single for a while."

"And be as happy as you?" She rolled her eyes mockingly. "Get up."

"I am happy. And, I am not going to wingman for you." I closed my eyes again.

"Why not?" she demanded.

"Because, I'll get stuck with one of his friends. I'm not interested, not this time."

"Oh, what a horror to get stuck with one of his hot friends. The last time I wing manned for you do you remember what I got stuck with?" she frowned.

"That was years ago, and it didn't stop you from boinking him," I reminded her crassly.

"That's it! Get up. Besides, you owe me. I paid for your trip." She pulled on my arm causing my chair to tilt menacingly towards the sand.

After an overdramatic eye roll, I asked, "Really? Now I have to work for my vacation?"

"If you want to call it work." She smiled mischievously. "While we're at it, I bet that blonde next to McDreamy could take your mind off of the Wolfman."

I narrowed my eyes at her. "What, now you're my pimp, too?"

"Don't be such a buzz kill." She pulled me to my feet. "We came here to have fun, and get you out of this love funk. So, let's go have some fun."

I sighed loudly, but didn't move from the safety of my lounge-chair. "Has it possibly occurred to you that I am happy? That I like being alone for once in my life, and it has nothing to do with Eric? I am *so* over him."

She gave me a knowing look. "Sure, you're happy, and I'm a virgin. Now, get up." Wiggling her eyebrows, she said, "I've got a husband to catch."

Nine

Barbie confidently strutted her perfect spray on tanned body toward the water's edge and the poor sap she had targeted to be the next love of her life. Muttering under my breath, while wandering why I let her talk me into these things, I reluctantly slid up from my chair. Once I caught up, we slowly made our way down the beach. Barbie was pointedly ignoring my muttering as she considered the best scheme to meet the buff brunette standing merely feet away.

Interrupting her train of thought, I asked, "Uh…Barbie, have you noticed that people are beginning to stare?"

"No. But, I have noticed that since you left Seattle you've turned paranoid and grumpy," she glared at me.

"That was harsh!" I frowned before asking, "Am I really that bad?"

"Yes." She gave me a frustrated sigh. "Okay, here's the plan. Once we start to pass the guys, I'll pretend to fall so McDreamy there can help me up," Barbie explained.

"That's your plan?" I gave her a questioning glance.

"Yeah." She nodded.

"That's stupid."

"Do you have any better ideas?" Her voice was tense.

I shrugged my shoulders. "Not really."

She nodded. "Okay then, that's the plan."

The closer we got to McDreamy and his friends, the worse the sinking feeling in the pit of my stomach got. "Do you have any idea how embarrassing this middle school ploy is? We are intelligent and attractive women, we shouldn't be stooping to these juvenile techniques to meet men."

"Hey, this 'ploy' as you called it has been working for me since the seventh grade." Barbie shrugged off my complaint.

"That's exactly my point. Don't you think it's time to start using grownup tricks to meet men?" I asked.

Keeping her eyes on the prize, she asked, "What do you want me to do? Take off my top and jiggle my boobs?"

With a sigh, I rolled my eyes. "Don't you ever get tired of being a slut?"

We were practically face to face with McDreamy and his friends. As their attention turned our way, Barbie spun around to give me a mischievous grin, said, "Nope."

Someone behind us yelled loudly. Barbie ducked to the side. A sudden pain shot through my left temple. My vision blurred, and my balance faltered. The world was slowly coming into focus around me when I realized that I was mid-fall. My body moved in slow motion as I clumsily clutched at the air, careening into Barbie. A deafening screech echoed in my right ear as we fell in a tangled heap at the feet of Barbie's future ex-husband and his friends.

After a brief moment of disorientation, I disentangled myself from Barbie, brushed at the sand sticking to my sunscreen covered limbs, and self-consciously peered up at the quickly gathering crowd above us. My cheeks felt like they were on fire, a sure sign that I was turning bright red from my chest to the roots of my hair.

"Are you alright?" It was one of McDreamy's friends. His voice was sexy with a rough and difficult to understand lilt.

"I think so." I rubbed my sore temple. "I'm not sure what just happened."

The guy Barbie had her eye on crouched down in front of us. "You were hit in the head with a volleyball. You should 'ave been paying attention." He spoke with the same rough lilt to his voice.

Barbie was practically melting as he checked to be sure that she wasn't hurt. I gave him a weak smile. "I'll keep that in mind for next time."

Our group of onlookers laughed as a couple of the hotties helped us to stand. As soon as my rescuer let go of my arm, a draft slid up my boobs signaling that my bikini top had become loose. I grabbed at the thin triangles of fabric moments before flashing the whole beach, but not before giving the group around us a sneak peak of my girls.

Barbie rolled her eyes. "Jessie! This is a family beach!"

"The strings must have gotten pulled when he helped me up. Did anyone see?" I could feel the heat on my face intensify.

A redheaded guy to my left said. "Just us blokes. Don'cha worry lass, not a one of us is complainin'."

While Barbie flirted with McDreamy and friends, I attempted to slip away, unnoticed. I was experiencing a desperate need to nurse my embarrassment anywhere but here, covered with sand, and surrounded by a bunch of strangers who had just seen me all but naked.

"Where ya goin' pretty?" Another redhead from the group asked in the same lilting tones as his friends.

I motioned back down the beach. "I'm a little tired. I'm just gonna go up to my room and never come out again."

His laughter was disarming. "Don't let Seamus here upset you. He means no harm."

I gave him a weak smile, wishing that I could disappear.

"Right, I didn't mean nothin' by it." A roughly handsome redhead, and obvious leader of the group, gave me a warmly disarming smile. "Name is Seamus McGreary. This here is my brother Tad." He pointed to the other redhead. "These two blokes are our cousins Shaun," he motioned to the blonde, "and Amos." He motioned to the brunette.

Barbie smiled warmly at the group of men. "Pleased to meet you. I'm Barbie O'Grady." With a quick motion towards me, she said, "This is my cousin Jessie Hart."

The men exchanged surprised looks as Amos repeated, "O'Grady?"

"Our grandparents' parents came from Ireland." Barbie shrugged.

The men turned to me, taking in my freckled skin, green eyes, and dark auburn hair. The moment stretched into an uncomfortable silence. Seamus finally broke the silence by asking, "Do you know where about in Ireland they hailed from?"

Barbie and I exchanged looks as we worked to understand his thickly accented English. Not sure if I was answering his question, I responded tentatively, "Somewhere near Dublin?"

The men looked at each other, then nodded. "This calls for drinks, cousins!"

"Cousins?" Barbie and I asked at the same time.

The men grinned as Amos said, "We're O'Grady's, from near Dublin."

Barbie and I looked at each other in shocked surprise. "Really?"

Seamus motioned to Tad. "Honest be to God. Our mother were an O'Grady before she married our father."

With a smile, I whispered to Barbie, "Guess you're gonna have to find a new future ex-husband."

"I guess so." She shook her head in disbelief. "We go to Thailand, and the first people we meet are long lost cousins from Ireland? No one is going to believe this."

"I'm not sure I believe it," I agreed.

"Why don't you lovely lassies join us for a cruise?" Seamus asked.

Barbie perked up. "A cruise?"

He nodded. "We were just getting ready to take a run around the sea. Have you been out there?"

I shook my head. "We just flew in a few hours ago. We're still a little jet lagged. That's probably why we didn't see the ball coming at us, jet lag."

"That's right, jet lag." Barbie gave me a 'stop talking' look.

Tad smiled warmly, and said, "'Tis settled. We're taking the Americans for a cruise."

"How did you know we're Americans?" I asked.

The guys laughed as McDreamy answered. "'Tis clear as the day is long, lass."

Barbie and I didn't speak while following our newfound cousins to a group of WaveRunners. She was too busy being charming. As the guys each climbed on a WaveRunner, I pulled Barbie's arm to get her attention. Barbie had started to turn toward me when Seamus turned and held out his hand to her.

"Are ya comin' lassies?" he asked, with a grin.

I leaned forward to whisper into her ear. "I'm not sure about this. We don't know anything about these guys."

"Sure we do. They're O'Grady's." She climbed up behind Seamus, giving me a look that said 'get with the program and board a WaveRunner'.

I took a deep breath before climbing up behind Amos. As we headed out to sea, something caught my eye. I turned toward the beach where a man stood by the water's edge, staring sinisterly towards us.

Where had I seen him before? His skin was unnaturally pale, and he had a thin wiry build, with white blonde hair, and deeply hooded eyes. I couldn't place him, but his stare was so hard that it felt as if he was looking straight through me, causing a familiar yet foreboding chill to race down my spine.

Our newfound cousins parked the WaveRunners along the side of a large yacht, with the word *Tempest* written on the side, before helping us to climb aboard. When we reached the deck, we were surprised to find it filled with people laughing, talking, and drinking.

"Are you having a party?" I asked.

Seamus shook his head. "Na, tis just Monday."

The men around us laughed heartily as Seamus led the way through the throng of people. My intuition antennae were raised, along with the hairs on the back of my neck. If Barbie was experiencing any discomfort, she wasn't showing it. She appeared to be in her element in the center of the group. She hadn't even noticed that I had eased toward the back. While I struggled with my discomfort, Seamus and our new cousins stopped in front of a door, ushering us inside to a large sitting room. As I approached the doorway, Amos stepped in front of me.

"Why don't we go someplace private, lassie?" He murmured huskily, running his hand sensually down my arm.

I blinked in surprise. "What? I thought we were cousins."

He shrugged while making eye contact with my breasts, and said, "We're all part of the family of God." Moving his hand to caress my neck, he added, "If things work out, you could be my lady. You would have a very comfortable life, by my side."

I was speechless and standing in shock with my mouth open when a similarly redheaded guy, wearing European swim trunks, multiple tattoos across his chest and arms, leather sandals, and a large cross on a rough cord tied around his neck, stopped in front of Amos.

He didn't appear to notice me as he spoke. "Good, you're back. Get the boys and come to the office."

"What's up?" Amos asked, with one eye focused on my top.

I moved to step inside with the others, but Amos had a grip on my arm. I tried to slip out of it, but he just pulled me in closer. The other guy continued the conversation, as if I wasn't there.

"News is, we've hit the big time." he said, with a confident grin.

"The big time?" Amos asked, with awe in his voice.

The other guy nodded, "Our guy says the yanks are sending an operative." His grin widened, "a female operative."

Amos turned to me, his posture suspicious. "Who do you work for?"

"Me?" I gave him a confused look.

His grip tightened uncomfortably.

"I'm unemployed. I live with my parents," I cried.

"And your friend?"

"She's a divorced heiress. She doesn't have to work," I mumbled in pain.

"It's not her, Amos," The other man sneered, looking at me for the first time. "You know who she is."

Amos' hard gaze seemed to look into my soul before he loosened his grip. "Sorry 'bout that lassie. You can never be too careful." He patted my partially exposed butt cheek, leaning in to whisper in my ear. "Offers still good."

Speechless, I just stared at him.

Without a word, he leaned inside the door. "C'mon you blokes, we've been summoned." They filed out as Seamus ushered me inside saying, "Relax and have a drink, 'til we get back."

Once we were alone, I said to Barbie, "Your future ex-husband just felt me up and propositioned me."

"It's okay if you want him. I'm not interested anymore." She winked past the drink in her hand.

I gave her a hard look. "He rubbed his hands on me while inviting my breasts to go someplace private."

Barbie considered my words before saying, "He'd be a distant cousin. I'm not sure if it counts as long as you don't get married or, god forbid, pregnant. You can't tell me he doesn't make you all warm inside."

"Then, he got weird and demanded to know who we work for," I told her. "He hurt my arm," I said, rubbing away the memory.

"What did you tell him?" She asked, surprising me with her calmness.

"The truth. Then, he patted my butt, and said that the offer was still open. I'm telling you he's certifiable."

"You're being paranoid again," she said, as she inspected the room.

I bit my lip, wondering if I really was being paranoid. They thought I was paranoid when Jim went missing, too. Was I? No. "I'm not so sure these guys are our cousins, Barb. When I said something about it, he gave me some nonsense about us all being part of the family of God."

"That is so lame," she said.

If I didn't know better I'd think Barbie was looking for something the way she was so obviously snooping. I shook my head. I really was paranoid. "Yeah, it is," I agreed.

"I mean, who pretends to be related to someone to get laid. We were already going to sleep with them." She was still busy with the room, and hadn't noticed the shocked look on my face.

"Barbie!"

"What?" She gave me a surprised look.

"What do you mean *we* were going to sleep with *them*?" I squeaked.

"Come on, it's not like you're that particular. I've seen some of the guys you've slept with. Anyway, you said you'd take one for the team." She reminded me.

"Yes, but that was before we found out that they were cousins. And, I never agreed to have sex with the team!"

"Don't be such a prude." She wandered across the room avoiding my repulsed glare.

"Barbie, I know you think I'm paranoid, but just hear me out." I gnawed my lower lip. "Something doesn't feel right. The chance encounter with long lost cousins, all of these people on the boat, the way they all jumped when they were summoned to wherever, Amos' paranoia. And, did you see the creepy guy watching us as we left the beach?"

She shook her head. "No, but come check this out."

I walked over to the window Barbie was staring out of. There were three women servicing a man in a lounge chair on the deck. "Oh My God!"

Reaching into her bikini top, Barbie frowned. "It's like watching porn, except he's all flabby. He'd look a lot better with more clothes on."

"You watch porn?" I gave her a questioning look.

"No. Well." She shrugged. "If it's got a good plot."

"Eww..." I cringed at the thought.

"What you've never watched one?" she asked.

"No."

"I don't believe you." She shook her head as she began snapping pictures with the tiniest camera I'd ever seen.

I turned away from the window. "That is disgusting. Why are you taking pictures, and where did you get that teeny tiny camera?"

With a noncommittal shrug she replied, "Posterity," she answered, ignoring my second question.

Who are these people?" I asked rhetorically.

"I'm pretty sure the porn star out there is the President's right hand man. Rumor has it, he's planning to make the Oval Office his next home."

I took a second look. She was right, there was no mistaking those eyebrows. "What is he doing here?" I asked.

"Ruining his career and probably his marriage," she smiled.

"And you're taking the pictures?" I shook my head.

"Of course." She smiled. "Think of it as a public service."

"How is taking dirty pictures a public service?" I asked.

"Once these pictures get into the wrong hands, the public will be served by his retirement from politics." Her face lit up at the thought.

"You would ruin a man's career, just like that? With no thought of who else it might affect?" I asked with surprise.

She shrugged before saying, "I'm not the one playing half-dressed tonsil hockey with someone who's not my wife, and her little sister."

"No. You're taking the pictures." I glared.

The look on her face was devoid of responsibility, or even the smallest hint of guilt, as she shrugged her shoulders. With a roll of her eyes, she said, "Don't get too excited. I'm about to make a bundle of cash off of these pictures. I'll give you a cut."

Fighting down nausea, I left the window. A group of items on the coffee table stopped me in my tracks. "Is this what I think it is?"

Barbie left the window to investigate. Peering over my shoulder, she said, "Probably, if you think it's cocaine."

A shiver of fear surged down my spine as I stood staring at a small bowl of white powder next to an assortment of mirrors, cut glass, and razor blades. We were on a huge yacht with a group of dangerous looking...cousins? Sex, drugs...what kind of mess had we stumbled into this time?

I raised an eyebrow in a silent plea for normalcy. "Maybe its sugar."

Barbie licked her finger, touched it to the white powder, then licked the finger again. "Nope, its coke."

I gave her a shocked look.

"Don't look at me like that. My third husband was an international drug king pin. Remember, that's why I divorced him." She frowned before adding, "That and a few other reasons."

"I thought you divorced him because he embezzled three million dollars from that bank."

"That was husband number two," she casually stated while taking pictures of the cocaine and drug paraphernalia.

"Because he was a double agent?" I asked.

"Husband number one," she corrected. "I guess I can tell you, Jonathan wasn't just a cross dresser, playing for the other team. He was also an international art thief."

"That explains the too expensive, even for him, artwork he gave you. It's like you're attracted to dirt bags."

"I couldn't pick worse if I tried," she admitted nonchalantly.

"You kept the art?" I asked.

"Had to give it up," she sadly shook her head.

"Even *Dogs Playing Poker*?" I asked.

"I'll get you a good reproduction when you finally get stable," she offered.

"Somehow, it's just not the same," I pouted.

"You'll never be able to tell the difference," she assured me.

A quick glance at the coke on the table reminded me that this wasn't a pleasure cruise. Taking my right hand, I wiped an inordinate amount of sweat off my brow. "Suddenly, I don't feel so good. I hope this is the bathroom." I opened a door to the back of the room. "Holy Shit!"

Barbie cautiously peeked around me into the tiny room. It was filled with rectangular packages, neatly stacked in rows, from the floor to the ceiling. There were so many packages that we could only get the door open about halfway. We stood side by side, open mouthed, staring into the room.

"If that's what I think it is, it's time for us to go," I nervously squeaked.

Barbie calmly stepped into the other room, returning with a letter opener. Without a word, she quickly poked one of the packages. We silently watched as the same white powder we had seen in the bowl poured out of the freshly made hole. Once again, she licked her finger to taste the white powder. With a quick nod, she pulled out her little camera. When she had taken pictures from every angle possible, she grimly closed the door and returned the letter opener to its previous location.

"Okay, I've had enough fun for today. Let's get out of here. And, don't try to tell me that I'm no fun," I said.

Barbie just nodded in silent agreement before leading the way out. Pausing at the door, she put a finger to her lips in the universal signal to keep quiet. There were voices on the other side of the door.

"…Was easy. Seamus and the lads found 'em roamin' the beach. Soon as they get enough coke in 'em, we'll find out where they stashed the jewel. Seamus said we can help with the interrogation."

"What will he do with them after?"

"I don't know how much we'd get for 'em. They're a little old to sell. Most likely, they'll have a boating accident." His laughter made me want to hit him.

"What about Leery?"

"What about him?"

"I hear he's looking for Red, too. He may turn up when he hears we have her."

"Thomas Leery is a petty thief, liar, and swindler trying to catch up to the jewel before the authorities catch up to him. He's not even a speck to McGreary, now. The girl snatching it from him was a lucky break for the bloke. Now, we won't have to kill him."

The voices trailed off as the men passed our door.

My eyes were bugging out and my composure was noticeably absent as I squeaked, "Barbie! Those men were talking about us. We've been kidnapped!"

"I don't think I like our new cousins." She frowned, picking something up from a nearby table.

I threw up my hands in frustration. "Barbie! I'm pretty sure they lied about being O'Grady's."

She gave me a worried look. "What have you stumbled into this time, Jessie?"

I gave her a blank look as my mind raced to catch up to the turn of events. "Me?! This was all your idea."

She gave me an intense look. "Who is Thomas Leery? What did you take from him? Do you have it with you?"

I shook my head in response. "I knew you shouldn't have eaten that cocaine. You're delusional."

Frowning, she sighed. "This is serious. Did Amos give you anything while he was chatting you up?"

"The heebie jeebies. For some reason, I doubt that's the jewel they were talking about." I frowned. Barbie had obviously ingested too much coke if she thought I was involved in this. I took another step away from the table, afraid I might breathe some in. "Okay, here's the plan. We'll make our way back to those WaveRunners and get the hell out of here, preferably without being noticed."

"I like that plan." Barbie nodded.

"Okay, let's go!" I pushed past her, giving the door a hard shove.

The door stopped with a sudden thud, pausing us in our tracks like deer caught in the headlights of a speeding car on a dark country road. My heart was beating so fast that I could hear it.

"Shit!" whispered Barbie.

I nodded in agreement. A moment later Barbie peeked around the door. Her pale face told me that whatever was back there, it wasn't good. Cautiously, I peered over Barbie's shoulder.

We hesitated in stunned silence, staring at a pale middle-aged man who was standing next to the wall. Blood was spurting out of his nose and down his bare chest. As we watched, the shock seemed to wear off. Suddenly, he began to scream in surprised pain, grabbing the attention of the other passengers. The fat man touched his wounded nose, looked at his left hand that was now coated in sticky red liquid, looked down at the blood slowly dripping down his chest, and promptly passed out. A couple of girls saw him hit the deck covered in blood, and started screaming that he'd been shot. No longer stupefied, Barbie and I slipped past the crowd in the confusion, thankful for the diversion.

Halfway down the steps that led from the deck to the abandoned watercraft, I nervously asked, "Do you know how to drive one of those things?"

"Sure." She nodded. "It's like riding a motorcycle on water except you don't have to worry about your balance."

"Okay, you're driving," I called out, heading for the nearest one.

"Coward," she teased pulling a handful of keys out of a bucket. She handed me a bunch of keys, keeping some for herself. "Find a key that works, and let's get out of here."

A quick movement on the deck caught my eye. Seamus was glaring down at us, and he had a gun. Great. Taking my handful of keys, I jumped on the nearest WaveRunner while trying to remember the Guardian Angel Prayer.

"Angel of God...um," A bullet hit the water beside me.

Another shot rang out. Instinctively, I ducked as the bullet whizzed past my head.

"I um...promise to go to church, and learn the prayers if you get me out of this!" I yelled to the heavens.

"Amen!" Barbie shouted in agreement.

Seamus was heading our way, waving his gun while yelling profanities in a thick working class Irish accent. "Give me the jewel, bitch!"

Barbie gave me a questioning look. I shrugged my confusion, then yelled back. "What jewel?"

"Fucking American bitches..." The diatribe continued, but his accent was so thick that we couldn't understand most of what he said, probably for the best. I didn't need to be distracted by his words as his intentions were obvious. Another bullet pinged off the WaveRunner that I was trying to start, just a quarter of an inch from my leg. The engine roared to life under me, catching me by surprise.

Barbie leaped over the WaveRunner that she had been attempting to fit a key into, and onto the back of mine, yelling, "Drive!"

"What?! I don't know how!" I yelled.

"Just give it some gas and go!" She shouted.

A bullet lodged itself in the side of the watercraft next to my foot, providing all the prompting that I needed. Barbie almost fell off when we shot forward. I almost fell off when we jerked back.

"Do something!" I shouted at Barbie, who was working frantically to untie us from the yacht.

"I'm working on it!" she yelled. "GO!"

Without a second thought I gave it gas. We lurched forward, as I dropped the rest of my keys into the sea. Another shot rang out. From the corner of my eye, I saw Barbie toss something onto the boat. When another bullet bounced off the vehicle she haphazardly threw three more. One flew into an open window in the lower part of the boat. All of her other pitches landed on the deck with amazing accuracy for someone whose idea of playing sports was beer pong.

"Nice arm!" I gave her a surprised look.

"I dated a pitcher for the Mets for a few weeks last month." She grinned pridefully.

We roared away, just ahead of the shots delving into the sea behind us. Once we were out of firing range, I took a moment to look back. People were jumping overboard, climbing into nearby boats, and floating on life preservers. I glanced at Barbie in unspoken confusion. Before she could speak, an indescribably loud noise came from deep inside the boat causing even more people to leap into the clear blue water.

"What the…?" My words were drowned out by a deafening blast, moments before the yacht exploded into a fiery ball.

Barbie hollered above the clamor, but I couldn't make out her words.

Idling the WaveRunner among several other watercraft that had gathered to rubberneck, we watched three speed boats approach the steaming wreckage.

I whispered to Barbie, "What did you throw onto that boat?"

"I thought they were flares, you know the old kind that flame up after you light them, but maybe there weren't," Barbie shrugged, staring at the quickly sinking wreckage.

"Flares?" I blinked. "What did you light them with?"

"I picked up a lighter and cigarette from the table. It was next to the cocaine." She frowned holding up a cheap plastic lighter in one hand and a bent cigarette in another.

"I thought you quit." I glared at her.

She shrugged her shoulders. "I did. But, I've been under a lot of stress. I need a cigarette!"

"You have got to be kidding me!" I rolled my eyes.

"I wish." She looked longingly at the cigarette, frowned, and tossed it into the sea. "You don't understand. You've never smoked. Quitting is harder than you think."

Ten

We sat watching the commotion at the yacht until it became obvious that there was nothing to see, then fired up the WaveRunner and headed for the beach. Parking it where it could easily be found, we left the key in the ignition. It was bad enough we had blown up a boat and probably killed someone. I didn't want to be accused of stealing.

Hoping no one would know we were involved, we hurried to our hotel. On the way to our room, we stopped by the bar so Barbie could pick up a bottle of Coconut Rum, Tequila, fruit juice, Coke, and some limes.

"We're about to be arrested for destruction of property and murder, and you're making drinks?" I asked.

She shrugged. "It's medicinal. Besides, I was planning to share."

Once we were safely inside our rooms, Barbie mixed drinks while I flipped through the news stations looking for coverage of the yacht. I found a station that broadcasted in English, and we sat down to watch. The anchorman was reporting in the background while scenes from the day's events were flashed onto the screen.

"...The explosion occurred aboard a yacht known to belong to members of an alleged Irish organized crime ring. As you can see from the police footage, two unidentified women were seen leaving the scene minutes before the explosion. Police say shots were heard as the women sped away. It is unknown at this time why those shots were fired or who the women are. The police tape shows passengers and crew alike jumping into the Andean Sea as a series of explosions overcomes the vessel. Remarkably, no one was hurt, and local police were able to rescue all of the survivors. Officials have said that the police arrested thirty-two people on charges of prostitution and drug trafficking during today's raid. Authorities are still looking to apprehend the two women seen fleeing from the scene. If you have any information call..."

An enlarged picture of the backs of Barbie and me riding the WaveRunner was plastered across the screen. I muted the television as we watched an angry Seamus being lifted out of the water onto a small boat. An officer immediately handcuffed him, like they had done with several others already in the boat. The camera panned across the wreckage to show a bunch of neatly wrapped packages floating on the water. Officers were carefully fishing the packages out of the sea with hand held nets.

Barbie and I sat on the couch silently staring at the television. Her phone rang, causing us to both jump. Looking at the screen, she sighed before handing it to me.

"I don't know how he does it, but he always knows when something's going on," she said, sliding off of the couch.

I looked at the caller ID, '*Greg*'.

Barbie carried our empty glasses to the bar. "I'll make more drinks. I have a feeling you're going to need them."

I rolled my eyes while mumbling, "Whatever" under my breath. Plastering a fake smile on my face, I took a deep breath, and answered the phone. "Hey, big brother. How's it going?"

"It had better be going dull and boring. Because, right now, I'm developing an ulcer, and it's all your fault," he grouched.

"Now Greg, you can't go blaming all your problems on me."

"Little sister, I work for the United States Government. Not much happens, without us knowing about it," he sighed. "So, tell me what you two were doing on the McGreary yacht."

"I don't know what you're talking about," I denied.

"Is Barbie with you?"

I nodded, forgetting for a moment that he couldn't see me, then quickly added, "Yeah, hang on while I put you on speaker." After locating the speaker button on the unfamiliar phone, I somehow managed to turn up the volume. "Okay, you're on speaker," I announced once I had finished.

"Okay you two, talk," Greg grumbled.

Barbie sucked down half her glass before speaking. "There's not much to tell. We're just relaxing in our room and having a couple of drinks, aren't we Jessie?"

"Barbie, is that you?" Greg demanded.

"Hey cousin." She made a face. "How's the *real estate* business?"

Greg is an undercover FBI agent. That means that almost everyone, including Barbie, thinks he's a corporate real estate agent. I only found out that he worked for the FBI a few weeks ago, when he came to Seattle in official FBI capacity, to hunt down my ex-fiancé. He swore me to secrecy and, as far as I understand it, there are only a handful of other people, outside of the FBI, who know his real occupation. I guess that makes Greg something like a modern day superhero. He's a mild mannered, womanizing, real estate agent by reputation and a hot tempered, Rolaids popping, FBI agent in actuality.

"Booming, now tell me what's going on." You could hear the vexation in his voice.

"Well, the place is just beautiful! I have never seen skies so blue. And, the water, it's so clear that you can see straight through to the bottom, I swear." Barbie winked, causing me to stifle a giggle.

Greg took an audibly deep breath before loudly exhaling. When he spoke, it was slow and clear like he was speaking to a small child. "I saw the footage of the yacht. Jessie, you were driving that WaveRunner with Barbie on the back. Somehow, you two blew the damned thing up. I know it. You both know it. What I don't understand, is what you were doing on the yacht in the first place. Now, I am going to strongly suggest that you tell me everything, before someone else figures it out, and you two trouble makers end up in a Thai prison."

Barbie and I exchanged glances. She nodded her head.

With a sigh, I responded, "You're not gonna believe it."

"Try me." His voice was cold.

"Okay, but first let me say…"

"I know, it wasn't your fault. It never is." Greg finished my sentence for me.

Barbie laughed, as if that were funny. Making me wonder, what had she put in her drink?

I glared at her before finishing my drink, which was lacking whatever happy tonic Barbie had added to hers. Once the glass was down to the ice, I began the explanation. "Okay, we landed in Phuket Island this morning."

"The airport lost my luggage. All of it! Can you believe it?" Barbie interjected loudly.

"You haven't even been there a full day, and you two are already in trouble," Greg groaned.

Barbie and I traded guilty looks.

"When you say it like that it sounds bad." Barbie frowned into her drink before finishing it off.

I rolled my eyes at both of them. "After we checked into the resort, we decided to go down to the beach. We were happily sunning ourselves by the water, when Barbie saw a guy she just had to meet." I glared over at her. "This whole thing started when she forced me to go with her to say hello, using her middle school tricks."

"Jessie head butted a volleyball, knocked me down, and flashed her tata's to the whole beach. You should have been there. It was classic Jessie." Barbie grinned.

"Oh please! That's not what happened." I frowned at her. "My top got tangled up and…"

"Jesus, Jess!" Greg, interrupted. "Take me off of speaker. I'm getting an echo."

"Okay," I agreed, messing with Barbie's phone. "You're off speaker."

"First the airport and now the beach! What is wrong with you? It is seven o'clock in the morning. I walked into the office, and this nonsense was waiting for me. I haven't even had time to enjoy my coffee yet, because of you. My desk is piled high with paperwork from my last assignment. I need to get ready for my next assignment. In short, I have a long day ahead of me. Are you actively trying to make my life that much worse? Because, no one could cause as much trouble as you do on accident."

I glared at Barbie. "Like I was saying, it was an accident." I sighed, "Don't tell momma and daddy." I bit my lower lip. "Don't tell anyone."

"I won't tell mom and dad," he sighed. "They'll just blame me for not dragging you home like I was told. I should send someone out there to get you and bring you home," he muttered.

"Send the Wolfman!" Barbie grinned.

"Barbie? I thought you took me off speaker!" He groused.

"I tried, but I'm not used to Barbie's phone," I said with a shrug, forgetting that he couldn't see me. "Don't send the Wolfman, I mean Eric, after me. I'm not an errant teenager you know."

"Wolf, you're not still seeing him? He didn't tell me you two were still together," he said, almost to himself.

"What, you've talked to him?" I asked, a little too eagerly.

"Not for a couple of weeks. He's been out of town on a job, but he's supposed to come over and play poker tonight."

"Poker? I'm banished to the place that time forgot, and you two are poker buddies? I introduced you to him. You didn't even like each other," I muttered jealously.

"No, I didn't like the fact that he wanted to sleep with my little sister, and he didn't like my attitude." He paused, deep in thought. "Maybe I *should* send him after you two."

"You wouldn't dare!" My eyes were shooting daggers into the phone. If there was one person who could actually make me leave, it was Eric. He has his own army, his own plane, and plays by his own rules.

"Yeah, you should. Tell him to bring his trunks and a friend, a hot friend. I'm dying to meet the guy that's got Jessie's panties in a wad." Barbie grinned at me.

"No, no, no! I do not need a babysitter," I protested.

"Knowing you two, you'd probably get him shot or something. Then, I'd be out another wingman," Greg grumbled.

"A what? A wingman? Did you say wingman? You and Eric have been picking up girls together?" At his words, my eyes had widened. I could feel the color draining from my face. I didn't like the idea of Eric picking up other women. Why? I wasn't sure. I could work that out later.

"Well no, not yet anyway. Something happened shortly after he returned to Boston. It must have been urgent because he left in the middle of the poker game, and he was winning. Whatever it was, I guess he took care of it because he sent me a text yesterday, asking if we were playing tonight. I was planning to see if he wanted to join a group of us at the bar this weekend. My best wingman just got married. I could use a new one."

I narrowed my eyes, bit my lip, and hung up the phone.

Barbie's eyes widened in surprise. "Why did you do that?"

I let out a low growl, moving to throw the offensive device, lying silently in my hand, out of the open patio door.

"No!" Barbie shrieked snatching her phone from my fingers. "What you need, is another drink. Get one for me while you're at it."

Barbie's phone rang, just as I reached the bar.

144

"Greg, now's not a good time. She's gone crazy," she said into the phone. "Okay, if you're sure." Barbie put the phone on speakerphone. "Okay, you're on speaker."

"Jess, I'm sorry. I didn't realize you two were still seeing each other. Wolf hadn't said anything so… Anyway, I just assumed that since you were in Oklahoma and he was in Boston or wherever, that it was over." He sighed loudly, "I won't use him as my wingman, if it's going to cause a problem."

I knocked back a shot of Tequila. My eyes watered and my throat stung, but it was better than the pain of knowing that I meant so little to Eric that he hadn't even asked about me since we'd parted.

"I'm fine, Greg. We're not together." I frowned down at the Tequila bottle in my hand. Another shot had magically appeared in my glass. "I haven't heard from him since he left me in Oklahoma, three weeks ago. I was just surprised that you two had such a budding bromance."

"Do you want me to have him call you?" he asked, ignoring the disdain in my voice.

Barbie shot me a knowing look and joined me at the bar.

I sadly shook my head. "No, he's obviously not interested." I watched her pour us another round. What had happened to the one that I'd just had? "I just don't want to hear about him, okay?"

"I'm sorry Jess. I didn't know." He paused to change the subject. "Tell me how you two ended up on the McGreary yacht."

"Like I said, Barbie saw a guy on the beach. She wanted to meet him, so we thoroughly embarrassed ourselves as an introduction. Then, they invited us to go on a cruise." I shook my head at the memory.

"What were their names?" he asked.

Barbie spoke up, "The red headed brothers were Seamus and Tad McGreary. Amos and Shaun O'Grady were their cousins. Amos is the hottie that started this mess. I could sink my teeth into that…"

"O'Grady?" he asked in surprise.

"After we introduced ourselves, they told us they were O'Grady's from Dublin. We all agreed that we must be related." I paused wandering if we had stupid written across our foreheads. "But, I think they were lying about being O'Grady's. I think they just wanted to win our trust, so we would go with them."

Greg was quiet, I could almost hear him thinking. "What happened after that?"

"Like we said, they invited us to go on a cruise on their yacht. Normally, we wouldn't take off with a bunch of guys we don't know, but since they were family, we agreed," Barbie explained.

I gave Barbie a 'You've got to be kidding' look. We both knew that it was nothing unusual for her to go off with a guy she doesn't know. She just shrugged and rolled her eyes at me.

I heard Greg groan. "You two took off with four strange men because they said they had the same last name as you?"

"When you say it like that, it sounds pretty stupid." I glared at Barbie.

She knew who that comment was aimed at and coolly met my gaze without responding.

Greg sighed, "It doesn't just sound stupid." He took a moment to calm himself before continuing. "Okay, that explains what you were doing on the yacht, but how and why did you blow it up?"

Barbie and I exchanged glances.

I asked, "Would you believe it was an accident?"

"I can't believe you two are allowed to walk around without an armed guard," he grumbled.

"They led us into a room off the main deck, to have a drink and celebrate being cousins or something like that. Just as we got there, they got called away. They said they'd be right back." Barbie explained.

"I was already feeling uncomfortable. While waiting, we looked out the window onto the deck to see some girls and a guy having a four way," I admitted.

Barbie jumped in, "That's when Jessie found the bowl of cocaine."

"Cocaine?" Greg asked.

"Yeah, I tasted it. It was definitely cocaine," Barbie verified.

"You tasted it? Don't tell anyone else that. I don't even want to know how you know what coke tastes like," he grumbled.

"Anyway," I interrupted, knowing her ex's drug habit was a sore spot for Barbie. "I had to pee so I opened the door to the bathroom. It was filled with more coke. The whole room!" I shook my head, remembering the neat brown packages stacked on top of each other until they filled even the smallest space.

She nodded, "That's when we started to think that we'd made a bad decision and should probably get out of there."

"It took you that long?" Greg asked with disdain.

"In my defense, I never wanted to go in the first place. This whole thing was Barbie's idea. I wanted to lounge on the beach and drink Fuck-it punch." I glared at Barbie.

"I told you I was sorry." She glared back.

"So, how did you end up blowing up the yacht?" Greg interrupted what had become a recurring argument.

"Well, we started to leave the room. Outside the door, there were guys talking about how they were going to get us high, then torture us to find out what happened to some jewel that they said Jess stole, which she says she knows nothing about." Barbie explained, without emotion.

"I don't!" I glared at her. "Back to the facts, we didn't want to turn into coke head prostitutes or end up dead, so we got off the boat as quickly as we could."

Greg whistled. "I don't know how you two stumble into these messes."

I shook my head. "Me neither."

"As we were leaving, Seamus showed up and started shooting at us over the railing. I pulled a couple of flares off of the little floating dock that was set up next to the yacht, lit them with a lighter that I found in the room where the coke was, and threw them at Seamus on the yacht," Barbie added.

"Why?" Greg asked.

"He was shooting at us," Barbie stated. "I had to do something."

"Of course you did," he was mocking us. "How many flares did you throw?"

"Four or five, I lost count." She gave me a smug look. "Only one landed below deck, the rest went straight to the target, Seamus."

"After we got out of range, we heard a loud noise, and the boat exploded," I finished the story.

Greg paused before asking, "Why did you leave the scene?"

"We thought we'd get blamed," I frowned.

"I wonder why you would think that," Greg said sarcastically.

"We didn't mean to blow anything up. They were flares, probably. We were just trying to leave, and then he shot at us, with a gun. Are we going to get arrested and go to jail?" I asked nervously. "I don't want to die in a Taiwanese jail."

"Don't worry. I've got a friend at the CIA who can take care of this. I just need to make a few phone calls. It shouldn't be a problem. They may have to send someone out to take your statement.

I'll let you know." He paused before adding, "In the meantime, stay out of trouble."

Barbie nodded, "We promise."

"Greg, thanks." I hesitated a moment before saying, "Wait! Don't hang up!"

"Don't tell me there's more," Greg sounded defeated.

"No, it's just…um…do me a favor. Don't tell Eric that I...um…well…asked, miss...no…like….no… I don't know," I stammered.

"I feel like I'm back in middle school again," Greg said, as the line went dead.

We sat staring at each other before I asked Barbie, "What time is it?"

"I don't know anymore. All I know is, it's been a day." Barbie frowned down into her empty glass.

"A horrible day. Well, my body says its bedtime. So, I'm going to bed. Maybe we'll wake up tomorrow to find out that today was just a bad dream." Unceremoniously setting my glass down, I headed for my room.

"Good call," Barbie agreed as I disappeared into my room.

Eleven

The alarm at my bedside went off, waking me just as the sun was emerging over the horizon. Gazing at the bright orb glistening off the water, I considered rousing Barbie. No, she had been very clear that she didn't want to get up to run. After pulling my hair into a quick ponytail, I dressed in blue running shorts, a white tank, and my seldom used running shoes with the pink flower on the side. Once I was dressed and ready, I considered going back to bed. A quick look at my too tight waistband was all the motivation I needed. Instead, I chugged a glass of water and headed to the beach.

I meant it when I said that I wanted my body back. I needed to get back in shape. I had begun to realize that my self-esteem and confidence were linked to my appearance. Right now, I didn't like what I saw in the mirror. If I wanted *me* back, I had to be happy with the girl on the other side of the looking glass.

Except for a handful of early risers like myself, the beach was deserted. I started off with a jog, thinking that things were working out even better than I had hoped for.

"I'm not as out of shape as I thought," I said to the mostly empty beach.

It wasn't long before I was full speed, running through the salty surf, with the wind in my hair, and sea gulls calling out encouragement behind me. My mind was blank. I was at one with the sea.

While dodging a pile of seaweed, my right foot slid through the sand, taking the rest of me for an impromptu swim. The cool ocean waves were a welcome relief for my sweaty body. With a giggle, I let myself float in the surf, taking a short break from my run.

"I just need to find a bunch of money and move here," I said to the surrounding waves.

Minutes later, I found myself moving rapidly away from the beach, the currents threatening to pull me under. Realizing the danger, my eyes widened. With a deep breath, I attempted to free myself from the rip tide that had claimed me. What had I read about rip tides? They can be big and people die in them. With renewed effort, I pushed against the tide that was intent on carrying me out to sea.

"Help!" I called out to the handful of early morning beachgoers, unsure if they would hear me over the crashing waves. Just as I was tiring, a strong arm grasped me under my chest.

"Quit struggling, before you drown us both," a deep voice said from behind me. "We're going to swim parallel to the shore, until we're free of the rip."

I struggled to turn, hoping for a glimpse of the man who had braved the currents to help me.

"Don't worry," he assured me, mistaking my struggles for fear. "I used to lifeguard in Southern California. Rip tides are pretty common there."

"Okay," I nodded, the salt water I had already swallowed making it hard to form any other words.

Once we reached the shore, I finally got a glimpse of my rescuer. He was shorter than me, but much more muscular, with gleaming ebony skin, and kind eyes. Helping me clear of the water's edge, he took a moment to be sure that I wasn't injured. Despite my violently coughing up sea water, he didn't appear to be concerned.

"You'll be fine. You've just swallowed a little too much of the ocean. Next time, be more careful. And remember, the rip can't hurt you if you don't let it. Swim along the beach until you're free of it, like we just did. Don't fight against it."

I nodded my understanding, saying, "Thank you."

"No problem. I'm just glad I was here to help," he said with a smile.

With a wave, I headed back to the resort. I'd had enough of the beach for one day. Half an hour later, I stumbled back into the hotel room, heading for the kitchen and a glass of OJ. Looking at the time, I wondered if I should wake Barbie.

"Why yes, I did actually go. No, it wasn't as uneventful as one could hope, but... You're doing it again." I sighed. "I need more friends or better conversationalists as friends or just friends who get out of bed." I shook my head. "You have got to stop talking to yourself," I said, turning to the refrigerator.

The all but empty refrigerator reminded me that I was on vacation with Barbie. I couldn't pick someone to travel with who cooks or at least buys food for me to cook? The only thing looking back at me was some leftover soda and sandwiches from yesterday. We hadn't bought any juice. We hadn't bought milk. We hadn't bought cereal, lunchmeat, or bread. We hadn't bought anything. I let out a long sigh as I grabbed my room key and purse from the counter.

It was almost two hours later when I stumbled back into the suite with three bags of groceries. I carefully unloaded the milk, juice, carrots, celery, yogurt, apples, bananas, and other fruits that I wasn't sure I recognized, but was willing to try. Now, it was time for breakfast. I ate my yogurt and banana while fantasizing about a stack of pancakes, eggs, and bacon, dripping with sugary syrup. When I was done, I washed it down with a glass of OJ, pretending it was a big thick glass of chocolate milk. Barbie wandered in just as I was finishing my breakfast.

With a confused look, she asked, "What are you doing?"

"Eating breakfast," I replied just before swallowing the last gulp of juice from my glass.

"Breakfast?" The confused look waited around a moment before evaporating into a suspicious frown. "Breakfast sounds like a good idea. What are we having?"

I pointed to the refrigerator knowing she wouldn't approve of my healthy diet shopping spree. Cautiously, she pulled open the refrigerator door. Her face fell as she surveyed its contents.

"I'm on a diet," I said, with a shrug.

"But, I'm not." She frowned into the refrigerator as she warily selected a fat free yogurt.

"I know, but you know how diets work. If there's anything else in the house you'll eat it, even if you don't like it, just because you're not supposed to." I poked at my muffin top. "I have got to get rid of this thing."

She contemplated the contents of the refrigerator again, looked me up and down, then sighed. "Let me get changed, and we'll get started."

I rolled my eyes at her. "It's almost ten o'clock. While you lounged in bed all morning, I was up at the crack of dawn running the beach. After I finished my run, I went to the grocery store. I would have never found what I wanted without the shuttle driver; that guy is incredible. Now that I've had my breakfast of low fat, low cal good for you food, I'm going take a nap on the terrace."

"No, you're not. I refuse to eat health food for the remainder of this vacation. Let me get changed and we'll hit the gym." She disappeared down the hall.

I frowned down at my belly, why not? A little more exercise certainly wouldn't hurt me. Since I had already had my run today, I could skip the treadmill, and go straight to the weight machines. Barbie came out about ten minutes later wearing a high ponytail, black spandex capris, a hot pink sports bra that paired with her surgically enhanced DD's left little to the imagination, and a pair of gray and hot pink Nike's. She looked like her namesake. Looking down at my belly pudge, I couldn't help but feel second-rate. If I'd known I was going on vacation with Exercise Barbie, I would have kept my body in better shape.

She shot me a knowing look. "Don't worry, you just need to re-tighten some muscles and lose about five pounds of fat. After that, you'll look great. Fortunately, it's only been a couple of weeks. I'll have you looking like me in three days."

Frowning my concern, I followed her out the door. "Three days? What are you gonna to do, surgery?"

With a laugh bordering on sadism, she stepped into the elevator. "No. CrossFit."

"CrossFit? I've heard of it, but I've never tried it. It sounds a little...intense." I winced at the idea.

"It's a lot intense, if you do it right. Lucky for you, I'm a level one CrossFit trainer, certified to mold you into a sex goddess like myself," Barbie said, with a smile that served to fuel my misgivings.

"Since when are you a CrossFit trainer?" I asked, as I followed her into the resort's gym.

"I've been doing CrossFit for about four years now. About a year and a half ago, I decided to get certified as a trainer. It's fun, and I'm in phenomenal shape. I'm thinking about making a DVD." She frowned as she glanced around the traditionally outfitted gym. "Let's see what we can do with this."

As Barbie walked around the gym, planning our workout, she began to explain the fundamentals of CrossFit to me, causing my anxiety to intensify. This did not sound like fun. It sounded like some kind of crazy torture thing. Unfortunately, I was the victim.

Once Barbie had finished her assessment of the gym, we began our workout with some yoga stretches. By the time we'd finished warming up, Barbie had a whole class, instead of just me, trying to keep up with her. After about ten minutes of loosening up, we started the morning's circuit with some fancy sit-ups and regulation push-ups.

"I'm sorry for doubting you, cousin. This isn't nearly as bad as I expected," I said between breaths, noting that Barbie hadn't broken a sweat yet as I wiped a stream of it from my forehead.

"I thought you'd like an easy warm up. Now, let's get to work!" Barbie grinned.

"Warm up? That was just the warm up?" I groaned.

"Of course. You didn't think we were just going to do a few boring exercises and call it a day. Did you?"

"Ummm..." I wanted to say yes, but my old friend pride wouldn't let me. "No, of course not. Let's do this," came out of my mouth instead.

"I knew you'd love CrossFit!"

Barbie's squeals made me want to grab my pride by the throat and strangle the life from it. While I was having a stern talk with pride, Barbie quickened the pace. This was unreal. I'd never exercised like this before. I wanted to die as we moved from deadlifts, to jumps, to body squats, to kettlebell lifts. This was obviously some kind of punishment for my whiny attitude the past few weeks. I wanted to quit, but my pride wouldn't let me.

My eyes silently begged the other vacationers, who had joined us in Barbie's torture workshop, for help. No one noticed. I considered crying, but needed all of my energy to keep up. Twenty minutes into the circuit, the contents of my meager breakfast unceremoniously erupted from my mouth. Fortunately, I made it to the trashcan, which was a step up for me these days. Immobilized with embarrassment, I was debating whether or not Barbie would notice if I slinked back to our rooms when a much older man came over and gave me a kind smile.

"This must be your first time." He put a kindly hand on my shoulder, leading me back to my spot. "Don't worry about it. We've all been there. Don't let it beat you. You can finish this," he said, with an encouraging pat to my shoulder.

I felt a single tear slide from my lashes as he steadfastly walked me back to my spot, all the while spouting encouragement. Then, like a bad dream or a flash mob, the rest of the group began to cheer me on. I couldn't help but sigh. Everyone would know that I had quit if I left now. What did it matter if they knew I quit; that what seemed easy or at least manageable to them was too much for me? They were strangers, people I had never seen before and probably would never see again.

With a sinking feeling in my stomach, I knew that for some unexplainable reason it did matter. Pride was back, and she had made me her bitch. Just like that I was peer pressured into finishing the circuit. Resolutely, I slid into position, willing my body to perform the duties requested of it by the sadistic woman in pink standing at the front of the group. My only pleasure came from knowing that I wasn't the only one suffering, just the worst off.

As soon as I heard Barbie call a halt, I collapsed into a heap on the mat, unable to move. It had been thirty minutes of sheer hell and public humiliation. The others helped put the gym back together. Not me. I was busy laying in the middle of the cold gym floor, in a pool of my own sweat, gasping for air, while desperately trying to catch my breath, wondering if I was going to die.

Barbie looked unfazed by the workout as she discussed the morning's routine with her new admirers. How could they stand, let alone speak, after that? I tried, unsuccessfully, to protest as I heard Barbie invite them to join us later tonight for another workout and again tomorrow. If I was going to die, I wanted to do it before tonight. I wasn't sure that I could handle another workout like the one that I had just experienced.

Once everyone had stumbled out of the gym, Barbie half carried me off of the mat, out the door, and down the hall. It took me a while, but with her help I was able to painfully limp from the elevator, down the hall, and into our suite.

"So, what did you think?" she asked, after guzzling a quart of water.

Laying half on the counter and half on the floor, I gulped my own glass of water. "It was hell, pure hell." I gasped. "Why did you do that to me? Do you hate me? I *WILL* get even you know. Someday, somehow, when you least expect it." All I could think about was revenge; I wanted the perky sadist in pink to feel my pain.

She laughed, watching me stumble towards a chair. "You've been saying that since elementary school. Don't worry, a few more workouts and you'll come to love it. Now, let's get showered and hit the beach."

Twelve

After my shower, I felt almost human again, except for the part where I could barely walk. I don't know how I managed to get my swimsuit on or hobble down to the crowded beach, but I did. We found a couple of empty chairs resting beneath the shade of a white umbrella next to the water. Barbie watched, without sympathy, as I practically fell into one.

"Don't you think that you're being just a little melodramatic?" Barbie asked.

"You don't understand how much I hurt right now." I groaned. "My body is broken, irreparably broken."

Barbie rolled her eyes as she motioned for a server. "I know just what you need to cheer you up, lunch!"

"Lunch? I'm dying, and you want lunch?"

"You're not dying." She rolled her eyes. "I intentionally took it easy on you."

Jenn Brink

"That was easy?" I moaned, worried about a repeat performance.

As the server approached our resting spot, Barbie greeted him with a huge smile. "Two margaritas on the rocks, don't skimp on the Tequila or salt. We're in room three-fifteen, charge it to the room," Handing him a large bill and shooting him a big smile, she added, "Keep the drinks flowing, and we'll be your best friends."

With a smile and a nod he pocketed the bill, heading towards the hotel.

"A margarita! I can't drink that. I can't drink anything but water. I'm on a diet." I frowned down at my belly bulge.

"Yes you can, drama queen." Barbie gave me an annoyed look. "You burned plenty of calories between your run and the CrossFit this morning. And, don't forget, we're going work out some more this evening. You're going to need to take in more calories if you expect to keep up."

"Oh, why are you trying to kill me?" I groaned. "Haven't I been through enough? I can barely move, let alone exercise."

She gave me a look that implied I wasn't being very bright. "That's what the Tequila's for. After a little of the hard stuff, you won't even feel those muscle aches."

"A little of the hard stuff, and I won't be able to exercise for a whole different reason. Barbie, that is the worst idea you've ever had," I groaned.

"Fine." She shrugged. "Don't drink it."

162

"Oh, you know I'm gonna drink it. At this point it's medicinal." I closed my eyes. "But, you may have to cancel class tonight."

She laughed. "Nope, you're just going to have to tell your body who's calling the shots around here."

"May I sit?"

We looked up to see an older man standing over us. His speech was slow, deliberate, and laced with an unfamiliar accent. Without waiting for a response, he carefully lowered himself to the edge of an empty chair, as if he was carrying the weight of the world.

Barbie and I exchanged surprised glances. Neither of us had noticed his approach.

"Of course." Barbie gave me a look that asked, *'Do we know this guy?'* "Is there something we can help you with?"

The stranger had a thin wiry build, unnaturally pale white skin, thinning white blonde hair peeking out from a large hat, and deeply hooded, colorless eyes. He looked uncomfortable in his ill-fitting khaki shorts and cream colored linen shirt. Even though he appeared to be harmless, his presence was causing the hair to stand up on the back of my neck. Patiently, we watched as he dug a cigarette and lighter from his shirt pocket.

Once his treasures were in hand, he looked up asking, "Do you mind?"

Barbie shook her head. "No, not at all."

With a frown, I silently added that I minded, but it was too late to protest.

"Thank you." He gave us a thin lipped smile resembling a grimace. "I apologize for the interruption. I will be brief."

"Thank you," Barbie said, as if creepy strangers sat down to chat with her every day. "What can we do for you?"

"I am investigator with Interpol," he began. "I wish to speak about the incident from yesterday evening time." He spoke as if it was a great effort to use English.

Barbie nodded warily. "Greg said someone may need to talk to us."

Frowning, I bit my lower lip. Greg had also said that he would let us know if someone else needed to take our statement. Unless I had missed something, he hadn't done any such thing.

"Yes, I am that someone." His lips turned up into what I could only guess was supposed to be a smile, but looked more like he had to go to the bathroom, badly. "What can you tell me about the...incident?"

Barbie shrugged. "Like we told Greg, they told us that they were long lost cousins and invited us to take a cruise on their yacht. We quickly realized it was a bad idea and left. Then, the boat exploded."

He sat quietly, processing the information that Barbie had just given him. "Of course, of course. Did you give them...anything?"

Barbie and I traded confused looks before simultaneously shaking our heads.

"Perhaps in trade for…cocaine?" he prompted.

"No!" I exclaimed. "We didn't even keep the WaveRunner. We left it parked at the beach with the key in the ignition and turned ourselves in, as soon as we realized the police were looking for us. We don't want any trouble, we're on vacation."

By 'turned ourselves in' I meant that we admitted our involvement to Greg, after he called about it. It was almost the same thing. The stranger turned his focus to Barbie. She nodded her head in support of my statement.

After a moment of quiet thought, the man asked, "You have spoken with the authorities?"

"Yes." I narrowed my eyes, giving him a suspicious look. "Isn't that the reason you're here, to take our statement, in person?"

"Yes, of course, the statement. It is what I am here for." He paused a moment, looked me in the eye, and said, "You know a man by the name of Ivan Burkov. You will say where to find him."

Barbie and I shared a confused look.

"Was he on the boat?" I asked.

"I am understanding that he gave you," his colorless eyes bored into mine, "an item. Yes, to keep safe, for him. I am in need of that…item." His voice had turned sinister, causing my bad guy radar to scream *RUN*!

With a confidence I didn't feel, I shook my head. "I'm sorry, I don't know any Ivan. Even if I did, no one has given me anything."

"Do not play with me." His voice was harsh and cold. "We know that Ivan passed it to you, for safe keeping, some days ago. Now, you have brought it to Thailand, to him. It is beautiful and deadly. The rightful owner wants it," he paused before adding, "returned."

The surprise I was feeling must have been evident to everyone on the beach.

"Listen, I don't know this Ivan guy or have whatever it is your looking for. We're on vacation. Anyway, you said you were investigating the yacht blowing up." I said, impressed at my ability to hide the fear that was building in the pit of my stomach.

The stranger looked at me with an attitude matching his colorless eyes. "I must be mistaken. It seems that everything is in order. Thank you, for your time." He abruptly rose from the chair while speaking.

"Wait, you didn't show us a badge, or tell us your name. Do you have any identification?" I asked him.

"I am sorry. I am undercover, and do not carry such things. Good day." He nodded towards us in cold dismissal.

As we watched him walk away, Barbie and I exchanged glances.

"Did that seem weird to you?" I asked, replaying the conversation in my head.

Barbie nodded her agreement. "Uh huh." After a moment, she said, "Jess, you'd tell me if you had it, wouldn't you? I mean, if you had it, I wouldn't judge you." She paused, then said, "I wouldn't." Earnestly, she looked me in the eye.

"Of course I would! But, I don't." Unable to drop the subject, I said, "I'm sure it's just some sort of mistaken identity. But, maybe we should call Greg."

"Mistaken identity," she said to herself. "I'm sure you're right." She relaxed into her chair.

"We'll call Greg later tonight. Right now, it's the middle of the night in Boston, he's probably sleeping," I said, more to myself than to Barbie.

Barbie nodded. "I should make some calls too."

Thirteen

"What did you do now?" The voice on the other end of the line grouched.

"Nothing," I rolled my eyes at the phone in my hand. "We had a visit by some weird Interpol investigator today. We talked it over and decided that we should let you know."

"You had a what?" I could hear the confusion in Greg's voice.

"You know, the international police, Interpol."

"I know what Interpol is. Are you saying that you talked to an Interpol investigator, about the McGreary situation?" he asked.

"Yes," I answered.

"What made you think he was with Interpol?" His voice told me that I had his complete attention now.

"That's what he told us." I shrugged into the receiver.

"Did he show you a badge? What was his name?" There was an urgency to Greg's voice that hadn't been there before.

"He said he was undercover so he doesn't carry a badge. He didn't give us a name, either." I mutely cursed myself for not getting his name. "Your friend can tell you his name. He sent him, right?" My voice begged him to say yes.

"Jess, Interpol doesn't investigate crime. The local authorities do that." His words and voice lacked the reassurance I desperately wanted to hear.

"They don't?" I asked in a quiet voice, while my stomach flip flopped. I really hate it when my gut is right.

"No, Interpol helps the local agencies with specific types of crimes. Although they have been an active part of the McGreary investigation for years, they would not have sent an agent to talk to you about it. What did the guy look like? What did he say he wanted? Tell me everything." He had his cop voice on.

"He was thin, but muscular, and really pale, with almost colorless eyes, and he spoke with a strange accent. He was creepy." I cringed at the memory of those colorless eyes boring into me.

"The Albino." Greg sounded surprised. "What would he want with McGreary?"

"I don't know, but I saw him standing on the beach when we rode to the yacht with McGreary. I remember because it looked like he was watching us. I know I hadn't mentioned it before. I thought it was just me being paranoid."

"And today, he asked you about McGreary?" Greg asked.

"Not really. He didn't seem very interested in McGreary or the yacht, even though that's what he said he was there to talk about. He was more interested in some guy named Ivan something or other. He was sure that the guy had given me something. He really wanted it."

"What?" he asked.

I shrugged, then remembered he couldn't see me. "I don't know. That's all he said. When I told him I didn't know the guy or have anything, he seemed angry. Then, he left. The whole thing seemed odd. Honestly, I called you so you could tell me I'm just being paranoid."

"This time, I don't think you're being paranoid. I'll call my friend at the CIA and see if he knows anything. Until then, stay away from the Albino," he commanded.

"If he's not Interpol who is he?" I asked.

"An international thug. If you see him go directly to the police. Don't let his appearance fool you Jess, he's deadly. Stay away from him. And please, try to stay out of trouble."

Fear caught in my throat, blocking my words. *Deadly?* I'd had enough of deadly to last me a lifetime. After a moment, I realized that there was no one on the other line. Greg had hung up. I was alone in the room, and somewhere out there, a deadly international thug wanted something that I didn't have. Something he was convinced that I did have. Where was Barbie with our food, and why do these things keep happening to me?

Fourteen

Randall was carefully laying me on the couch in our suite after the second CrossFit workout of the day. Meanwhile, his wife, Hillary bustled around the room making sure that I had everything I needed. Randall and Hillary were enjoying their second honeymoon while celebrating their fortieth wedding anniversary. We had met them about an hour ago, and they were now our surrogate parents.

They had heard about the CrossFit class from another couple who had been in the morning class. Halfway through the circuit, my muscles had given out on me, causing yet another embarrassing scene in my life. When I collapsed on the floor with a shriek, Hillary had volunteered her husband to carry me up to our rooms, which were conveniently located down the hall from theirs.

"Are you sure you don't want someone to stay with you, dear?" Hillary asked me, for the fifth time, as she fluffed the pillow under my head.

171

"No, thank you. I just want to laze on the couch, and watch a little TV." While I die, I added silently.

"I can stay," Barbie offered.

I shook my head, willing them all to leave me to die in peace. "No! Just go, and enjoy drinks with the class. I'll be fine, really."

"Are you sure?" Barbie asked.

"Yes." I sighed my frustration. "Go, have fun."

"If you're sure you're sure…" Barbie gave me a guilty look.

"I'm sure." My words were exasperated.

"Okay then, I'm off to the shower," Barbie called over her shoulder, as she disappeared down the hall.

Randall looked at his watch. "Let's go dear. Jessie just needs to rest her muscles. She'll be fine by morning, a little sore, but fine."

I smiled up at them. "Doctor Randall's right Hillary, I just overdid it a little. I'm feeling better already," I lied through the pain.

She gave me a motherly look. "I don't know. Maybe, we should stay for just a little longer. I hate to leave you here all by yourself and not able to get up. What if you need something? What if you need to go to the little girl's room?"

"No! Really, you've both done enough. I appreciate the help. I'll be fine. I'll probably just take a nap in a minute," I insisted.

"Sec Hillary, she'll be fine. She doesn't want us sitting around mother henning her. Now, let's go get changed so we can meet everyone downstairs." Randall walked towards the door.

"She's just saying that because she doesn't want us to feel obligated. Look at her, the poor dear needs us. We can't leave her alone, not like this." She gave him a pleading look across the room.

Randall sighed in resignation as I closed my eyes in defeat. There was no way to politely get rid of them, and I couldn't bring myself to be rude. They were just too nice.

Ignoring my plea to be left alone, Hillary scurried off to the kitchen to make me a snack. I could hear her banging around, opening and closing cabinets, the refrigerator, and the freezer.

Easing himself into the nearest chair, Randall gave me an apologetic look, and said, "She means well. Do you want to watch the game?"

With a confused glance at the television, I asked, "What game?"

His face lit up, "You haven't seen the game? It's great!" Grasping the channel changer, he began to flip through the channels, searching for the show he wanted. "They have three teams of one and the object, I'm not sure what the object is, other than to win. There aren't any subtitles. But, it's great! Oh, here it is!"

The television showed three contestants in brightly colored jumpsuits standing quietly in front of a man in a dark suit. Since I don't speak Thai, and there were no subtitles, it was hard to follow. Despite the language barrier, it sucked me in. Before I knew it, the show was over and I had eaten half a sandwich.

173

I looked down at my sandwich, and asked, "Where did this come from?"

Hillary looked up from her chair and smiled. "You girls don't have anything but yogurt, fruit, and alcohol in your kitchen. I snuck down the hall and made you a quick sandwich and a glass of milk."

"Oh," I said, looking down at the sandwich in my hand. "Thank you. I didn't even know I was hungry."

She smiled, and said, "You're welcome dear."

"I'm ready!" Barbie called out as she entered the living room.

Hillary looked torn, "I'm sorry, but we can't possibly leave Jessie here all alone."

I nodded, "You can. I mean, I'll be alright. I have my sandwich," I held up the half eaten sandwich for everyone to see, "television, and milk... Honestly, I'll be fine." I gave them a reassuring smile.

"Oh, no dear. We don't mind, do we Randall?" She gave him a look that didn't give him the option of contradicting her.

"No, of course not," Randall sighed.

"Hillary, this is your second honeymoon!" Barbie admonished. "You cannot spend it mothering Jessie."

"Oh, it's not a problem," Hillary insisted.

"Not for you." Barbie gave her a sly look. "But, what about your devoted husband? After all these years of commitment, only to you. He's worked long hours, sacrificing time he would have liked to spend with the kids and grandkids, to take care of you. He retires, like

174

you asked, and brings you here as a celebration of his love, to you. And, how do you repay him? By putting someone else's needs above his?"

"It's not like that," Hillary protested, with a guilt-ridden look.

"Of course it isn't dear," Randall said. "We can always go out tomorrow."

"No," Barbie shook her head. "We can't let you put your relationship in jeopardy for us. How do you think we'll feel if you two end up divorcing, after all these years of a happy marriage? It would be our fault."

I nodded my head in agreement, "Barbie's right. You should listen to her. She's been divorced more than anyone I know."

Barbie nodded, "It's true. You never know what little thing can fracture your relationship."

"Randall?" Hillary asked, worry across her face.

He smiled, and said, "Honey, I love you. Nothing could change that, but I would like to go out with the class. Jessie will be fine."

"Okay, let's go then." She smiled at me, and said, "If you need anything, just call down to the bar, dear."

With a smile, I said, "I will. You kids have fun!"

As Barbie followed them out the door, she turned and winked.

Fifteen

It had been four days since we stepped off of the plane and onto the island. My CrossFit pains had dulled to a tolerable ache. The past two days, there had been no sign of fake Interpol investigators or sex starved Irishmen demanding stuff I didn't have. We were happily in full vacation mode.

The majority of our time had been spent sunning ourselves on the beach, shopping our way through the local towns, and partaking in the nightlife. Currently, we were lounging on the beach, after spending the morning parasailing in the cove with a couple of cute guys we had met at a local bar the night before. Enjoying the contenting feel of the sun's rays warming my back, I debated whether or not to move. My thirst won out, causing me to languorously roll over. I picked up my cup and peered hopefully inside. There was a little bit left. I took a sip of ice cold water from the glass of melted ice beside me. This is what I came for. No wonder they call it paradise. A furtive glance down at my waist made me smile.

Pointing at my gut, I glanced over at Barbie. "All that running and working out in the gym seems to be working. My belly doesn't look so jelly anymore."

Barbie glanced over at me. "Just don't quit again when you get home."

I bit my lip, considering my words before I spoke. "I'm thinking about not going home."

"What? Where are you going to go?" She gave me a panicked look. "You're not planning to stay here are you? Because, I don't think that would go over well with the family. They'll all blame me, and then everyone will be mad at me, and then where will I go at Christmas? I love Christmas!"

"You are such a drama queen." I rolled my eyes. "No, I'm not planning to stay here. It wouldn't be any fun lying on the beach by myself. Anyway, I'd need a job. I have a feeling it would be pretty hard to get hired to do anything here since I'm not a five foot nothing size zero."

"So where are you going to go? It's not going to affect my holiday plans is it? I've never been single over the holidays before. What will I do? Where will I go if you get me banned by the O'Grady's and the Hart's? You're going to ruin Thanksgiving and Christmas!" she shrieked in a full-fledged panic.

Willing the stress to leave my body, I leaned back, closing my eyes. "I don't know. I could go to Boston and stay with Greg. He knows a lot of people. I'll bet he could help me get a job." I frowned, then said, "No. I'd end up running into Eric on poker night. That would be awkward. I could go to New York or…"

Barbie jumped up with a shriek. "Really, you would move to New York? You could live with me! It would be so great!"

"Maybe." I bit my lip, knowing it would only be great until she met a new guy, then I would be the third wheel. "I don't know. I just don't think that I want to stay in Oklahoma anymore. I'm afraid I'm gonna come home one day to find the preacher in the backyard with the whole town waiting to marry me off to some bubba who lives down the road from my parents. In five years, I'll be fat with a herd of kids hanging on me, and a husband that I'd rather shoot than sleep with." I shuddered at the thought.

"That sounds horrible." Barbie wrinkled her nose at me. "You can come live with me. It would be so much fun to be roomies." She giggled with excitement.

"Until you found husband number… How many times *have* you been married?" I asked.

"Oh, shut up." She glared at me.

"I don't know. I could just close my eyes, put my finger on the map, and let that be my new home." I sighed.

"You can't afford it." Barbie shook her head. "You need a place to live until you find a job. That's going to you cost more than you have in your checking account. Besides, with your luck, you'd end up someplace cold and miserable."

I narrowed my eyes at her. "You know, Barbie, this is why nobody likes you. You're a dream crusher."

She laughed at me, and said, "Whatever, everybody likes me. You're just pissy because you know it's true."

I sighed. "Yeah, my life sucks."

Barbie suddenly sat up in her chair and shrieked so loudly that people up and down the beach turned to look. "Ohmigod! Do you see him?"

I rose up, looking around, trying to see what Barbie saw. There were a lot of men on the beach in front of us and even more on the water. My eyes followed Barbie's finger, but I still couldn't tell which him she was all worked up over. There were just too many possibilities to choose from. It didn't help that Barbie's tastes in men are very accepting. As far as I can tell, her only qualifiers are male, legal, and preferably rich.

"Can you be a little more specific about which him I'm supposed to be seeing?" I motioned to the crowded beach.

"Him!" She hissed, pointing to the left and down the beach. "The swarthy beach god walking this way. That, cousin, is my future ex-husband."

I pulled my sunglasses down to get a better look. He was walking by himself, wearing brown leather sandals with a pair of form fitting, short, black, European style, swim trunks that would have looked indecent on most men. Sodden dark hair dripped tantalizingly down his golden brown neck and shoulders to his muscular chest and

179

rock hard abs. His only visible adornment was a braided leather necklace with a metal dart pendant, resting sensually against his collarbone.

I raised an eyebrow at Barbie before sliding my sunglasses back over my eyes and leaning back into my chair.

"Barb, wipe the drool off your face. Sure, he's hot. But, do you really want to get into a relationship this soon? I mean, you just got divorced. Besides, your last future ex-husband turned out to be a sleazy bad guy, who wanted to drug us up so he could torture us about some fictional jewel, then turn us into sex slaves on the company yacht or worse."

Barbie didn't take her eyes off of the man walking down the beach. "Oh, I'm sure."

Glancing his way again, I couldn't help but give him a closer look. Removing my sunglasses, I leaned forward. "Wait a minute, I think I know that guy."

"If you tell me that it's your mysterious Wolfman, I am going to hurt you." She fluffed her hair as she eyed the handsome stranger making his way up the beach.

"No," I sneered. "It's not Eric."

"Good, because if you tell me that you see that man, or his men one more time, I swear I'm going to call him and tell him to get his hot ass over here so you'll shut up about him," she threatened.

I smiled at the thought of seeing Eric in a pair of tight European trunks, walking the beach… I shook my head, clearing the vivid mental picture from my brain. He didn't seem like the European swimwear type. That was too bad, I had really enjoyed the mental picture.

Barbie looked over at me. "Oh my god, you're thinking about him again! Aren't you?"

"No." My cheeks blushed crimson as I denied the accusation.

"You are too." She narrowed her eyes at me. "How do you expect to get over him if you keep thinking about him?"

"I don't know." I sighed. "I may need a support group."

She frowned at me. "It's really not that difficult to get a man out of your head. You just have to focus on all the things you don't like about him. You'll start to see him in a negative way. Pretty soon you won't be interested anymore. One day, you'll suddenly realize that you're over him. It never hurts to spend some time with other guys who fawn all over you either."

I was willing to take her advice. If anyone knew how to get over a man, it was Barbie. There was only one problem.

"You don't understand. He's perfect. There's nothing that I don't like about him," I admitted dejectedly.

"What about his chauvinism? He wouldn't let you drive your own car. He's overprotective. He left his rent-a-thugs to spy on you all of the time. He's jealous. He got upset every time you talked to one of his men. That sounds like jealousy, and not the good kind. Let's see what else, oh…he hasn't so much as butt dialed you since he left you with your parents, but he's hanging out with your brother, playing poker. What about that?" she asked smugly.

Leave it to Barbie to keep a list. "Sure those things annoy me." I frowned, knowing she wouldn't like my next statement. "They're also a part of his charm. I've never had a guy refuse to let me have my way before. They usually fall over themselves trying to do and say what they think I want them to do and say. To be honest, it was damn sexy when he'd pick me up and set me in the passenger seat while we argued about who was driving." I smiled at the memory.

Barbie sighed in defeat. "You're not trying." She moved her gaze back towards the beach. "There is no way your Wolfman could be hotter than that dreamsicle walking this way."

I looked up, unable to not compare the two men. While we were talking, Barbie's dream guy had gotten closer. Abruptly, I sat up.

"Hey, I do know that guy!"

"Really?" Barbie blinked.

"Yeah, that's the guy I told you about from the airplane. It was dark the last time I saw him, and he was wearing more clothes." I gave him another look. "I'm almost positive it's him."

"The one that jumped the security line at the Oklahoma City airport, just to meet you?" she asked.

"Yes," I nodded distractedly.

"The one who told the stewardess that he was your husband so that the annoying girl sitting next to you would switch seats with him because he didn't get your name?" she frowned.

"Yeah, that one." He was close enough that I was sure now.

"The one that you talked to through the entire flight from Dallas to New York City?" she asked.

"That's the guy." I nodded in agreement.

"The one that you shared a cab with when you left LaGuardia. Then, he took you out for drinks on Fifth Avenue until two in the morning?" she asked.

"Yes, he's the one." This was getting annoying.

"The one that gave you a deep, sensual kiss that made you forget all about the Wolfman, and get naked with him in the coat closet?"

"No! That did not happen." I gave her a shocked look.

"If it had been me it would have." She licked her lips as he bent over to pick up a kid's Frisbee.

"Eww! Yuck! Gross! I think I just threw up in my mouth a little bit," I gagged.

"Tell me again why you didn't tap that? He is super yummy hot." She smiled while her eyes drank in the sight of him.

"Yes, he is hot, but...he's not. I mean, don't get me wrong, I liked him, but...he wasn't." I bit my lip, trying to put my feelings into words. "What I'm trying to say is, I was attracted to him, but at the same time I wasn't attracted to him. He was handsome, smart, funny,

183

and interesting, but…" I sighed again. "I don't know what I'm trying to say."

Barbie rolled her eyes. "I do. You're saying that, although you were attracted to him, it wasn't enough to make you forget the Wolfman."

I sighed. "I don't know. I guess that's it."

She gave me a pitying look. "Jessie, you're just hurting yourself. You've got to let him go. He's gone back to his life, and you aren't a part of it. You do know if he cared for you, he would have called, right?"

"Yeah, I know." I bit my lip to prevent a tear from welling up. "Don't worry, it's just a crush. I'll be fine."

Barbie sat quietly a minute before asking, "So, do you want him? You did see him first."

"I know, and he is hot." I shook my head, trying to figure out what my problem was. He really was gorgeous. I sighed, "I'm just not all that interested. I guess you're right. I'm still stuck on Eric."

A lot of good that was doing me. He seemed more interested in Greg. Maybe he was gay? No. He was definitely not gay. I knew that for a fact.

"Don't worry." I sighed. "I'll meet someone, when I'm ready. Right now," I paused, "I'm just not ready. I have more important things to worry about, like where am I going to live, and how am I going to pay my bills?"

"Well then, don't just sit there. Introduce us!" she demanded. "I don't have to worry about any of that stuff, and I'm not carrying around a bunch of emotional baggage like you."

"You've been married twenty times, how can you say you don't have emotional baggage?" I asked.

"Baggage doesn't suit me. I let the exes carry it around," she said, with a smile.

Feeling just a bit sorry for Random, I shrugged. "Why not?"

We stood up, slowly walking toward the water, timing it so that we just happened to cross paths.

He spoke first. "Jessie, I thought that was you." His smile was warm and friendly.

"Random, what are you doing here?" I asked conversationally.

He was still smiling down at me. "I was really hoping that I'd run into you."

"You were?" I couldn't help but smile back.

"Yes."

Before I could step away, Random put his hands on my shoulders, looked me up and down, then pulled me to him. His hands roamed my backside as I struggled out of the unexpected hug. With a frown, I noticed a mischievous twinkle glittering in his eyes.

"You left too soon the other night." He frowned. "I went to pay the bill. When I got back to the table, you were gone. I didn't even get to kiss you good-bye. You missed out." He paused, adding in a stage whisper, "I'm a great kisser."

My eyes searched out Barbie, hoping for a rescue, as I worked to disentangle myself from Random's overly ambitious and uninvited embrace.

He merely grinned at my discomfort before continuing to speak, "I didn't get your number, then I remembered that you said you were on your way to Phuket Island. So, I flew out; hoping that, if I wandered the beaches long enough, I would find you."

I didn't know what to say. He was coming on uncomfortably strong. "Oh, okay. You followed me here?" I stumbled over the words, and out of his embrace.

He shrugged. "Yes and no. I told you my grandfather has some property here. I pretty much live here, taking care of his investments, since he died." He smiled, his eyes twinkling in the sunlight. "I must admit, I was hoping to run into you, and here you are. I guess *chance* really is on my side," he said, with a grin.

Barbie pinched me.

"Ow!" I rubbed my arm. "This is Random Chance." I motioned to him.

She smiled at Random, and said, "It sure is."

I rolled my eyes. "Random, meet my cousin..."

"I know who you are," he interrupted.

Barbie and I looked at each other in confusion.

"You do?" I asked.

"Of course, I'm a big fan." His smile rivaled the sun. "This must be my lucky day."

"A fan of what?" Barbie asked, not even trying to hide her confusion.

He winked at Barbie. "Why, I'm a fan of you, Ms. Jons."

"Hey Random!" A couple of guys called out from down the beach.

Random turned away as Barbie and I traded confused looks.

"Over here, I want to introduce these two beautiful women to you," he yelled back. As the group of men neared, Random gestured back at us. "Guys, this is Jessie Hart and her cousin Jennifer Jons."

Barbie blinked her surprise as my mouth fell open. Random thought Barbie was Jennifer Jons, the movie star? I looked at the group of men fawning all over Barbie. One of them was even asking her to sign his chest. Why would Random and his friends think that Barbie was one of the most reclusive and sought after movie stars in Hollywood? I tilted my head to the side, focusing on my cousin as she forged the movie stars signature over some guy's chest hairs. She was eating it up, smiling and flirting with her new admirers.

I tried to remember exactly what Jennifer Jons looked like. She had starred in that movie a couple of months ago, what was it called? The one about the cop, that fell for the girl, who murdered her boyfriend. It had been an okay movie. I only remembered it because Jim had gone on and on about how sexy she was.

Once I had a mental picture, I carefully scrutinized Barbie's features. Her ocean wet hair was in its naturally wavy/curly state instead of straightened with a flat iron like she usually wore it, and her skin had been bronzed by liberal amounts of tanning oil and the sun, giving her a vaguely Mediterranean appearance. Tilting my head to the other side, I took an even closer look.

"I suppose she does kind of look like her. Why haven't I noticed it before?" I asked no one in particular, earning an odd look from a woman standing a little too close for comfort.

Well, that explained the deferential treatment we'd been getting the past few days. I had just thought that the people here were really nice. Someone said my name, reminding me that I hadn't been paying attention. Pasting on a smile, I turned my attention back to the others.

"That sounds like fun, we'll meet you there," Barbie was saying to Random.

"Great! We'll catch you babes later." He gave us a wink, then turned to leave.

"Yeah, we'll see you." I waved as Random and his group of friends strolled back down the beach.

Barbie was grinning like the Cheshire Cat with a belly full of mice. Once the guys were out of sight, she grabbed my hand, dragging me back toward our chairs.

"Can you believe this?!" she shrieked.

Trying to catch up, I blinked. "What?"

"This! They think that I'm her! She is so pretty! Don't you think she's pretty? Am I really that pretty? I always wanted to be a movie star," she giggled.

I had a bad feeling about this. "Wait a minute. You can't go around letting people think that you're her."

"Why not?" she asked.

"Why not?" I frowned. "Because, it's lying. It's wrong to pretend that you're someone else."

She cocked her head to the side and looked at me. "Wait a minute. Just a few weeks ago, you let everyone think that you were dead. You lied for days, to the whole family, and the rest of the world, about being dead. Now, you're telling me that it's wrong to lie?"

"I didn't actually tell anyone that I was dead. The news did. I just didn't tell anyone that I wasn't dead. Anyway, that was different. The FBI made me do it, so they could catch my stalker," I reasoned.

"I know it was different. It was worse, much worse. I thought you were dead!" She glared at me. "Besides, I didn't tell them that I was her. I just didn't tell them that I wasn't." She looked me in the eyes, daring me to argue.

Nervously biting my lip, I said, "Barbie, my gut is telling me that this is a bad idea."

"Since when has that stopped us?" She grinned. "It'll be fun, you'll see."

I shook my head, and said, "I don't think Random and his friends are the only ones here who think that you're her. Have you noticed that people have been treating us well…different, since we got here; giving us stuff and taking our picture?"

She thought for a moment, then said, "You know, you're right. I just thought everyone here was super friendly."

I nodded. "Yeah, me too. Now, I don't think that's it. I think there are a whole lot of people here who think that you're her."

"Why?" She gave me a confused look. "I mean, no one in the states has ever thought that I was her, and I live in the Big Apple itself. The only place with more movie stars is Hollywood."

I paused a moment while staring closely at her. "I think it's your hair. You haven't straightened it since we got here. Normally, you don't wear your hair wavy, like she does. Also, your clothes...you don't dress like her at home, but here you're just wearing a bikini, like everyone else."

"You think so?"

I tilted my head, trying to see her as Jennifer Jons. "The tan helps too. You usually have really pale skin. We've spent so much time tanning the past few days that your skin is more of a golden color. It gives you that Mediterranean look that she has."

She looked at her arm, shrugged, and said, "I guess that makes sense."

Sixteen

We sat deep in our own thoughts, enjoying the warm breeze that was blowing lightly across the crowded beach in silence. My mind emptied as I became mesmerized by the sounds of the waves crashing against the sand. As the sun began to dip beyond the horizon, I drifted off under the shade of the white umbrellas.

The next thing I knew, I was being chased by a man with no face. I dodged through the white umbrellas, heading for the safety of the building in front of me. Reaching the entrance, I jerked at the door. It was locked, and I had lost my room key somewhere on the golden beach, well beyond my pursuer. With an evil laugh, he raised his gun. I felt the bullet hit me in the forehead. Crying out, I fell out of my lounge chair.

"I can't take you anywhere," Barbie's voice dripped with sarcasm.

After a quick moment of panic, I realized that I was lying on the beach with Barbie. "I must have dozed off." I squinted up at the sun. It was starting to set.

"You did. What time do you think it is?" Barbie asked, as if reading my mind.

"I don't know." I looked up at the sun again and yawned. "We should ask someone."

We looked around for someone who might have a watch or a cell phone with them. I noticed an older man walking toward us with a little boy. It looked like a grandpa and his grandson out for a day at the beach. The kid with him was cute, probably three or four. The man was a little shorter than me and a lot heavier with close cut white hair. The sun caught my eye, off of the metal band of his wristwatch.

"I'll go ask him." I motioned towards the man. "It looks like he's got a watch on." My body protested as I heaved myself up from the warm sand.

"Wait," Barbie said, giving me a strange look. "Is that bird poop on your forehead?"

Hoping she was wrong, I gingerly felt the spot where I had dreamed the bullet had struck me. Sure enough, there was a sticky white substance on my hand. Giving Barbie a despondent look, I said, "This just isn't my week."

"No, it isn't," Barbie agreed.

After wiping off my forehead, I headed over to the man and little boy. Flashing them a friendly smile, I asked, "Excuse me, do you know what time it is?"

They stopped walking while the man looked at his wrist. I couldn't help but notice that he had on a very nice and expensive looking watch. Who wears an expensive watch to the beach?

"It is half past the seven o'clock," he responded in stilted English.

I smiled at him. "Thank you."

He smiled back. "It was my pleasure. Is there anything else that I may do for you?" He wiggled his eyebrows.

"What?"

"Then, you will do for me?" He smiled a skanky smile as he ran his eyes down my body, in a very ungrandfatherly way.

"What?" I must have had too much sun.

"I would like very much to spend some time with you." He wiggled his eyebrows again as he reached out with his right hand to run it down my exposed stomach. "How much for one hour?"

"Um, no, that's all I needed!" In horrified shame, I backed away, tripping over a sunbather. "I'm so sorry!" I squealed. Scrambling to my feet, I tripped over someone's drink, then stepped into a bowl of something gooey. "Oh no! I'm very sorry." Shrieks of anger followed me across the sand as I quickly headed back to the lounge chairs where Barbie was waiting for me. Sitting next to

Barbie, I shook my head in disbelief and began to rub the gooey, sand covered gunk off my foot. "Next time you get to go ask."

"What happened?" she asked.

I wrinkled my nose. "The old man propositioned me! I guess he thought I was a prostitute or something. He tried to feel me up in front of the little boy! Didn't you see it?"

"Eww…that is so gross!" Barbie made a face.

"It's not like I invited him to touch me. I just asked him the time," I complained.

"Maybe he thought that was code for something else," Barbie offered, trying not to laugh.

I frowned. "A yacht full of murderous cocaine and sex dealers, a deadly Albino, new stalker, and now this? This really is the worst vacation ever."

"The view is delish," Barbie countered as a group of buff men sauntered past us. "So, what time is it?"

"Oh, it's about seven-thirty," I answered dismissively. I was still a little freaked out by the old man trying to feel me up.

"Really? Get your things! It's time for us to go upstairs and get ready!" She jumped up excitedly.

"Ready for what?" I turned my attention to Barbie.

"Remember, we're going to meet those guys in Patong tonight." She grinned in anticipation.

"Those guys? You made a date with my new stalker?" I asked, following her lead and gathering up my things.

194

"And his friends. Anyway, he's harmless and super cute!"

With a sigh, I rolled my eyes. "You think every cute guy is harmless."

"That is not true and you know it." She smiled, and said, "Random is too sweet to be a threat. You're just paranoid." Flashing her *'I win'* smile, she asked, "Anyway, have I ever been wrong?"

I threw up my hands in frustration, and exclaimed, "Yes!"

"Whatever," she blew me off. "What did you bring to wear?"

Frowning, I realized that I had nothing to wear to a club. "I told you before, I just brought beach clothes. You know swimsuits, shorts, tank tops, a sweatshirt, Oh! I have a cocktail dress and heels!"

She looked me in the eye. "Seriously?"

"Well, what did you bring?" I glared at her.

"Everything," she gloated.

I rolled my eyes. "That's right. You brought five huge suitcases, to the beach!"

"Of course I did. I may be on vacation, but I still need to be prepared for anything. I can't believe you just brought that little carry on."

I sighed, realizing we had gone back to arguing over packing. "Okay, Boy Scout Barbie, we've been over this. I'm cheap, and it costs a fortune to check bags these days. Besides, I hate lugging a bunch of bags around."

"Yeah, that part does suck." She nodded in agreement.

Like she would know. I just shook my head, knowing that Barbie had never lugged her own bags around. Not when some too happy to help simpleton would trip over himself for the pleasure of doing it for her. Usually, it was some poor slob who knew she was way out of his league, but couldn't help trying.

We stepped inside our suite. Barbie headed straight for her room to get ready. I considered doing the same, but I was hungry. Anyway, I didn't think this was a dinner date. My eyes fell on the hotel's phone.

"I'm gonna order room service. Do you want anything?" I called down the hall.

"Good idea, I'm starved. Anyway, we don't know if there will be food at the club where we're meeting the guys," she called back.

"That's what I was thinking. What do you want?" I asked.

She stuck her head out the door. "Something light, I never eat a heavy meal before partying. A heavy meal before a night of drinking always makes me sick."

I shrugged, thinking that sounded almost too reasonable to have come from Barbie. A quick look over the room service menu was all I needed to make up my mind before I picked up the phone. I was listening to it ring when Barbie stepped out of her room and into mine.

"It's a good thing they found my luggage. I'd be pissed if all we had to work with were your beach clothes."

"You liked my beach clothes the first two days we were here, when it was all you had to wear," I reminded her.

"Whatever." She headed back into her room. "Just order room service and get moving." A panicked look spread across her face. "We started getting ready too late! We've got to figure out what we're going to wear! Jennifer Jons and her entourage wouldn't go out in just anything."

"We have hours. You are not Jennifer Jons. And, I am not your entourage!" I called out.

She stuck her head around the door, rolled her eyes at me, and flippantly said, "Details."

I rolled my eyes back at her as she disappeared into her room. Smiling, I picked up the phone, for the second time that night, to dial room service. I had to admit that Barbie was right, this could be fun. I would never admit it to Barbie, but I kind of wished that I could be the one mistaken for a famous actress, instead of her.

Barbie called out from her room, "Ask them if they have any tabloid magazines that they can send up. I want to look as much like her as possible."

Rolling my eyes, I couldn't help but mutter, "Diva," under my breath.

By the time we had eaten our sandwiches, showered, and finished dressing it was getting late. Barbie stepped into my room, twirling around in a circle. She was wearing her hair in long curly waves and makeup that looked like she'd carefully applied it, with a spatula.

"What do you think?" She held up a magazine picture next to her face.

I had to admit, she was looking more and more like the actress she was pretending to be. She gave me another self-satisfied twirl before gesturing to her outfit. She had on a blood red mini dress that was tight on the bottom and loose on the top. The dress had been paired with multiple strands of large white pearls hanging long around her neck, and a set of matching pearls covering her wrists. I couldn't help but notice that she had painted her nails and lips the same shade of red as her dress. A pair of blood red, five inch hooker heals finished off the outfit.

It took me a minute before I could speak. "You look like a lipstick."

"A lipstick? This dress is a Lydia. I picked it up in Paris at her summer collection show. You have no sense of style." She blew me off as she looked at herself in the mirror. "I look hot. Rarrr," she purred to herself.

I stepped up to the mirror. "How could you say that I have no sense of style?"

I gave myself a once-over in the mirror, just to make sure that I hadn't crossed the line from 'Hey there sexy mama' to 'For Sale'. I had also put on a full face of makeup; although, mine wasn't caked on like Barbie's. Just for fun, I shook my head from side to side.

"Look," I said to Barbie. "Nothing happens when I shake it." I giggled. "It just...stays there!"

Barbie had artfully piled my hair on top of my head, securing it with half a can of super hold hairspray and a handful of bobby pins, allowing just a few loose curls to hang alluringly down my neck. The curls didn't move either. I smiled at my reflection, deciding that I would have to wear my hair like this again. With a quick turn, I checked out my backside and smiled.

"I look cute." I informed my cousin.

"Cute?" Barbie rolled her eyes at me while continuing to spray hairspray on the inside of her mini dress to keep it from riding up. "Put your big girl panties on cousin. We're going out with men not boys."

Deciding to ignore her, I continued my pre-party appraisal. The leopard print dress I'd found in Barbie's room fit me like a glove while accentuating all of my best assets. It probably went to her knees, but it was a mini dress on me. For accessories, I had added a short gold shrug, thin braided leather belt, thick gold wrist circlet with colorfully mismatched thin bracelets on both sides, chunky gold necklace, and a pair of brown leather knee boots. The boots were a size too small, because they were Barbie's, but they looked good. I could deal with cramped toes for a few hours.

I smiled at my reflection. "Take that back, I look hot!"

Barbie glanced over at me. "Everything you're wearing came from my closet. I even fixed your hair."

199

"Together *WE* have a great sense of style," I said, smoothing an imaginary wrinkle from my dress.

Barbie put down the hairspray to peer into the mirror with me. "Damn, we look good!"

"Yes, we do." I grinned at her. "Are you ready to go play movie star?"

She grinned back at me, and said, "I was born ready."

Seventeen

The resort shuttle drove us into Patong to the club where we were meeting Random and his friends. Easing to a stop, the driver motioned to a building on our right.

"You go in there," he said.

Barbie and I peered apprehensively out the shuttle door. The area was noisy with people and music from the different bars, and restaurants. Street vendors peddling their wares, added to the commotion. The building he pointed at, and its immediate neighbors, shared a seedy, rundown appearance. Between the lights, music, and people; I felt as if I'd stumbled upon a sordid street party.

Frowning, Barbie turned back to the shuttle driver. "There must be some mistake."

The driver shook his head, then in broken English said, "No mistake lady. This is Patong club district." He pointed to the right. "That is place."

Barbie and I looked at the building he had indicated. Were those prostitutes standing in front of the doors? I was pretty sure they weren't the only vendors selling sex at this block party.

We looked back at each other before Barbie asked the driver. "Are you sure this is the right place?"

The driver nodded impatiently and pointed again. "Yes. This is place. You go in there."

She looked at me and shrugged. "We're here. We might as well check it out."

Unconvinced, I said, "Sure, why not."

Before we could change our minds, he drove away. Standing on the sidewalk in front of the club, I had to admit that I was out of my comfort zone. Knowing my comfort zone is pretty narrow, the knowledge only bothered me a little. Turning to my up-for-anything cousin, I was suddenly concerned. Barbie's confidence seemed to have left her. Now, I was worried.

Barbie gave me a questioning look, then asked, "What do you think?"

I looked at the club behind Barbie. "Is that a strip club?"

She was looking at the building like it was infected with an incurable disease. "I don't know, maybe."

We stood in front of the building, looking up and down the street, unsure of what to do next. After a few minutes Barbie whispered, "Hey Jess, all of these clubs look like sex clubs, either that or they're letting prostitutes hang out in front of the doors."

Having just come to the same conclusion, I nodded my agreement. Up and down the street, in front of most of the doors, stood scantily clad Asian women, trying to persuade the men passing by to come inside. Every few attempts they would be successful, and a man would enter the club with the woman.

"The girls seem to be working out of the clubs." She paused before adding, "I'm not sure that they are sex clubs. I've seen groups of both men and women going in and out the doors." She pointed to an older group of men and women coming out of a club to our left. "It seems like if they were strip clubs or brothels it would be just men going in. They wouldn't be taking their wives and girlfriends inside with them."

"I guess the women could be gay." I shook my head, then added, "That doesn't make sense. Every woman here can't be gay."

Barbie nodded her agreement. "I think you're right." Barbie's famous confidence was quickly returning, "We should go in, and check it out. I mean we're already here, so why not?"

I inhaled sharply. "Barbie, look over there, but don't be obvious."

She turned to my left. "What am I looking at?"

"The big guy on the side of that building. Do you see him?" I motioned with a jerk of my head.

"The one in black?" she asked guardedly.

"Yes! Don't look like you're looking. You'll spook him," I hissed.

Barbie rolled her eyes. "I'll spook him? What is he, a horse?"

"No, he's one of Eric's men," I whispered.

"*He's one of Eric's men?*" She raised an eyebrow in disbelief.

"And, I bet he's not alone." Ignoring her tone, I scanned the crowd.

"Are you saying this because he's wearing black, or because you've met him?" Her tone was irritated.

Wrinkling my brow, I bit my lip.

"You had better tell me that you've at least seen that guy with the Wolfman." She put her hand on her hip in annoyance.

"Well...no." I fidgeted under her stare. "I haven't seen that specific guy before. But, look at him! He's big and scary looking and he's dressed all in black, standing like a sentinel on the street corner."

"Jessie, look around you! There are lots of guys like that out tonight. Everyone is standing outside. It's a nice night, and black is a very popular color." She waved her arm towards the crowded sidewalks.

"Barbie, look at him!" I begged. "I admit that I've been wrong, a lot, but I swear, that is one of Eric's men. Do you think that he might be here, too?" I continued to scan the crowd, eagerly searching for Eric.

Barbie took a deep breath. "I told you already, I am not having this conversation with you again. Give me your phone."

I shook my head. "I can't. I left it in the hotel room, in my suitcase."

Cerulean Seas

"What? You didn't bring your phone?" She looked at me as if I had just admitted to a heinous crime.

"Why would I bring it with me? I can't afford to turn it on outside of the states. Roaming charges are exorbitant. Some of us aren't made of money," I explained. "Besides, if you looked closely you would see that I didn't bring my purse with me either."

"I hadn't noticed." Reaching into her purse, she said, "Whatever, just tell me his number. I'll call him."

I gave her a bemused look. "What about the expense?"

She shrugged. "It doesn't cost me that much. I have an international plan because I travel so much, for my job."

I silently stared at her, before saying, "Barbie, you don't have a job. I'm not sure that you've ever had a job."

"Well, if I did have a job, it would be one that required me to travel internationally, then I would need an international phone plan." She brushed off my logic, leaving me to wonder, once again, how much money Barbie actually had.

A familiar voice abruptly ended our conversation.

"Ladies, I thought I saw you out here." It was Random, looking us up and down while smiling like he was about to eat something tasty. "You two are absolutely stunning! Let us go inside, and get you lovelies some drinks."

Before we could answer, he slid between us, draping his arms across each of our shoulders. Inside, it was packed. There were tourists from every country, mixed with locals. In the middle of the

Jenn Brink

club was a dance floor where three pretty Asian girls, dressed in lingerie and plastic stripper heels, were grinding against each other while one of them sang 'Material Girl' in heavily accented, and off key, English.

Staring at the girls on the stage, I asked no one in particular, "Are they strippers? Is this a strip club?"

One of the girls turned around to reveal a paper with the number twelve stuck to her back.

"What's with the number?" I asked.

Smiling in obvious fondness, Random looked up at the girls on stage. "That is one of the things that I love about Thailand. You can buy and sell sex as easily as alcohol, but unlike the alcohol and sex, the show is free."

Both his words and attitude surprised me. He hadn't come off as that kind of guy earlier, or maybe he had and I just hadn't been paying attention.

Frowning my disapproval, I asked, "What is this place? Did you have us meet you at a brothel?"

He laughed at my indignation. "No, it's just a club. Thailand has some interesting views on what constitutes prostitution, and those views are loosely enforced. Most of the clubs here have girls for sale, both outside and inside, and rooms to rent on sight. Some of them have stages where girls strip or sing. It's just a show, unless you want it to be more." He gestured around him. "Most of these girls can be bought for anything from sex to playing darts, and everything in

206

between. Many of the clubs, including this one, number them to make it easier on the customer when picking the girl of his choice."

As if to lend credence to his explanation, an Asian girl, who couldn't have been more than fifteen, walked past us wearing the number eight on her back, a shiny gold tube top that barely covered her small breasts, matching sarong skirt that hung low at her pelvic bone with a slit up the left leg, and clear plastic stripper heels. I couldn't help but notice that the skirt barely covered her butt cheeks.

I frowned up at Random. "I don't know what kind of girls you think we are, but we are not the kind of girls that hang out in strip clubs, brothels, or whatever you want to call this place."

His face was grave as he stared deep into my eyes. "Pardon me. It was not my intention to make you uncomfortable or offend in any way. I just assumed that you ladies knew what the clubs were like here in Patong. Look around, both men and women come here to socialize, like any American club. Having the girls in the clubs is just the way that they do things here. The invite was not meant as disrespect."

Barbie and I did as he suggested. Taking a good look at the other patrons, we saw many of the same men and women that had been outside on the street with us sitting at tables, drinking, talking, and paying no attention to the bar girls. Suddenly, Barbie smiled warmly up at Random with a look that I knew too well. Knowing what would happen next, I couldn't help but sigh.

"Please excuse our naiveté." Barbie placed a hand on Random's shoulder and murmured, "We should have known."

When Random looked away, Barbie gave me a look that asked me to stay. I shrugged my shoulders. She mouthed '*Thank you'*, then linked her arm through Random's. Once she had reclaimed his attention, she looked up, and said, "I believe that you promised us a drink."

Random grinned while motioning to the bar girl. After ordering in Thai, he wrapped his arms around our waists and led us to the back of the room, where a group of men and women sat around a large table. As we approached the group, Random draped his arms around our shoulders.

As an introduction, he asked the group, "Does everyone remember Jennifer Jons and her cousin Jessie?"

The men nodded, saying "hello". The women ignored us. I noticed that there wasn't a bad looking guy in the crowd. The women were dressed in almost non-existent outfits, pegging them as bar girls. The men all wore Khaki shorts and short sleeve button down shirts, with sandals. I felt a little overdressed. Barbie was too deep into being a famous movie star to care.

Our drinks arrived while we were completing the introductions. Slowly, we were making our way to the end of the table where there were three vacant seats waiting for us. Random slid into the middle seat, leaving Barbie and I to seat ourselves on either side of him. Almost as soon as we sat down, the man in the chair next to me rose to excuse himself and his Asian friend. I watched curiously as she led him through an unmarked door behind us.

"Are they leaving?" I asked Random.

"No." He smiled. "She is taking him upstairs."

"What's upstairs?" I asked, straining to see through the rapidly closing door.

Random shot me a lecherous glance. "I love your innocence. It is what attracted me to you at the airport the other day."

"I don't understand." I gave him a confused look.

"Really Jess?" Barbie rolled her eyes. "They went upstairs." She paused, adding, "To be alone."

I gave her a blank look and shrugged my shoulders. I still didn't get it.

"You know, *ALONE*," she said it slowly, stressing the last word.

"Oh!" I exclaimed.

Barbie shook her head while Random and the other guys at our table laughed at my flaming cheeks. I took a big drink from my glass, to hide my embarrassment.

"Do you like the drink?" Random asked, watching me practically drain the glass in one gulp.

Not wanting to admit that I hadn't bothered to taste it, I contemplated the liquid before answering, "Yeah, it's fruity. What is it?"

"It is a specialty drink they sell here on the island. The translation is difficult. If you like, Lucas will get you another one." He motioned to a beefy blonde guy at the end of the table.

Lucas stopped beside Barbie. With an Australian accent, he asked, "May I bring you another as well?"

Taking in his perfect hair and muscular build, Barbie smiled coyly. "Yes, thank you, Lucas."

The Asian girls came and went. Glasses were emptied and refilled. I lost track of how long we sat there listening to the music, dancing, flirting, and talking. Barbie was playing the part of the flamboyant actress on vacation so well that even I was starting to believe it. As I finished another drink, I realized that somewhere along the way Random seemed to have switched his interest from me to Barbie. He was hanging on her every word. I wasn't upset about it. I mean, he was pretty, but like I had told Barbie, I really wasn't interested.

I just couldn't get Eric out of my mind. Since I had met Eric, I found myself comparing every good looking guy that I met to him, and finding each one lacking. Part of me said that everyone was right; I should move on. He had told me that he wasn't interested in a relationship, and since we had parted, he hadn't called. He hadn't even asked about me. As Barbie had pointed out, he hadn't so much as butt dialed me. Taking another swallow of the fruity drink, I frowned. He sure hadn't acted like he wasn't interested in Seattle.

Then, at the airport, he had said that he didn't want any other man to have me. That didn't sound like a guy who wasn't interested, did it?

Thinking about Eric, and the way he smiled at me, I couldn't help but smile. Was it possible that he could be just as confused as I was? He seemed to have it all together, but what if he didn't? Maybe, Barbie was right. Maybe, I should give him a call when I got back to the states. But, what if he wasn't confused? What if he really didn't want a relationship? What if he had just used me for sex? Then, I would look like a fool.

I frowned at the thought. Boston isn't that far from New York City. I could just stop by on my way home. Yes, I could do that. Greg lives in Boston. I could stop in, to visit Greg, and just happen to run into Eric. Didn't Greg say they were playing poker at his house? I could show up on poker night. That way, if he had forgotten all about me, I wouldn't embarrass myself. I nodded, silently congratulating myself on the plan.

"Jessie, snap out of it!"

I blinked, it was Barbie. She was snapping her fingers in front of me with an annoyed look on her face.

I gave her a confused half smile, and said, "I'm sorry B...um...Jennifer." Everyone at the table was looking at me. "I'm feeling a little...I guess I'm just a little tired."

Barbie gave me a weird look. Everyone else at the table nodded, then went back to what they were doing.

I flashed a quick smile at Random. "If you'll excuse me, I need to go to the ladies room." I motioned with my eyes for Barbie to follow.

"Oh, yeah, me too. We'll be right back," Barbie said, as we stood up from our chairs.

Once we stepped into the bathroom, Barbie's smile was replaced by a frown and a cross look. "Jessie, what is wrong with you tonight?"

Leaning my hair against the cool wall, I said, "I don't know. I'm having a hard time focusing." Turning my face against the wall, I let the stones cool my cheek. "I must be coming down with something." I put a hand on my stomach. "I've got a little bit of a headache, and my stomach is unhappy. Whatever was in that sandwich didn't agree with me." I gave her a pleading look, then asked, "How about we call it a night?"

Barbie gave me a sympathetic look. "I hate to agree, but my stomach is a little queasy too, and my head is starting to hurt. I was just ignoring it, thinking that I was getting one of my migraines."

I blinked a couple of times, then shook my head to clear it. I really didn't feel good. I blinked again, then squinted at Barbie. "Hey, there are two of you!" I closed my eyes tight. After a moment, I slowly opened them again, trying to fix my vision. "What was in those drinks?"

"Wait a minute." Barbie's voice had an edge to it. "My vision is also a little blurry. Like I said, I just thought I was getting a migraine."

I grabbed ahold of the sink, to steady myself, suddenly alarmed. "Barb, something is wrong with me. I feel weird!"

Barbie gave me a concerned look as I struggled to stay on my feet. "I don't feel that great, but I'm not as bad off as you are." She stood quietly, thinking. After what seemed like a really long time, she started thinking aloud. "We felt fine when we got here. Neither of us has had that much to drink." She frowned. "At least I haven't. I'm pretty sure that you've had at least one more drink than I have."

I nodded in agreement, unsure of how many drinks I had ingested, but sure that I had had more than her. Burping loudly, I added, "We haven't eaten since those sandwiches in our room. That was hours ago. So, I don't think its food poisoning. Although, I do feel like I've been poisoned."

"Fuck me!" Barbie snapped. "Those jerkoffs put something in our drinks."

"What?" My brain was working at half-speed.

"They drugged us," she scowled.

"Shit!" I bit down on my lower lip. "Now Greg will get to say, '*I told you so*'."

"Somehow, I suspect that Greg is the least of our problems tonight." She frowned. "We felt fine when we got here. Those guys have been getting our drinks all night. That has to be it. It's the only answer that makes sense." She frowned at me as I lay slumped against the wall. "I don't know what they're up to, but I don't think we want to wait around and find out. Let's find a back way out of this place, and get back to our rooms."

"Back to our rooms, at the resort? How are we gonna do that? I can barely stand, we don't have a car, and we're in the wrong town," I reminded her.

She waved off my objections. "It'll be easy to get a taxi once we get out to the street. They were everywhere when we got dropped off. I'm sure that all of the taxis around here know how to get to the resort."

"Sure it'd be easy, if we'd just had a little too much to drink, but have you forgotten that we've been drugged?" I was panicking. "Drugged people pass out. Then, bad stuff happens to them. I had a friend in college who…"

"Calm down. Don't tell me you've never been drugged before?" she asked.

"What? No! Have you?"

She gave me a *'get real'* look. "I've been going to New York City bars since I was fifteen. I lived in Greenwich Village for five years, and majored in partying in college. Of course I've been drugged before. It's no big deal. I thought everyone had been drugged at least once." Giving me a sympathetic look, she said, "Just calm down. It's going to be okay. All you have to do is focus on walking and staying awake, until we get to a cab. I'll do the rest. Don't worry, you'll be alright."

"Okay." I took a deep breath to calm myself, then another, because the first one didn't work. "So how do we get out of here?"

"Just stay with me," she said, heading out the door like she knew what she was doing.

I followed Barbie out of the bathroom, down a dark, narrow hallway, and through an unmarked door that led into a small kitchen. The workers angrily yelled at us in Thai as we hurriedly pushed through to the back door. By the time we emerged into a back alley, confusion and disorientation were descending upon me. It seemed as if all of the sounds and lights were melding into one very scary dream.

Barbie said something, but I couldn't make out the words. Carefully, I shook my head, working hard to concentrate on the world around me. Dizzily, I watched as the images surrounding me shifted back into focus, just in time to see Barbie spewing bile into the alley. Eww...the smell! With a grunt, I turned away, fighting my body's reaction to the odors wafting over me. As I swallowed back the bile in my throat, Barbie said something that sounded like water rushing through a tunnel.

Sweat dripped down my hairline, catching in my painstakingly crafted up do. Swaying unsteadily, I leaned my head against the rough stone wall. The cool dampness felt good against my skin. Time stood still, as the wall held me up. From far away, I could hear my name being called. The voice was familiar. A face moved into my line of sight. It was Barbie. Her lips were moving with rapid urgency, as she tried desperately to tell me something, but what? Her words were just a swooshing noise, rushing through an underwater tunnel. My head began to hurt as the images and sounds around me merged into each other like a bad dream, one I couldn't wake up from. Once again, I carefully shook my head, hoping to clear it.

Barbie grabbed my wrist, pulling me off of the wall. With her leading the way, we stumbled away from the back of the club, moving towards the noise and lights of the main street in front of us. Seemingly hours later, we fumbled our way to the end of a long dark tunnel. An eternity had passed by the time Barbie finally hauled me into the neon lit street. It was so bright!

The sounds and lights reverberated through my head with a disconcerting rush, blurring together into a frightening, roaring nightmare. Holding tight to my cousin's arm, we staggered through the crowd. My only thought was that if I were to let go, I would be lost forever in the lurid noise and confusion.

Stumbling down the street, I struggled to remember what it was that we were looking for. I needed to ask Barbie. She would know. Slowing, I tugged on her arm to get her attention. It didn't work. I tried to speak. It sounded like gobbely gook. Suddenly, she stopped and turned towards me. I looked around in confusion. Why had we stopped? Where were we?

I tried to speak, again. It was useless, my lips weren't working right. Watching Barbie pull hard at my arm, I wondered why I couldn't feel it. She put her face in front of mine, allowing her tears to fall on my cheeks. I watched, detached from the scene, as her lips moved faster and faster. Faintly, I could feel her shaking me from somewhere far away. I could see words tumbling from her lips. Why was there no sound? Something was very wrong with my hearing. Without warning, the sounds around me became one loud noise rushing through my head with no rhyme or reason.

I blinked. The images around me separated, my vision clearing. Suddenly, I remembered what we had been looking for, a car. Who's car? I wasn't sure. Why? I couldn't answer. Barbie was now motioning frantically as she spoke. Hard as I tried, I couldn't understand the words she was saying. I leaned back, gazing up at the unfamiliar world spinning dangerously out of control around me. What had happened? Where was Barbie? Abandoned, in this crazy place, I began to cry.

Strong hands appeared from the darkness. Roughly, they grasped my arms before effortlessly pulling me to my feet. I looked down at my feet in confusion. I couldn't remember sitting, let alone lying down. With effort, I looked up at the dark figure in front of me.

He was holding me up by the arms. Why was he holding my arms so tight? What did he want with me? I tried to wiggle free. He was saying something. All I could hear was the loud noise rushing through my head, again. I blinked, trying desperately to focus on his faces. Why did he have so many faces? Abruptly, the rushing noise stopped. All at once, his many faces molded into just one. The sudden

217

silence was equally as terrifying as the noise had been. Blinking away my confusion, I worked to focus on the lips moving above me. Where was the sound?

"Are you all right?" The sound came from far, far away.

I licked my dry lips as my tired eyes blurred shut. Feeling myself falling, I tried to speak, unsuccessfully. I seemed to fall for the longest time. Before my body could touch the ground, those strong arms caught me. The world tilted upward, as muscular arms roughly pulled me upright until I could look at him, face to lips? The lips said something. It was no use, I couldn't understand. For a moment, I stood on my own before feeling myself begin the long descent to the ground, again. The man in front of me reached out, instinctively wrapping his strong arm around me, protectively holding me upright, against the black material covering his chest. Again, I attempted to raise my head to look at his face as a mixture of confusion and relief enveloped me.

"Eric?" I heard myself ask, no louder than a newborn kitten.

He didn't seem to hear me. He was speaking to one of the faces. Then, there was just one face. My heart fell as the panic returned. Warm liquid trickled out of my eyes and down my cheeks. It wasn't him. It wasn't Eric.

"Where's Wolf?!" My panic stricken voice loudly demanded.

Unexpectedly, the rushing noise returned preventing me from hearing his response. Anxiously, I tried to focus on the words floating around me. I blinked again. It was no use. His features merged together into a jumbled Picasso of lips, eyes, and nose. The world was spinning too fast, causing me to feel sick. I hate to be sick. I closed my eyes. It didn't help. I opened them just as the rushing noise faded.

Painfully, I tried to speak. All that came out was an almost imperceptible, "Help!"

The stranger holding me against his chest tilted his head towards mine. Was he speaking to me? His mouth was moving. I could feel his chest vibrate, but there was no sound. Hopeless tears seeped from my eyes. I couldn't hear. I couldn't understand. I reached up to him. He was so far away. My hand fumbled in the air, just short of his features. I tried to focus on his face again. There were just too many of him. His heads turned. The moment, my chance, was lost.

I could hear deep voices in the air around me. The sound carried, as if it was created far away from me. Squinting my eyes, trying to focus on the faces around me, didn't help. They just kept multiplying. It was no use. The faces kept swimming in and out of focus. I was trapped in some kind of hell as all sight and sound stopped, just to rush at me again, preventing me from understanding anything. Panic caused me to push against my captor with a frantic need to escape.

"Officers...please...we've been drugged." Barbie's speech was sluggish and slurred.

Barbie! Where was she? I tried to turn my head, but didn't seem to have any control over my muscles. Taking a deep breath, I focused all of my energy on the once simple task. It was no use. Realizing my hands rested against his chest, I pushed myself upright. Finally, I was standing alone.

If I could just get my eyes to focus, I could find Barbie and get us out of here. I lifted my foot to take a step. Everything played in slow motion as the world tilted. A moment later, I was helplessly falling into the darkness. I could hear shouting voices, but wasn't able to discern the words. The rushing sound was louder than ever. It hurt my ears. I tried to reach out to cover them, but couldn't find my arms. Where were they? I had just used them.

A bed of hands seized me. Suspended midair, my hand scraped the pavement. Strong arms hastily lifted me higher until they cradled me close to a broad chest.

"Daddy?" I asked, in a soft voice.

"Everything is going to be okay. I won't let anything happen to you," he answered, cradling me like a small child. His voice was deep and soothing, resonating confidence.

I sighed my relief. My head was so heavy. I let it rest on his chest. Mmmm...He smelled so nice. Tilting my head up, I could see a trace of black fabric and dangerously dark eyes staring apprehensively into mine. Taking a deep breath, I allowed his scent to overwhelm me while my tired body relaxed into him. Aware only of the ground swaying rhythmically with his steps, I briefly wondered where he was taking me before the world went black and silent.

Eighteen

I woke up alone in my bed, with the worst hangover that I have ever experienced. My mouth was sandpaper dry. I tried to moisten my tongue with spit, but there was none. A noxious stench accosted my nostrils, causing me to gag. Wow! My breath reeked, enough that the smell was making me nauseous. Sticking my too dry tongue out of my mouth, I had to wonder what I had eaten. No, what did I drink that could cause such a horrible smell and taste? My mind was blank. I couldn't remember anything.

I put my hands to my head, trying to think around the hammering inside my brain. The pain was intense. I needed something for the pain. Gently pointing my body towards the edge of the bed, I prepared to stumble into the bathroom. Once I finally talked my eyes into opening, I quickly closed them again. The bright sun was piercing needles into my brain. My head was shrieking. I needed water and an Ibuprophin.

"Ooooohhh," I groaned as I crawled on my hands and knees out of the bed.

Somehow, I managed to get myself mostly upright and stumble into the bathroom, all the while shielding my eyes from the bright sun that streamed through the windows. Slowly, I turned on the tap, leaned down, and shoved my head under the faucet. After I had finished trying to drown myself, I scrubbed my mouth with toothpaste, crawled back into bed, and put a pillow over my head. That took care of the vile taste in my mouth, and the penetrating morning sun. If only the little alien hammering inside of my head would quit, I could die happy.

"Ooooohhh," I groaned again.

What did we do last night? All I could remember was a crazy nightmare. With a sigh, I crawled back out of bed and down the hall, into Barbie's room. Reaching her bed, I rose up on my knees to peer across the surface.

Barbie was passed out with her makeup smeared down her face, and her hair in a tangled mess. It wasn't a pretty sight. I decided right then that I was happy not to have her naturally curly hair. Was she breathing? I wasn't sure.

"Barbie," I whispered, gently poking her.

She didn't move.

"Barbie," I whispered a little louder, poking her a little harder.

She exhaled into my face. As the fumes of last night's liquor washed over me, a wave of nausea hit, forcing me to fight back the bile that was already seeping up from my belly. I really needed to go back to bed. I looked down the hall. My bed was such a long way away. Too far. I crawled around to the other side of the king sized bed, eased myself up, and closed my eyes.

The warm sun radiating through the windows felt good on my body as I drifted off to sleep. When I awoke, what seemed to be a short time later, I reached out, poking Barbie a little harder than I had before.

"Barbie, are you dead?" I whispered.

"I think so," she whispered back.

"Me too."

"Good to know," she replied.

"What happened last night? How did we get back to our rooms?" I whispered.

"Ooooohhh...I don't remember." She opened one eye, then quickly closed it. "You look like death warmed over."

"You're not going to win any beauty pageants either," I told her.

"Ooooohh..." Barbie groaned, reaching for her head.

"The last thing I remember, we were on the dance floor at that club, getting all kinds of attention from hot guys that we'll never see again. Then, I woke up in my bed, alone." I grimaced. "What happened? How did we get back here?"

She shook her head. "Ouch! I don't know. The last thing I remember, we were outside of the club, talking to a police officer.

You weren't doing so well. I might not have been doing so well either," she ruefully admitted.

"I feel like shit," I admitted. "No, I feel like shit that got run over, puked on, and then run over again."

"Me too," Barbie croaked.

"I really hope we had a good time. If we didn't, I'm gonna be pissed," I mumbled grumpily.

Barbie opened her eyes to give me a strange look. "Jess, we had a shitty time. Your dumbass friend and his cronies drugged us. We slipped out the back of the club, stumbled down a dark alley, and wandered into the street looking for a cab. Then, you laid down in the middle of the street. I couldn't get you to stand up. I don't know what would have happened to us if those police officers hadn't shown up."

"Damn." I frowned at the memory. "I thought that had been a bad dream."

"No, it really happened. You were in bad shape. I was better off than you, probably because I didn't drink as much as you, and I threw up." She closed her eyes. "Next time you get drugged, you have to remember to throw up. It helps to get the drugs out of your system."

"Right, I'll do that," I agreed.

I'm not sure how long we laid there in the quiet room with our eyes closed against the morning sun.

After what seemed like hours, I opened my eyes and looked down. Turning slightly, I looked at Barbie. "I'm in my bra and underwear."

"So?"

"So, what are you wearing?"

She slowly opened her eyes, peering under the covers. "My bra and underwear."

I closed my eyes against the bright light shining into the room. "I may not remember much about last night, but I know that I was wearing clothes when we left the club. From what I remember, and what you said, I'm pretty sure I passed out long before we reached our rooms."

Barbie nodded. "I can scarcely remember anything after getting in the patrol car," she agreed.

"So, if we were passed out, how did we get into the resort, up the elevator, into our rooms, undress ourselves, and get into bed?" I asked.

"I don't know. Truthfully, I don't care," she moaned.

"Do you honestly think the police drove us all the way back here from Patong, carried us up to our suite, undressed us, and put us in our beds?" I asked her.

"Well, I sure as hell hope it wasn't the bellboy," she grumbled. "I remember a couple of those policemen being good looking, but the bellboy is not, not even a little bit."

225

"No, he isn't." I paused. "Whatever happened, I guess I can live with it."

A loud growling noise sounded from the other side of the bed.

"I'm hungry." Barbie put her hand to her stomach.

"Yeah, I need hangover food," I agreed. "I need a combo burrito from Taco Crack and a Pepsi, like nobody's business."

"I think you're out of luck." Barbie gingerly slid a foot off of the bed. "I haven't seen a Taco Crack since we left New York."

"I hate Fuck-It Island," I grumbled, burrowing deep into the covers.

"I'll order room service." She slid her leg back under the covers.

"I'll have dry pancakes and Ibuprofen. Tell them to send up the whole bottle," I groaned, putting my index fingers to my temples.

Barbie picked up the phone by the bed. It was only fifteen minutes later when we heard room service knocking on the door. I was amazed that we managed to stumble out of the bed, down the hall, and into the living room. I guess that's the power of food. Once we reached the living room, I fell onto the couch, while Barbie opened up the door. The bellboy wheeled in our breakfast with a smile, even though the clock said it was well past lunch.

While Barbie dug through her purse for a tip, I glanced up at the bellboy from my resting place. He stood next to the food cart like a dolt, with a stupid grin taking up the majority of his face. Barbie was right, he was not attractive. He was scrawny, with scraggly hair, and a head that was too big for his body. I really hoped that he hadn't undressed me. The idea of him touching me made me want to throw up, or was that the hangover mixing with the smell of food? Cautiously, I moved my gaze to the food trays.

"What did you order?" I wrinkled my nose.

"Everything on the menu, I thought we'd pick our way through it," Barbie answered.

I slowly let out a breath, trying to calm my stomach. "Well, something under those lids smells horrible. Send whatever smells so bad back, it's making me gag."

Barbie looked at the bellboy. "What is that smell?"

"Fish."

Barbie's face turned green. "Take it back. Take anything that's fish back," she called, rushing out of the room with her hand over her mouth.

I looked at the Bellboy. With a shrug, I said, "We had a rough night."

"Yes, no fish. Fish all gone." He smiled, nodding, while stacking a handful of covered plates back onto the food cart.

I stood up, dug through my purse for some money, and handed him some cash. "Thank you."

I waited for him to leave, but he just stood looking at me, smiling, and nodding. With a big sigh, I waved him and the fish out the door, just as Barbie came back into the room. No wonder the bellboy had been smiling like a dolt. Neither of us had put on clothes or even a robe.

Giving Barbie a stricken look, I said, "We just opened the door to the creepy bellboy in only our bras and underwear."

Barbie looked down and shrugged. "This covers more than my bikini, and I go out in public in that."

My stomach groaned as I glanced down the hall at my bedroom. I hadn't noticed what a long walk it was to my closet. The smell of pancakes wafted up to me, causing a rumble deep in my stomach. Finally, I said, "You have a point. Okay, I'm starved." I began lifting plates, searching for those pancakes. "What are the sliced cucumbers for?"

Barbie picked up a pancake. Devouring it, she explained, "Our eyes, we're going to spend the day detoxing. After we eat, I'm going to mix up a guac facial, so don't eat the cucumber slices or the guacamole. We'll sit out on the veranda soaking up some vitamin D rays, in our facial masks and cucumbers, until the chiropractor gets here. Then, at two I've scheduled us for in room massages. At four we'll have mani-pedis. After that...I'm not sure. I just told the concierge to send up everything they have."

I looked over at Barbie. "You've done this before."

"Too many times." She sighed. "I think I'm getting too old for this party lifestyle," she said, popping a handful of Ibuprofen into her mouth.

She was attempting to put the lid back on it when I reached for the bottle. "Maybe, it's time to settle down, slow down on the partying like a rock star."

She gave me a dirty look.

"Think about it, you could date a nice guy that you like for more than just his investment portfolio, and be involved in a fulfilling and lasting relationship. You could even marry for love instead of diamonds, big houses, and even bigger bank accounts," I suggested.

"Love is fleeting. Only diamonds are forever," Barbie countered.

Nineteen

After finishing a light breakfast of bland food, we lounged on the veranda in our guac masks for an indeterminate amount of time. The door chimed, interrupting our lazy afternoon. Behind it stood an elderly Taiwanese man with short gray hair and his much younger looking clone holding a large portable padded table on wheels. The chiropractor had arrived. Watching him bend Barbie into strange angles did not entice me to let him crack my bones, but Barbie insisted.

Feeling like a sacrifice, I approached the padded table. He said something in Thai, which I didn't understand, while motioning towards the table the men had set up in the middle of the room. Copying Barbie's earlier moves, I climbed onto the table, put my head in the little padded hole, stared at the floor, and prayed the little old man didn't paralyze me.

"Crrrraaaacckkk…crack…crack..." My joints succumbed to the old man's strong hands.

For the next half hour, the old man twisted, pulled, pushed, and at one time jumped on my body. His every effort calculated to force my joints into submission. By the end, my body was pliant and without pain for the first time in years.

"Thank you! Oh wow! That was amazing!" I gushed.

"I've never heard someone crack like you did. There for a while it was almost musical," Barbie teased.

"I don't want it to be over," I frowned. "I like him, even if I can't say his name. I want to keep him. Can we keep him?" I pleaded.

"Listen to you! He's a chiropractor not a pet," she chided.

The clone approached me, "You come." He pointed to the floor that had been covered with a sheet.

"What?" I asked.

"You come, lie on floor," he insisted.

"More chiropractor?" I asked eagerly.

"No, acupuncture," he corrected.

"Acupuncture? Isn't that where they put needles in your body?" I asked Barbie.

"Don't worry, you'll love it." Barbie assured me.

"No. Um, no…thank you." I shook my head, "I'm fine really."

Barbie stared me down, warning, "You're letting your ignorant fears get in the way of our fun spa day."

"Hey, I tried the chiropractor. No one said anything about using me as a pincushion," I said, protectively wrapping my hands around my arms.

"It's fine. He just finished me, and I'm fine. Just give him a chance to work with you." While speaking she had artfully eased me over to the other side of the room.

I looked down at the sheet. "But, I don't like needles or pain. I'm fine, really." I took a step back.

"Just give it a chance. Your body will thank you," she cajoled.

"I just don't…,"

"Just try it. If you don't like it, he'll stop," she promised. "You'll barely be able to feel it. I took a nap."

"A nap?" I asked, doubt written all over my face.

"Have I ever steered you wrong?" She asked.

"Yes, the day we got here. Did you forget about the torture bent kidnappers on the sex boat full of cocaine?" I asked.

"Just trust me. I do it all the time. You'll feel great," she assured me.

The next thing I knew, I was lying on the sheet, trying to relax, while the clone used me as a human pincushion. "Why did I let you talk me into this?" I asked. "What if he punctures a lung? What if I die?"

"Relax. You'll dislodge the ones up in your neck. They aren't that deep," she cautioned.

"The ones in my neck?" I asked.

232

"Yes, while you've been stressing, he's been working. He's good isn't he?" She smirked next to me.

"I thought he was just touching my neck to feel for, you know...veins and stuff," I answered sheepishly.

"Just wait until he's done, you'll feel like a whole new person," She smiled, picking up a magazine from last night.

Half an hour later, I had to admit she was right as we bid our visitors goodbye.

"That was so cool!" I admitted, heading to the kitchen for a glass of water.

"I'm feeling better already," Barbie agreed, fixing herself a light snack of orange slices and grapes.

Next, the masseuses arrived for our two hour massages. They beat, poked, and prodded our sore muscles until it felt as if we didn't have any. When they were done, the day continued with a stream of tiny Taiwanese men and women appearing at our door, one after another. They lavished us with manicures, pedicures, deep skin cleansing treatments, hot oil treatments for our hair, fish to eat the dead cells from our toes, and glasses full of strange liquids all meant to make us feel and look better. Once the staff had finished pampering us, we moved out to the veranda to lie in the warm sun, soaking up vitamin D rays while catching up on much needed sleep. We were still on the veranda when I heard a door close.

Leaving my eyes closed, I turned my head towards Barbie. "Are we expecting anyone else?"

"No, they didn't have anything else to offer us," Barbie said groggily.

"I just heard the door close." I sleepily opened my eyes in preparation to get up and investigate.

"It wasn't our room," Barbie assured me. "You probably just heard the people next door coming back for dinner."

"It sounded like our room," I disagreed.

"It couldn't have been. I latched the security lock before we came out here. No one can get in without us opening the door from the inside, not even the staff," she insisted.

"You're probably right," I agreed as heavy lids closed over my tired eyes.

A shadow blocked the sun's rays just before a deep voice, full of concern, asked, "How are you feeling today, Trouble?"

My eyes shot open. I shook my head, but the apparition remained. I was obviously dreaming. Taking a deep breath, I closed my eyes, and silently counted to three. When they opened again, he was still there, gazing down at me with a bemused expression.

The man in front of me appeared to be about my age. He was significantly taller than me, with dark brown hair that curled just below his ears and fell softly across his thick brown eyebrows. I hungrily drank in the familiar sight of his kissable lips, high cheekbones, and the small cleft in his chin. He remained silent as my gaze moved down to his exceptionally broad shoulders, tight muscular frame, and washboard abs. Blinking, I realized he was wearing only a pair of leather sandals, blue and white swim trunks, a thick leather banded watch, and a look of concern.

"Mmmm...I don't know what your specialty is handsome, but if the resort sent you up as part of the pampering package, then I am absolutely going to have to come back here again," Barbie purred beside me.

With a quick look at Barbie, I sat up. "He's not with the hotel. You should be able to see that from his height and obviously Caucasian features," I growled.

Barbie gave me a confused look. "What's got you so pissy?"

Turning back to Eric, I ignored her. "What are you doing here?" I glanced into the living room towards the locked door. "How did you get in here?"

He flashed a set of even white teeth at me. "The door was open."

"No it wasn't. The door automatically locks when it shuts. Even if it for some reason it hadn't locked itself, it was latched on the inside," I argued.

He shrugged. "Alright, it was locked. Does it matter?"

Glaring up at him, I folded my arms across my chest. "What are you doing here?"

He crouched beside me, balancing on the balls of his feet, before answering my question. "I came to check on you. I know Doc said that you'd be fine, once the drug wore off." He paused before continuing, "I had to leave before you woke up. I wanted to see for myself that you were alright."

"You had to leave?" I narrowed my eyes at him. "You mean you were here?"

His expression was somber. "Of course, you don't think that I would just send you back with one of my men? Not in the shape you were in. You scared the hell out of me last night. I thought…I thought that I might lose you." He reached out, tenderly touching my face. "I couldn't think of anything but you, all day."

Pent-up hurt and rejection surged to the surface, pushing aside my longing for him. Knocking his hand away I growled, "You can't lose what's not yours."

Barbie sat up. "Wait a minute! You're one of the policemen from last night."

"Police? Are you sure?" I glanced over at Barbie.

"I'm a little hazy about the details, but I think so," she replied.

I couldn't help but notice his eyes race across her body, taking all of her in. Pursing my lips and narrowing my eyes, I watched him openly admire her nearly naked form. Unreasonable heated anger surged through my veins.

Barbie moved her gaze from the man beside me to my chair. "Who is this guy, Jess?"

"Eric Wolf," he answered, before I could respond. "You must be Barbie."

Barbie slowly smiled up at Eric. "So, you're the mysterious Wolfman that I've heard so much about?" She glanced over at me. "I owe you an apology, cousin. He is every bit as hot as you said he was."

My eyes, a vessel for the animosity growing inside of me, shot daggers into the chiseled form in front of me. How dare he show up here, drooling over Barbie, after ignoring me for the past three weeks? As I started to speak, those dangerous dark eyes turned to me. My anger was vanquished by the sound of my own blood pumping in my ears. In silence, I watched as, much more slowly, he looked me up and down. My face warmed under his smile. Suddenly, I felt underdressed.

"Barbie, we should go inside, and put some clothes on," I stammered.

"We should?" Barbie gave me a look that asked *'Why'*.

"Don't get dressed on my account. I'm enjoying the view." Eric lightly traced a finger down my bare leg.

I quickly drew in my breath, as my heart began to race and my body temperature soared. I was mad at him, wasn't I? Why was I upset with him again? I couldn't remember. I was having difficulty focusing. Pulling my legs up to my chest, I shook my head to clear it. I didn't want him to know what his touch did to me. His eyes followed my legs, resting on the newly exposed space between them. A decent guy would at least pretend to look away.

"Come on, Barbie." I stood up, forcing Eric to stand as well. "It's time to put some clothes on."

"Why? We've been dressed this way all week," she muttered, following my lead. "Besides, all you've talked about for the past month is the Wolfman. Now that Mr. Hotstuff shows up, you want to put clothes on?" she grumbled. "If it was me, I'd be taking some clothes off," she purred at Eric, while slinking around him.

"Barbie!" I almost shouted.

"Sorry, I couldn't help myself." She stepped through the glass doors.

My face was becoming uncomfortably warm, clueing me into the fact that I had turned bright red from the roots of my hair to my chest. I glanced up coyly, to peek at Eric's face.

"I'm all you've talked about?" he grinned.

"No!" I denied.

"Yes!" Barbie yelled from the room behind us.

I shot her a dirty look through the open glass doors. "Don't you have something else to do?"

She ignored me as she addressed Eric. "It's been unbearable. She keeps swearing that she sees you everywhere she goes, and she won't give any other guy the time of day." She shook her head. "There have been some damn fine men trying to give her the time of day, too."

"Really?" He was rocking back on his heels with his hands in his pockets and a self-satisfied smirk on his face.

"No, don't listen to her. She's just trying to cause trouble. I haven't thought about you since you left me in Oklahoma." I pretended to brush imaginary dirt off of my arm. "What was there to think about? We had our little fling, then we both agreed to move on. And, I have moved on, lots of times."

I moved to step around him. In a swift motion, he grabbed me by the waist pulling me to him. The smell of his cologne enveloped me. Against my will and better judgment, I could feel my body begin to sink into his.

His voice was rough with emotion, "I didn't agree to you moving on. I told you, in Portland, that I didn't want you to be with anyone else."

I forced myself to focus on the conversation and not his hand lightly wrapped around my waist. "But, you didn't want to be with me. I told you, it doesn't work that way."

"It doesn't?" His enticingly deep coffee colored eyes bored into mine.

"No, it doesn't." I struggled to step away from him.

"Then, why is your heart beating so fast? And, why did you call out my name last night, when you were in trouble?" His eyes searched mine.

I looked away. "I don't know what you're talking about."

He released his hold, allowing me to step back to put some distance between us. I needed some distance. I needed a whole football field of distance.

239

"Last night in Patong, we were getting ready to close in on our target when you fell down in the road. Your cousin couldn't get you back on your feet. When my man saw you two, he left his position to help, thinking that you were drunk or high or both." His face was grim. "Public intoxication is against the law here. Do you know what happens to tourists who get arrested in Thailand? They get thrown into a dirty jail and forgotten about, until it becomes convenient to remember them. Top is a softy. You reminded him of his little sisters. He didn't want you to get arrested, and thrown into a Thai prison to rot."

"Oh," was all I could say.

Barbie stepped up to the glass doors. "We hadn't been using drugs. Those asswipes slipped something into our drinks."

He nodded in response. All the while, his eyes continued to hold mine hostage. "As pretty as you two are, and the way you were dressed, Top was afraid that bad things would happen to you in jail. He radioed it in, then went over to help you. He managed to get you up and out of the street, but you could barely stand or speak. He was trying to decide what to do with the two of you when you looked at him and asked for me, using my full name. That's when he called me over. He didn't know who you were, but not too many people know me by my full name, especially not here." He caressed my hand as he spoke.

His touch was almost more than I could handle. Wherever his skin grazed mine, there was fire. Did he know what he was doing?

With a deep breath, I fought off an overwhelming urge to grab him and drag him into my room. Taking another deep breath, I said, "I need to get dressed. You can wait out here."

It didn't take me long to pull on a pair of shorts and a t-shirt. Before facing Eric, I needed a moment to collect myself. I willed my heartbeat to slow to normal as I looked at myself in the mirror. Once I felt more in control, I fluffed my hair, applied some lip gloss, and headed back out to the living room. Stepping into the room, I noticed that Eric was seated on the couch across from Barbie, who had put on a pair of white yoga pants and a matching t-shirt.

Barbie spoke as I came in, "He said he's been working all day, so I invited the Wolfman to dinner and ordered room service. I thought we could eat while we talk."

In response, I casually shrugged my indifference.

Eric's eyes were on me. He watched as I crossed the room, then calmly lowered myself to the cushions at the other end of the couch. I nodded in acknowledgement before sitting Indian Style on the comfy cushions and pulling one into my lap. I needed something between us. The cushion was the best I could come up with. I was having difficulty resisting the magnetic pull that I always feel when he's around.

His eyes bored into mine as he spoke, "Barbie was just telling me what she remembered about last night."

"It's not much," Barbie apologized.

"Barbie remembers more than I do," I said nervously. Why was I so nervous?

His face was grim, his expression revealing his concern. "You two were lucky that we found you when we did." He focused on me. "You left your purse in the room, so I didn't know that you had gone into Patong. If I'd known that you were in the city, I would have had a man on you inside the bar. This would never have happened." He paused. I could see anger, along with something else, in his eyes. "Patong, just like any unknown city, can be dangerous for two girls traveling alone." He paused. "Especially girls that go out drinking with strange men." There was a hint of betrayal in his voice as he finished the sentence.

I glared at him. "My purse? You bugged my purse?"

"I put a transmitter in your purse back in Seattle, remember?" he reminded me. "I just haven't gotten around to removing it."

"So," I took a deep breath, "you've been spying on me, since I left Seattle?"

"No. But, I have had some unforeseen personnel problems. The last few weeks, I've had a man watching you, protecting you," he clarified.

"Are you hearing this?" I pointed my finger at Barbie. "You thought that I was imagining things." Narrowing my eyes, I turned my attention back to Eric. "Spying or protecting, I'm not seeing the difference. Regardless, I don't need your protection." I waved him off. "I'm not in danger. Don't you remember? All of that nonsense
242

with Jim is over with. He's safely tucked away in jail, for a really long time. He's being tried for multiple murders, extortion, money laundering, kidnapping, stalking, and attempting to bribe a police officer."

He frowned, then said, "I'm sorry, Trouble. I should have told you, but I didn't want to worry you."

I gave him a questioning look.

"A few days after I left you with your parents, one of my men from the Seattle office went rogue. He thought that we were more than what we were. He made threats against you. I was afraid that he would follow through with those threats. While I looked for him, I had a man looking after you. It took me a couple of weeks to track him down and neutralize the threat."

"What did you mean by *'neutralize the threat'*?" Barbie questioned him.

Eric stared, unblinking, into her eyes, his face expressionless.

She turned pale under her tan and stammered, "Oh, uh...okay."

Feeling frustrated, I put my head in my hands. "You couldn't have just called and told me to be careful? Instead, you sent someone to spy on me? Who does that? What is wrong with you?"

"I know how well you listen. I wasn't taking any chances." His eyes implored me to understand. "If anything had happened to you, I never would have been able to forgive myself."

Barbie sighed like that was the most romantic thing that she had ever heard, causing me to roll my eyes. My frown deepened as I crossed my arms. What had I seen in this chauvinistic man who thought so little of me that he ignored me while employing someone to watch me?

"If it makes you feel better, he was miserable the whole time. He said it was hotter than hell, and there was nothing to do but watch the crows fly." He gave me a sexy grin that reminded me just why I liked him.

I shrugged my shoulders, trying not to grin back. "Of course it was hot. It is Oklahoma, in August." My eyes narrowed suspiciously. "What else did he tell you?"

"Let's see." He moved closer to me on the couch, his eyes holding mine hostage. "You went on some job interviews, but didn't get any offers. You spent a lot of time at a local bar with the same group of friends. You have a habit of changing clothes in the car, in broad daylight, speeding when it's not necessary, wandering around the mall without buying anything, and nude sunbathing when you think no one is around..."

"Ah...ah...," I choked on my emotions, unable to get the words out. "What I do in the privacy of my parents' home, when no one is around, is my business. Besides, I sunbathe on the balcony off of my bedroom. No one can see me up there. I mean, who are you people?" My hands raced to illustrate my displeasure, while fire raced from my cheeks to my toes.

On the other side of the room, Barbie was laughing so hard she almost fell out of her chair.

Eric ignored her. "After my man told me about the sunbathing, I told him to keep a reasonable distance, unless he had reason to suspect that you were in danger from something other than sunburn." His eyes raked over my body causing a warmth to flow to places I had almost forgotten I had. "I don't like the idea of other men seeing you naked."

"That is so sweet." Barbie grinned encouragingly.

I shot her a look that said 'S*hut up*'. She sat back in her chair, pouting.

"Okay, if you '*neutralized*' your problem, and your man stopped spying on me while I was in the states, then how did you know that I was here? What are you doing here?" I clenched my fist in annoyance.

"My man wasn't taken off of the case until you were in New York. He was in the airport waiting on his flight out when the two of you caught your flight out of New York," he explained.

"Is that so?" I asked, unconvinced.

We locked glances for a moment before he added, "I asked your brother where you were headed. He told me that you were staying here, with your cousin."

"Greg? Greg told you that I had gone to Thailand?" I was livid. "I knew he would send someone to spy on me! I told him, and

I'm telling you, I am perfectly capable of taking care of myself without his or anyone else's help."

"Yes, I noticed that last night." His words rang flat in the suddenly silent room. "I hate to disappoint you, but Greg didn't send me. We were at his place, getting ready to play poker. I mentioned that my man had spotted you at LaGuardia, then the news came on."

I exchanged glances with Barbie. We knew what he was going to say next.

"Imagine my surprise when I saw a woman, who looked like you, speeding away from an exploding yacht." He gave us a disapproving look before adding, "Greg filled me in on the details. What were you two thinking? Two women, traveling alone, are a target anywhere, especially in foreign countries, even at beach resorts."

I shrugged, quietly mumbling, "It wasn't our fault."

He shook his head as if to say that I was beyond hope. "Anyway, I was already scheduled to fly to Phuket the next morning, for a recovery job. After hearing about the trouble you had gotten involved with, I decided to bring an extra man to function as your security. I was hoping that he would be able to keep you out of trouble. He apparently underestimated both the importance of the assignment, and your ability to find trouble."

"Hey!" I protested. "Except for that little episode last night, which could have happened to anyone, we were doing fine on our own."

He gave me a look that said that he disagreed. "We got in around five yesterday morning. My man picked you up during your run. Do you really want me to go over yesterday with you?"

I glared at him, daring him to say anything. I have nothing to hide. Well almost nothing. Maybe he was bluffing. I hoped he was bluffing. In my mind, I quickly went over the events of yesterday. Let's see, there was the mortifying moment when I tripped in the surf, and got caught in a riptide, while jogging. Thankfully, there had only been a few witnesses. Then, there was the guy who had cornered me on the isolated patio, another misdirected weirdo who thought I had his jewel. Just as things were getting tense, the same jogger had walked up, startling my assailant into leaving. And of course, there was CrossFit. There aren't words to describe how bad that had been. There were lots of witnesses on site, including my helpful rescuer. Had anything else happened yesterday?

"I don't know what you're talking about," I lied unconvincingly.

He sighed in frustration. "Your brother was right. You don't just attract trouble. You are a magnet for disaster."

I rolled my eyes at him. "Really? Now you're just being mean."

He leaned toward me, forcing me to sink further into the couch cushions. "Trouble, by the time that I got to you last night, and I was only about a block away, you were done. Neither of you were in good shape; but, compared to you, your cousin was completely lucid and in control. You couldn't even stand without help."

I gave him the evil eye. "You are exaggerating."

"Trouble, as soon as I got there you passed out in my arms." He grinned as he added, "Calling my name."

I pursed my lips in annoyance. "That's only because I recognized you."

"That's enough!" Barbie stood up putting her hands on her hips.

Surprised, Eric and I turned our attention to her. "Jess, you know you've got it bad for hotstuff here. Your pride is just hurt because he said he didn't want a relationship with you, and then ignored you for three weeks."

I opened my mouth to protest, but she cut me off.

"No, you're going to listen, both of you." She turned her attention to Eric. "I know men. No man is going to pay someone to protect a woman that he's not interested in, when he doesn't have to. Bodyguards are expensive. Somehow, I don't think your Rambo clones come cheap."

He frowned, shaking his head. "I've been hemorrhaging money since I met her."

"Okay then, I have some questions that I'd like to ask, once you two are done jockeying for position. So, how about you two kiss and make up?" She gave us the same look my mother used on me and Greg to get us to behave across the room when we were children.

My mouth dropped open as I stared in horror at the traitor in front of me.

Eric winked at me. "That sounds like fun."

Before I could organize my thoughts into speech, the doorbell rang.

Barbie announced, "That'll be room service. I'll get it while you two work things out. I need to pee anyway."

Taking my hands into his, Eric looked into my eyes, and said, "I'm sorry. If you want me to go, I will."

"No, it's just...I mean." I paused, trying to organize my thoughts. "I hadn't heard from you, and then...you're here, and you've been watching me, but...I didn't think..." I shook my head, trying to clear it. "Never mind."

He scooted closer, invading my bubble. "You thought that I slept with you, then moved on. That I didn't care."

I felt something warm and wet slide down my cheek as I silently nodded.

Eric reached out, gently wiping away the tear. "Trouble, we have completely different lives. I thought if I didn't call or see you, it would be easier, but things didn't work out that way. I couldn't stop thinking about you."

I nodded my understanding. "Where do we go from here?"

"I don't know." He shook his head. "I hated the thought that my man was after you to get to me." His fingers tightened around my hand. "And today, I was so worried about you. I couldn't focus on the job. In my line of work, that could get me killed."

"So, you still don't want a relationship," I said, wanting him to correct me, knowing he wouldn't.

His face was expressionless. "I can't afford one," he paused before adding, "right now. Maybe not ever. What about you? Do you know who you are or what you want yet?"

I sat beside him, speechless, as a tear silently slid down my cheek. This couldn't be happening, not again.

He had a strange expression on his face as he leaned in and kissed me gently on the lips. "I should go." He stood up, giving me a forlorn look.

"Wait." I stood up, looking at him shyly.

He gazed at me expectantly.

I bit my lip, not sure how to say what I wanted to say. "You brought us back here, right?"

"Yes."

"So, you carried me in, undressed me, and put me to bed." It wasn't a question.

He looked confused. "Yes, I thought that you would be more comfortable."

"Um…Barbie, did you…?" My words faltered.

He grinned down at me, relief on his face. "Is that what you're worried about? No, I never touched her. You are the only woman that I've touched, since we met."

I smiled up at him. "Really?"

He nodded. "Top carried her up, and put her to bed, then he left." He paused. "I had Doc look at you both in Patong. He told me that you'd be alright once the drug wore off. You were so bad off... What I mean was, I was worried. I couldn't leave you. Anyway, I stayed as long as I could. I would have liked to have been here when you woke up, but I postponed the OP to get you to safety. We lost our target in the confusion. I had to get back to work."

"Doc?" I was confused. "You called a doctor for me?"

"Doc is one of my men," he explained. "He did two years in med school, dropped out, and then joined the army as a medic. He didn't like the army any more than med school, so after a few years he got out. I hired him six months ago to replace a man who left. He's a good man, and a good medic."

"You have your own EMT?" I asked.

He nodded gravely. "We always take a medic with us when we're doing a job, just in case."

"Thank you, for taking care of me, again. I know you didn't have to," I said softly.

He touched me lightly on the cheek. "You're welcome. Now do me a favor. Stay out of trouble for a few days, at least until I finish up my business here. I may not be around the block to come to your rescue the next time, alright?"

I nodded. "What about the man you assigned to protect me?"

"I fired him."

"Why?" I gave him a surprised look.

"He got sloppy, fell asleep on the job." His face hardened, "You could have been killed."

"So." I gave him a stern look. "No more spying?"

"No spying. That doesn't mean that I won't have a man watching you, protecting you." He stepped through the door. "I'd do it myself, but I have to get back to work."

"Wait!" I called out as the door began to shut.

The door stopped. Slowly it opened, allowing Eric to saunter back through it. He stopped at the table picked up a hamburger, then turned towards the door.

"Thanks for the burger." He said with a grin, as he sauntered back through the door and out of sight.

Barbie and I stood side by side, silently watching as the door slowly clicked back into place.

"That man is H-O-T, hot!" Barbie pretended to fan herself with her hand.

I gazed at the door, frowning. "He's unavailable."

"Don't think that I don't know it," she agreed.

I cocked my head to the side and looked at her. "What is that supposed to mean?"

"Can't you see it, Jess? He's as into you as you are him. I mean, the man barely noticed I was alive. He was too busy drinking you in."

I shook my head, frowning. "No. You were right before. If he was interested in me he wouldn't have left."

She gave me a surprised look, then laughed. "Cousin, you have a lot to learn about men. The Wolfman didn't leave. He just went back to work."

Twenty

After eating, we headed down to the gym to meet with our CrossFit class. It was the most strenuous thing we had attempted all day. I would have skipped it, except Barbie all but dragged me with her. I looked at the clock, hoping it was time to go back to bed. It had only been ten minutes, ten long minutes. My body was hating me. I, in turn, was hating Barbie.

Barbie was putting us through the most grueling workout yet, while chanting, "A hangover is not an excuse," over and over again.

Struggling to keep up, I considered throttling her. If she would only slow down long enough for me to catch my breath. Time stood still as I turned into myself, determined not to vomit or trip or fall or do anything, other than keep up and finish the workout without a commotion. A quick glance at the clock told me that there were only five minutes left. Satisfaction coursed through my veins. The circuit was almost complete!

"I'm going to make it," I gasped, in a barely audible voice.

That's when it happened. I was doing box jumps with everyone else when I received one of my most mortifying injuries ever. I jumped up like I was supposed to, but when I came down I missed my box, somehow landing on thin air. Panicking, I attempted to readjust my landing. All that did was make things worse.

My right foot just barely touched the edge of the box, throwing me off balance and causing me to spin sideways across the room. With unexpected force, I hit my head and shoulder on the edge of the weight rack. Then, instead of waiting for the stars to fade from my vision, I attempted to save face by pretending that I was fine. With my ears still ringing and my gait uncoordinated, I stumbled forward, inadvertently tripping over the hand weights before crashing to the floor with an unsettling cry of pain. That's when everything went black.

"Oh my god! Are you okay?" Barbie was leaning over me.

The entire class had stopped the circuit to rush to my side. Newly familiar faces stood over me with concerned eyes. I just lay on the cold floor, hoping it wasn't as bad as it felt.

"I'm fine. I just lost my balance," I somehow managed to murmur.

Tony helped me into a sitting position before quickly examining the huge knot that had just appeared on my temple. Once his examination was complete, he said, "You're going to have a pretty good sized goose egg in a couple of hours. You may want to take it easy, and call it a night."

I nodded, I didn't want to admit it, but my head was the least of my worries. My body hurt in places that I didn't know I had. Taking a deep breath, I decided that I could mark stunt double off of my career ambitions.

"Do you need some help getting up?" Tony asked me.

With a dazed expression, I focused on him. Until now, Tony hadn't so much as looked my direction. He was cute, a couple of years younger than me, about an inch taller, with muscles to spare, intelligent eyes, and a hyper vigilance that most vacationers lacked. When we had arrived for the class, he had been in the middle of his evening work out. After a brief introduction, Barbie had flirtatiously invited him to join our growing CrossFit group. Before we got started, I overheard him tell one of the other guests that he was from Boston, vacationing here with his brothers. I had met his type before and had my suspicions of who his brothers were.

Tony stood above me, holding out his left hand to help me up. Trying not to look like a wimp, I accepted the help. As he pulled me to my feet, a searing pain raced through my right knee causing me to cry out in anguish. Quickly, he pulled me against him, taking the weight off of my knee. While I struggled to balance on one foot, I looked up to see beads of sweat pooling on his forehead. He was nervous. I was pretty sure I knew why.

Leaning into him, I almost imperceptibly whispered, "You had better not tell *him* about this."

Tony's face paled under his tan, confirming my suspicions. Silently, he waited to see if I was badly hurt, avoiding my piercing gaze, while Randall crouched down to take took a look at my knee. After a few tense minutes Randall stood up.

"It feels like a mild muscle injury. It's not serious. You will need to take an anti-inflammatory and stay off it for the rest of the night, probably tomorrow too. You'll also want to take care of your head. That was a pretty hard hit that may have resulted in a mild concussion," he said, with concern. "I wish I had access to an X-ray machine. Since I don't, I'm going to insist on you taking precautions to avoid further injury."

I nodded my thanks. "I can do that. It's good to have a doctor in the group."

He shook his head fondly, "If you keep this up, I'm going to have to start billing you."

"Randall would you mind taking Jessie upstairs again?" Hillary asked.

I found myself surprised at the relief I felt for their concern and help.

He sighed, then said, "Of course not. Let's go child."

Randall effortlessly picked me up, while Hillary led the way to the elevator. I looked back to see Barbie talking to Tony. His expression had gone from morose to cheerful. I was pretty sure that she had offered to personally raise his spirits. As the elevator started to close Barbie eased inside, grinning like the cat that ate the canary.

"Did you thank Tony for me, cousin?" I asked, with a knowing smile.

She grinned back at me. "Since you're not going to be much fun tonight, do you mind if I go and thank him more thoroughly?"

I shook my head. "Of course not, go and have fun." I leaned forward and whispered, "You should know, he's one of Eric's men."

She gave me a surprised look. "Are you sure?"

"Pretty sure." I nodded.

"Even better." Barbie's grin got bigger.

When the elevator stopped, Barbie walked ahead of us to open the door. With Barbie leading the way, Randall gently laid me on the couch.

With a grateful smile, I said, "Thank you."

Barbie smiled sincerely at Randall and Hillary. "Yes, thank you both so much. I don't know what we would do without your help."

Randall smiled kindly. "We don't mind, you girls need a keeper."

Barbie grinned and turned towards the hall. "I'm going to go and get cleaned up real quick, my date is supposed to meet me downstairs in just a few minutes."

"You do that dear, we'll take care of Jessie." Hillary was bustling around, making sure that I had a pillow, the remote, and a glass of water.

"Hillary, it's time to leave Jessie alone. She needs to rest." Randall gently prompted his wife to go.

"I don't like leaving her alone like this. Barbie has plans." She frowned, "We should stay with Jessie, just in case she does have a concussion. Would you like that dear?" she called from across the room.

I shook my head. "That's not necessary. I'll be fine."

She looked torn as Randall gently guided her toward the door. "Come on dear, it's time for dinner."

"But, what about Jessie's dinner?" she asked, with a frown.

"I already ate," I said. No one was listening to me.

"If we leave who's going to take care of her?" She looked pleadingly at Randall.

"I'll take care of her," a familiar voice said from the door.

Everyone turned to look at the man, dressed head to toe in Rambo black, who had just stepped through the open door. Randall gave him a parentally assessing look as Hillary slowly let out her breath. I mentally rolled my eyes. He even had that effect on older women.

Eric held out his hand to Randall, and simply said, "Wolf."

"Doctor Randall Jones from Detroit. This is my wife, Hillary," Randall replied warily, firmly grasping the proffered hand.

"Nice to meet you Doctor and Mrs. Jones," Eric replied politely.

Randall narrowed his eyes, and asked Eric, "Are you a guest here at the resort?"

Eric's face was expressionless as he answered, "No, I'm here on business."

Randall and Hillary exchanged a glance, then Randall spoke to Eric. "Thank you for the offer Mr. Wolf, but it won't be necessary. Hillary and I don't mind staying and taking care of Jessie." He paused for effect before finishing, "She's like a daughter to us."

I watched Eric's mouth twist into a slight smile. "Don't worry Doctor Jones. I've had a lot of practice looking after Jessie. I'll take good care of her."

The atmosphere was tense as the two men stood silently sizing each other up. The room was quiet when Barbie stepped into the living room. She had taken the fastest shower in history, piled her wet hair on top of her head in a loose twist, and changed into a pair of dark green capris, a pale yellow tank top that showed off her girls, a pair of gold strappy hooker heels, and a ton of jewelry.

"Eric!" She squealed with delight, rushing over to give him a big hug.

Eric disentangled himself, then smiled down at her, he said, "Barbie, don't you look lovely."

She grinned up at him. "Why thank you, I've got a hot date."

He frowned down at her. "I came to talk to you about that."

She gave him an innocent look as she peered up at him through her lashes. "Really?"

His frowned deepened. With a sigh, he said, "Now I see the family resemblance."

"I am so sorry, have you met each other?" Barbie looked past Eric at Randall and Hillary.

Randall was frowning. Ignoring him, Hillary smiled warmly before saying, "Yes, we have. Is this a friend of yours, Barbie dear?"

"I guess you could say that." Barbie glanced over at me. Laughing at the expression on my face, she said, "You might say he's Jessie's boyfriend."

My mouth fell open in shock as my face caught fire. Leave it to Barbie to make things even more uncomfortable than they already were. Silently, I reminded myself to have a talk with her later. Right now, all eyes were on me. My mind went blank. I struggled to speak, but my tongue was made of stone. How I was going to explain this to Eric?

A high pitched voice, which I barely recognized as my own, said, "He's not my boyfriend. He's a friend. Just a friend."

Eric gave me a strange look, as if he was debating the idea.

Hillary shifted her glance from Eric to me. "How long have you two been *friends*, dear?"

"I don't know, a month?" I asked Eric.

His face was unreadable. "Something like that."

Hillary gave me a knowing look. "In that case, we had better be going now, shouldn't we Randall?"

Randall was still eyeing Eric. "I thought we had decided to stay, and look after Jessie."

Hillary expertly edged him towards the door. "Jessie will be just fine. Now, let's go get you something to eat." She looked over her shoulder to call out, "It was a pleasure meeting you, Eric. You kids have a lovely night. We'll see you girls tomorrow." We all watched as she gently, but firmly, guided her husband out the door, shutting it firmly behind them.

"I don't think he trusts you." I grinned over at Eric.

"Not even a little bit." Eric grinned back at me.

Barbie scrutinized him a moment before pronouncing, "It's the clothes. All of that black makes you look intimidating."

He gave her a level look. "That's the point. Now, about your date, it's cancelled."

Barbie's face contorted into a hideous vestige of its normal self. "What!"

"My men are not here for your enjoyment. They are working. At least they're supposed to be." He sighed, looking at Barbie's outfit.

"But, he said he had the night off," Barbie pouted.

"Yes, he has the night off, to go back to the FOB and get some sleep. I need my man rested and able to focus on his duties in the morning. He can't do that if he spends the night with you. I won't have you work your way through my men like it's a sale at Nordstrom's." He gave her a knowing look.

Barbie walked over to me, demanding, "What did you tell him about me?"

"Almost nothing," I said honestly.

"So, how do you explain this?" she demanded.

"I told you how unreasonable he is, don't you remember?" I asked.

She turned back to Eric, narrowing her eyes. "You can't cancel my date. I'm going down to the lobby. When I get there, I will expect to see..." She looked at me. "What was his name again?"

"Tony." I rolled my eyes.

"I will expect to see Tony waiting for me. Do you understand me?" She angrily stared up at Eric.

Without expression, he calmly said, "As of fifteen minutes ago, Tony has been reassigned. He asked me to give you his apologies. It has been explained to him that you two ladies are off limits. I need you to understand, I expect you to leave my men to do their job. That means that you will neither date, nor initiate contact with, Tony, or any of my men, for the duration of this job." His dark coffee colored eyes bored deep into Barbie's bright blue ones. "Do *you* understand *me*?"

Barbie narrowed her eyes at him. Her voice shaking with anger, she quietly said, "Get out."

He raised an eyebrow, responding with, "Excuse me?"

Sensing a fight, I somehow managed to stumble off of the couch and across the room. Wincing through the pain in my knee, I put a hand on Barbie's shoulder.

"It won't do any good," I told her.

She glared over at me, and growled, "You're taking his side?"

Wincing again, as another stabbing pain shot up my leg and into my back, I said, "Of course, I'm not taking his side. But, I know Eric. He's not going to budge on this. Remember, this is the same man who, instead of calling me to tell me that I might be in danger, sent a man to follow me around the countryside." I glared at Eric.

He shrugged, unapologetically.

With an aggravated sigh, I said, "It's already done, and honestly you weren't that interested in him. You couldn't even remember his name," I reminded her.

Barbie pursed her lips. "Maybe you're right, but I might have been more interested in him later."

I shook my head. "We both know that you were just going to sleep with him, then move on to the next guy to pass close enough to smell your perfume. Think about how that would have affected things with me and Eric."

"The last I heard you were ready to help him drop dead. Do you honestly think things could get worse than that?" she asked.

Eric gave me a startled look.

Ignoring the both of them, I sighed. "Barbie, don't be such a child about this. Eric's men don't share women. That means that if you slept with Tony, then later met another one that you liked more than Tony, you wouldn't get a shot at him."

She frowned angrily. "That's not fair. He has all of those sexy guys, and I don't have any."

I rolled my eyes. In some ways, Barbie had never really left adolescence. "How about this? Eric agrees that after this job is done, and he doesn't have to worry about his men being distracted, you can have one?"

"Well, I guess that would be fair," she pouted.

I looked at Eric expectantly. "Well?"

He gave me an incredulous look. "I can't believe that you are even having this conversation. My men are not toys to be passed around. They are men."

"I'm just asking you to allow any of your men who might be interested to go out with Barbie after y'all finish your job here, that's all."

After a slight hesitation, he nodded his head. "If one of them asks her out, after the OP is complete, I won't interfere. For the record, I don't like the idea of your friends and family dating my men."

Barbie smiled dangerously, "I guess I can live with that." She frowned, looking from herself, to Eric, then to me. "Now, I'm all dressed up with no date. Well, I'm not hanging out in the room watching television all night with a chauvinist and a crip. I'm going down to the bar to get something to eat." She pointedly looked at me, and said, "Do *you* want to come with?"

Taking a sharp breath, as another twinge of pain grasped ahold of my knee, I said, "No, I barely made it across the floor. I'm going back to the couch for the rest of the night."

Barbie grabbed her purse from the counter, then slowly turned to look at Eric. "This isn't over," she said, sashaying out of the door.

"Are all of the females in your family this difficult?" Eric gave me a questioning look.

"Barbie is not being difficult. You did just cancel her date. Under the circumstances, I think she's handling it quite well." I did my best to look refined as I slowly hobbled towards the couch.

Eric watched me for a moment before shaking his head. An instant later, I was being lifted off of the ground. His scent engulfed me. I found myself remembering what he looked like without all of those clothes on. I was thankful when, a few steps later, he gently sat me on the cushions. Once I was settled, he gave the bump on my head a concerned look, then carefully examined my knee.

"Randall checked it out. He said it was a minor muscle injury, but I should stay off of it," I volunteered.

With a quick nod he got up and walked across the room. Was he leaving? No, he was heading down the hall.

"Where are you going?" I called after him, but he didn't answer.

A short time later, he reappeared with my bathing suit in his hands. Walking over to the couch, he effortlessly scooped me up, cradling me against his chest.

"What are you doing?" I asked, panicked at being skin to skin with only our clothes between us.

"Taking you downstairs to the hot tub. The warm water will be good for your knee," he answered, heading for the door.

"Wait a minute!" I exclaimed.

"What?" He gave me a confused look.

"I'm okay with the hot tub idea, but I think that I should change here first." I pointed to the room.

"That's probably best." He carried me back across the room, lowering me down to the couch, and asked, "Do you need help?"

I felt my cheeks turn crimson under his glance. "No, thank you. I can manage."

Shooting me a sexy smile, he sat down to wait.

"Uh uh." I shook my head. "I need some privacy while I change."

His eyes flickered over my body, causing me to feel exposed. "It's not like I haven't seen it before."

Frowning up at him, I said, "It's been awhile, and things are different, now."

"We should change that." He said, with a sexy smile.

Rolling my eyes, I pointed to the door. "Out! I'll call you when I'm ready."

Fifteen minutes later, we were seated side by side in the hot tub; me in my bikini and Eric in a pair of black silk boxers. He looked just as I remembered, mouthwatering. He was leaning back with his eyes shut, letting the heat soak into his tired muscles. Over the next few minutes, I watched him visibly relax, transforming from the tough warrior Wolf to the man that I knew as Eric. I couldn't help but wonder how many other people got to see this side of him. I bet it was a short list. As I watched the warm water dampen his hair with steam, his eyes opened. He met my gaze.

"How's your knee?" he asked.

I glanced toward the knee. Seeing him in just boxers, I had forgotten all about my knee. "It's better. Thank you, for bringing me down here. It was very sweet."

He gave me a small smile. "You're welcome.'"

"I mean, it was nice of you to give up your plans, to take care of me," I stammered.

"What plans?" He gave me a blank look.

I shrugged, self-consciously babbling, "I'm sure you were heading somewhere when you came up to tell Barbie about her date."

He slowly shook his head. "I'm done for the night. I stopped in the lobby to talk to Tony before his shift was over, and get his report. But, I was already heading up to your room. I wasn't about to miss out on spending the night with you."

I raised an eyebrow in surprise. "Who said you could spend the night?"

He reached over, his hand seductively edging up my side, towards my breasts. My heart skipped a beat as he slowly leaned over to gently brush his lips across mine. My thoughts stopped, signaling that my brain was no longer in control, as my body melted into his. Of their own accord, my fingers reached for him. I felt him moan with pleasure as his warm tongue urgently sought out mine.

After a moment, where time stood still, he lifted his mouth from mine, and asked, "Can I spend the night?"

Stupefied from his embrace, I just smiled.

"Is that a yes?" he asked.

"Knock, knock."

There was a strange man, dressed all in black, standing on the other side of the glass door. Eric sighed before stepping out of the hot tub. Once Eric opened the door, the man in black quickly stepped inside, without looking my way. That was fine by me. I had a feeling he was the bearer of bad news.

"Sir," he paused, then added, "We've got him."

Eric glanced back at me. "Are you sure?"

"The team has identified a number properties on the island owned by a Sigrid Coulthurst. Top is convinced he's hiding out in one of them." He looked expectant.

Wolf frowned. "What makes Top so sure? We've tracked down dozens of false leads over the past few days because of his aliases."

The man in black smiled. "Sir, this isn't another alias. Sigrid Coulthurst was his grandfather. The old man recently passed, leaving behind two resorts, three bars, half a town, and a villa on the island. Due to probate, all of the properties not under rental contract are currently vacant."

Wolf silently considered the man before him, before saying, "Have Henderson sent over to run protection for Jessie."

"Yes, sir." The man in black stepped outside, closing the door behind him.

I raised an eyebrow in anticipation of an explanation.

He was already a world away when he answered my unasked question. "I have to go. Henderson will be here in twenty. Stay out of trouble."

Before I could speak, he was gone. I was alone in the hot tub, with a bad leg, and no Eric. Flexing my knee and releasing a frustrated sigh, I submerged myself in the warm water. When I came up for air, I wasn't alone.

"What are you doing here?" I asked, venom in my voice.

"Looking for you," he replied with a smile.

"Take a hint, I'm not interested," I glared.

"That's too bad. I've gone through so much to find you. This time, I'm not leaving until I get what I came for," he held his hand out to help me out of the hot tub.

I sighed, "The stalker routine is getting old. Go away."

A creepy smile flitted across his face, making him look demented and causing a cold chill to run up my spine.

"I'm trapped in here with a maniac!" I whispered into the bubbling water.

A movement caught my eye. I looked up, just in time to see a bottle of Tequila pummel my intruder across the back of the head. Random's eyes crossed as he sank to the floor. I had to move quickly to catch his head before he face planted into the hot tub beside me. As I held his face mere inches from the bubbling water. Barbie grabbed the back of his collar, and tossed him towards a chair. I cringed at the sound of his head thumping against the wall. I didn't envy the headache he was going to have when he woke up.

Barbie reached down to pick up the bottle. "Good, he didn't break my bottle. That would have pissed me off."

My mouth hung open, waiting for my brain to decide what to say.

"Are you alright?" Barbie looked at me with concern.

I nodded. "Yeah. What are you doing here?"

She shrugged. "Besides clobbering the perv? I saw the Wolfman heading out the door with Batman. Seeing as you'd just been ditched, I figured you'd want a drink. So, I grabbed a bottle of Tequila and some limes." She pointed to a little bowl of limes on a table by the door. "When I came in, stalker boy was already here. Maybe I was a little rough on him, but I'm still pissed about being drugged." She gave him a swift kick exclaiming, "Asswipe."

271

I held a hand up, and she helped me out of the hot tub. Wrapping a towel around myself, I asked, "What do we do with him?"

With a glance toward the unconscious man, she said, "We'll send security after him, but first let's get you upstairs. He's not going anywhere."

Twenty One

The sun's first rays were just beginning to shine through the open window, bringing with it the sweet smell of the sea. What had awoken me, my alarm? No, I hadn't turned it on. I wasn't going to be running the beach today. I should really get up, but the bed felt so nice and smelled like…cologne? A strong arm snaked through the covers, pulling me into a warm embrace.

"What time is it?" I asked drowsily.

"It doesn't matter." Eric gently stroked my cheek. "I'm sorry for waking you, but I wanted to do this." He leaned forward, allowing his moist lips to caress mine while his hands explored my naked form.

"Time for CrossFit!" Barbie stood over me, looking way too happy for it to be morning.

"Huh…what…?" I stammered my confusion.

"CrossFit, you know that thing we do every morning after your run, but before we hit the beach? Speaking of the beach, I was thinking we could skip it this morning and go shopping instead. The bartender was telling me about these handmade dresses his sister makes just a couple of miles away. What do you think?" she asked.

"What happened to Eric?" I asked.

"You mean after he abandoned you in the hot tub last night? I don't know, and you don't care, remember?" She stood in front of me with her hands on her hips, daring me to argue.

"That's right!" He had left me half naked and defenseless in the hot tub. This morning had just been a dream. I pulled the covers over my head. "You should have let me sleep. I was having a good, no great, dream. It was the closest I've come to getting lucky in weeks."

She frowned, and said, "CrossFit will make you feel better."

"No, it won't. With my lack of coordination, it'll just maim me further. I'm not going. I didn't run this morning, and I'm not going to CrossFit today, or ever again," I groaned.

Barbie frowned down at me in silent judgment. "Why not?"

"Did you forget about my leg? I could barely walk last night. From the pain shooting through it every time I move, I don't expect today to be much better. Besides, Randall said to stay off of it."

"But, what about shopping?" she asked petulantly.

"We went shopping Wednesday and Thursday. Today, I'm following the doctor's orders and lying on the beach."

"Fun-sucker." With a frown, Barbie flounced from the room.

The door slammed shut as I stumbled into the bathroom. I wasn't too worried about Barbie. I knew she would be her bubbly annoying self after an hour of playing sadistic exercise guru.

By the time I dragged my wrinkled body from a long hot soak in the tub, my knee had stopped twinging. Now, it only hurt a little, when I put all of my weight on it. I still wanted to rest it for the day. I was hoping some Ibuprofen and a warm beach would help. I didn't want to waste what was left of my vacation being an invalid.

Half an hour later, Barbie came in covered in sweat with a smile on her face. "You missed a great class!" she exclaimed. "I mean, you were so right to sit this one out. Randall said to tell you to take it easy today, and not to do anything to put too much strain on your knee for the rest of the week. How are you feeling? Are you up to some serious beaching?"

I smiled, "I've got my swimsuit, sunscreen, and a gossip mag. I was just waiting for you."

"Great! Give me a minute to get myself together, and we'll head out," she called behind her, heading to her room.

Thirty minutes later, we were lying under a shade umbrella drinking Phuket punch, gossiping, and looking forward to a boring day in the sun.

"Do you think you'll feel better tomorrow?" Barbie asked.

I thought a minute, lifted my knee, flexed it, then replied, "Probably. It doesn't hurt nearly as bad as it did last night."

"Great!" Barbie looked at me and grinned. "Let's go on an elephant safari!"

"An elephant safari?" I glanced at my knee. "I don't know."

Barbie's face fell.

"I want to go," I clarified. "I'm just worried about my knee. Do you think it will be okay?"

"Sure, it's better today. Anyway, I asked Randall about it after class. He said that as long as you didn't overuse the knee it should heal quickly. We'd be riding the elephants, so it shouldn't bother your knee at all."

"Okay, let's do it!" I grinned. "It's our last day on the island, before we go home, we should do something extraordinary."

"Epic last day of an unforgettable vacay!" Barbie squealed. "I'm going up to have the concierge book it for tomorrow. This is going to be so much fun!"

I couldn't help but smile watching Barbie practically skip up to the resort. Barbie stopped to chat with a tall, dark haired man, my most recent bodyguard, Henderson.

Closing my eyes to the bright sun, my thoughts turned to Eric. I knew I should be upset at him for leaving me alone in the hot tub last night, but I also knew that he was just being him. He wasn't the kind of guy who was ever going to act the way I thought he should. Anyway, it wasn't like he had completely abandoned me. Henderson had knocked on our door, just minutes after we had stepped inside, to make sure that I was okay. Then, he had gone downstairs to take care of Random. Ever helpful, Barbie went with him. Barbie came back a little over an hour later to tell me that Random had left before they got back to the hot tub.

"Jessica", a strange voice whispered my name.

I opened my eyes, yawning. Crouched next to me was a petite blonde, wearing a blood red bikini, covered by a gauzy black sarong.

"Do I know you?" I asked her.

"No, but I know you," she replied.

"Who are you?" I asked, wandering if I could still be dreaming.

"No one of importance," she answered, with one eye on the surrounding beach. "Listen up, I'll just be another beach dream if you hand over the jewel. If not," she gestured to a thinly disguised knife sheathed in the edge of her sarong.

"Not the jewel again," I groaned. "How many times do I have to tell you people, I don't know what you're talking about?" I asked grumpily.

"You want to do this the hard way?" she asked, grabbing my bag and frantically dumping the contents into the sand.

"Give that back!" I screeched.

Dropping the bag into the pile of sunscreen, brushes, lip-gloss, and beach towels, she exclaimed in frustration, "It's not here!"

"That's because I don't have it!" I yelled.

Grabbing my hair, she yanked me up from the chair, just as Henderson flew out of nowhere, all six feet and two hundred pounds of him. Hair ripped from my scalp as he tackled the strange visitor. In shock, I saw a handful of red hair clutched in her palm. Feeling the back of my head for blood, I quickly stepped away from the scuffle.

Barbie slid up next to me, "I've got twenty on the blonde."

"What?" I asked incredulously.

Barbie shrugged, "She fights dirty."

I shook my head, "Henderson can take her. He's a big guy."

The blonde wriggled out from under Henderson as more spectators surrounded them. Henderson grabbed her by the ankle, just as she started to flee. Jerking her leg from his grasp, she kicked him in the nose.

"That's got to be broken," I winced at the sight of Henderson's blood-stained nose.

Shaking it off, Henderson sprung at her. The crowd stepped back, avoiding the blood decorating the sand. For a moment, the two silent combatants merged into a weirdly shaped creature made of bare legs, arms, and long blonde hair.

It was looking like Henderson was about to win when somebody called out, "Watch out! She's got a knife!"

Henderson jumped back. The blonde had unsheathed a long, thick knife, with a jagged blade and she was now circling Henderson. Crouching into a fighting stance, Henderson slid a long, smooth blade from his boot. The crowd watched breathlessly as the two combatants circled each other.

The blonde clumsily thrust her knife at Henderson time after time, just to have him dodge it. Frustration began to show on her face, as her victim artfully escaped each calculated lunge.

"My guy's winning," I smugly said to Barbie.

"For now," she granted, "but it's not over yet."

As she spoke, Henderson swept his long leg across the sand, bringing down his victim. Before she could react, he pounced on the tiny woman. In an instant, he had her pinned to the ground. Sweat dripped from his face onto his opponent.

"You owe me twenty bucks," I crowed happily.

Barbie rolled her eyes and said, "Wait."

Pinned under the big man, the blonde was cursing in what sounded like three different languages. Henderson called out for someone to call the police, while he held the fuming woman. With his attention diverted, the blonde jerked her hand out of the big man's grasp. The onlookers gasped loudly as they watched her knife slice up the tendon in his forearm. A moment later, they were shocked into silence at the sight of blood pouring down from his arm.

Free from his right hand, she smiled before kneeing Henderson in the groin. A groan of empathized pain echoed through the men clustered around. Surprise mixed with pain on Henderson's face as he briefly fell to one knee. Taking advantage of his injury the tiny blonde rolled away from her opponent. Springing forward, she landed spryly on her feet.

Suddenly, a high pitched whistle pierced the air, signaling the arrival the authorities. The crowd quickly dispersed as a small group of heavily armed men made their way through the throng. A panicked look crossed the blonde's features. She turned to run, but Henderson grabbed her by the hair, roughly pulling her backwards. A shriek of pain pierced the air behind us as Barbie pulled me to the back of the crowd, leaving Henderson and the blonde at the mercy of the patrol.

"What are you doing?" I asked.

"I think it's time for us to leave," she said, pulling me back towards the resort.

"What about Henderson?" I asked, concern in my voice.

"Don't worry about him, he'll be just fine."

"But," I protested, "You don't understand, he was protecting me," I explained, pulling away from her.

Tightening her grip on my arm, she continued leading me towards the nearby building, "Doesn't matter. We don't want to get caught up with the authorities."

I glanced back, guiltily. "But,"

"Come on, we can get lunch at that great little place in town, then go find those handmade dresses the bartender was telling me about," she insisted, leading me into the resort.

Conceding, I agreed, "Okay, but for the record, I feel bad about Henderson."

"He'll be fine, once he gets that arm looked at. By the way, you owe me twenty bucks."

Twenty Two

I woke up, alone in my bed.

"Mmmm…" I'd just had the best dream. With a smile, I opened my eyes to greet the day.

"Ayyyyyyy!" I screamed.

"Ayyyyyyy!" Barbie screamed.

Gasping, while squeezing in a ragged breath, I jumped up, clutching my heart. It felt like my chest was about to explode. "Barbie! What is wrong with you?"

Barbie's eyes were wide as she, too, clutched her chest. "You scared me."

"I scared you? I opened my eyes and you were a half inch from my face, staring at me," I grumbled.

"You were so still and quiet, I thought you were dead." Barbie gave me an accusing look.

"Barbie, I know the past few days have been a little crazy, but…dead?"

"I came in to wake you up, and you were unnaturally still," she insisted, with a frown.

"Why did you want to wake me up? Is everything okay?" I asked.

"I've been up for hours. I've already had a pot of coffee mixed with some weird energy drink," she buzzed.

"Hours?" I looked at the clock. It wasn't even nine yet. "Are you okay?"

"It's our last day here. I didn't want to waste any of it sleeping." Her words merged together in her excitement. "We have to be downstairs in an hour to catch the taxi. I'm so excited!" she shrieked.

I grinned back at her. "Me too! I've never been on an elephant safari before."

An hour later we were dressed in shorts and tank tops and heading out the door. Barbie had put on a pair of gold sandals that tied to her ankles, bangle bracelets, and a pendant necklace with an etching of the sun that she had bought from one of the street vendors. Her eyes widened in undisguised disapproval as I pulled on my favorite red cowboy boots.

"Boots?" She questioned my footwear choice.

"There might be snakes. You'll want to put on some real shoes," I added.

Barbie raised an eyebrow. "There won't be any snakes. We're at the beach."

"The elephant safari is in the jungle," I reminded her.

"I know, but it's connected to the beach. Anyway, this is a resort island," she shrugged.

"What is that supposed to mean?" I asked.

"You know." She gave me a look that said she expected me to understand.

I shook my head. "No, I don't."

She waved the thought away, "There are no snakes at resorts."

I gave her a '*You have got to be kidding me*' look. "Please, tell me that you don't actually believe there are no snakes here, just because it's a vacation paradise. Do you think they said, 'Sorry Mr. Snake, this is a resort now. You'll have to relocate to the mainland.'?"

She shrugged, then said, "If there are snakes, I'm sure there won't be any on the elephant. Anyway, I look cute."

Rolling my eyes and shaking my head, I dutifully replied, "Of course you do. I know how much more important it is to look fashionable than to have on the appropriate footwear."

Ignoring the sarcasm in my voice, Barbie smiled her agreement. I looked her over. Something was different. She was wearing her hair curly and a lot more makeup.

"Wait a minute!" I frowned. "You're not planning on playing actress again, are you?"

Barbie fidgeted under my stare.

"Are you?" I asked, with an edge to my voice.

"Well, you have to admit all that attention is fun. I don't see what the harm is." She stared at her nails as she spoke.

"You don't see the harm!? Have you forgotten the last time you played actress? I haven't! We were both drugged and narrowly escaped who knows what? Then, we spent the entire next day recovering from the worst hangover that I ever hope to have. That was NOT fun."

"You have to admit, the spa treatment was nice, and you got to see the Wolfman because of it. Anyway, it would be different this time," she smiled.

"No," Frowning, I crossed my arms. "I don't like being drugged."

"You're no fun," Barbie pouted.

"Maybe that's because in the past thirty days I've been stalked, kidnapped, moved back home with my parents to the land that time forgot, spied on, shot at, drugged, stalked some more, and almost broken," I groused.

Barbie thought a minute before conceding, "Well, I guess that's enough to make anyone cranky."

"It's working for me." I agreed as we stepped into to the elevator.

Several hours later we were eating airplane peanuts and drinking bottled water while sitting on the back of our elephant, Bessie. We named her Bessie because she reminded me of a difficult cow my parents had when I was a little girl, and we couldn't pronounce her Thai name. It seemed to fit.

"It's no use. There is nothing but dense jungle everywhere you look," Barbie complained.

I frowned, popping another peanut into my mouth. "I just don't understand how we could have lost the rest of the tour. I mean, we're talking about losing fifteen people, on elephants. Big elephants!"

"Don't look at me." Barbie gave me an accusing look. "You were driving Bessie. I was just enjoying the never-ending forest bumping along under me while trying to see if anyone had posted about seeing Jennifer Jons on the island." She paused to look around again. "Whose idea was this? This sucks."

"Yours," I reminded her.

"Right. Well, I'm not the one who lost the rest of the tour," she pouted.

"It's not my fault." I bit my lip. "It never occurred to me that she wouldn't stay with the other elephants. The guide should have warned us. I mean, we obviously don't know anything about elephants, or we wouldn't have rented Bessie for the day."

She gave Bessie a repulsed look, and said, "That's the truth. How did you lose the tour, anyway?"

I shrugged. "Honestly, I don't know. We were riding along, at the back of the tour, when Bessie stopped to eat a plant or something on the side of the trail. I was watching these cute little monkeys play in the trees, trying to get a good picture." I paused, holding up my camera for Barbie to see. "Look at this! Aren't they the cutest things you ever saw?" I smiled at the picture on my camera.

"Adorable," Barbie sneered. "Can we focus on the problem? It's almost happy hour time and we're lost in the jungle on an elephant named Bessie."

I nodded, and said, "You'd think that she would head back home. It must be getting close to her dinner time."

As one, we both peered up through the treetops at the brilliant blue sky. I leaned back, trying to see where the sun was. It was no use, the surrounding forest was too dense. With a sigh, I popped another peanut in my mouth. Bessie reached up her trunk and took the bag from me.

"Bessie! That's our last bag," I protested to no avail.

"How many peanuts has she had?" Barbie asked.

"I had five of these little bags when we left. I saved them from the airplane," I answered.

"No wonder she's not worried about dinner." After a long moment of silence, Barbie sighed her frustration. "Where are our guides? Shouldn't they have noticed that we're missing by now?"

"Let's try again," I said.

"It's not going to work. She's too stubborn," Barbie said, with a frown.

"Just try." I insisted. "We need to get back."

"Yeeeee Hawwww!" Barbie shouted, loud enough to make me jump.

Bessie didn't even twinge.

"Let's try the kicking thing they showed us," I suggested.

Barbie nodded. "On three. One, two, three."

Simultaneously, we cajoled her with the Taiwanese words our guides had taught us while kicking our legs against her leathery hide. After a few moments, the large elephant under us made a loud noise, tossed her trunk from side to side, and lowered herself to the ground.

"That's it! I'm getting off. I've got to pee," Barbie announced.

"Me too," I agreed.

Barbie grabbed ahold of the saddle to gracefully slide off of the big elephant's back. That looked easy enough. I started to slide down, just as Bessie decided to rise. The movement caused me to lose my grip, and fall clumsily down the elephant's spine. Letting out a startled screech, I slid haphazardly across her left flank while grasping at the blankets across her back. I was fearfully clinging to a thin blanket when Bessie looked back to see me desperately trying to retain my grip. With a firm shake, she took a step, causing me to lose my tenuous grip. A loud thunk echoed in the trees when I hit the hard ground.

"Ouch!" I yelled.

I landed hard on my back, in a dirt pile, next to the grass where Bessie had been gorging. Still in shock after being ejected from my elephant host, I dumbly held up my hand. It was covered with elephant slime. Barbie was bent over, laughing so hard that she couldn't speak. As I checked to make sure nothing was broken, the earth started to shake. Barbie and I looked up at the same time to see Bessie take off sprinting, down the dirt path.

"Shit!" Barbie yelled.

Without a second thought, we jumped up, racing after her. It wasn't long before my bad knee twinged with pain. A few more strides and the pain was shooting up and down my leg. Then, my knee gave out, collapsing me in a heap. It wasn't long before Barbie came back for me, without Bessie.

"I can't believe this. I was out run by an elephant," Barbie complained.

"Don't beat yourself up. That elephant was speedy." I peered down the path in front of us, hoping to see Bessie stopped ahead munching grass. There were no elephants in view. This was not how today was supposed to go. Bessie was out of sight, leaving us to trudge down the wide path in a desperate attempt to follow her footsteps back to civilization. We were quiet as we slowly hiked down the path, me with an improvised tree branch for a cane.

Half an hour later, Barbie looked at me, and said, "Next time I go on an elephant safari, I'm wearing sneakers."

"Me too," I agreed.

"Let's take a break." Barbie motioned toward a rock on the edge of our path.

"I have a better idea, why don't you call someone to come get us?" I suggested.

"I don't have my phone, or I would." Barbie sighed miserably.

I tilted my head. "Of course you do. Remember you were checking Facebook with it earlier."

"No, I was tweeting," she corrected me.

"Okay." I shrugged. "You were tweeting earlier. So, call someone to come get us, anyone."

"I can't," she said. "I don't have it anymore."

"Where is your phone?" I asked slowly.

Barbie frowned. "In my purse, with Bessie."

"You didn't grab your purse?" I asked accusingly.

"I was just going to find a tree to pee behind. I didn't think I'd need it." Barbie threw a small rock at a tree.

"Don't worry about it. It'll be okay," I said.

Suddenly, Barbie smiled. "Wait! You've still got the Wolfman's transmitter in your purse telling him, and his merry band of rent-a-thugs, where to find you, right? He's probably already realized that we're missing, dropped what he was doing, and gathered the other superheroes to plan our rescue. I'm sure he'll pull up in the Batmobile any minute."

Guiltily, I bit my lip and looked away. To distract from the quiet, I said, "I think you're mixing up your fairy tales. The Wolfman doesn't drive the Batmobile, Batman does. Batman works alone, and Robin Hood is the one with the merry men."

Ignoring my sarcasm, Barbie looked closely at me before slowly asking, "Where is your purse, Jessie?"

"Bessie has it." I gazed down the path the elephant had taken.

"Shit!" Barbie exclaimed.

I nodded in agreement. "It looks like we're on our own. Come on, let's move."

We headed back to the path, following in Bessie's huge footsteps. It seemed like we had been walking for hours. Barbie began to sing. I didn't know the song well, but once she got to the chorus, I joined in. With no other options, we followed the trail, optimistic that it would lead us somewhere soon.

After what seemed like hours, we had sung every song we could remember. Bessie's footprints were long gone. It was getting dark and we were tired, tired of walking and tired of singing. I kept hearing something. It sounded familiar, but I couldn't place it.

"Do you hear something?" I asked, nervously scanning the fast growing shadows of the forest.

Barbie listened carefully. "Is that running water?"

I tilted my head. "I hope so. We ran out of water hours ago. Let's go see."

Barbie looked around with an unsure expression on her face. "We must be close to the elephant safari place. I don't think we should leave the path"

"We've been thinking we're close for hours. Face it, we don't even know if we're on the right trail anymore. We might as well get some water," I insisted.

"I can't argue with that logic," she agreed. "We'll get something to drink, and then head back to the path. Even if we aren't on the right trail. Sooner or later, we're bound to run across someone with a car, phone, or something."

"I don't think it matters." I tilted my head, following the sound. "I don't think anyone is looking for us. They'd have to realize we're missing first. With our luck, Bessie went home and everyone assumed we did too."

"No, Bessie wouldn't do that to us. And, if she did, the group would have to notice they'd lost someone. I bet it takes lots of water for the elephants. That's what we're hearing. They're watering the elephants. We're almost there!" Barbie perked up excitedly.

"I bet you're right!" I exclaimed, desperately wanting her to be right.

With renewed spirit, we pushed our way through the jungle until it abruptly ended. As we surveyed the area, I exchanged a confused look with Barbie. There were no elephants, no tourists, no local tour guides, and no buildings in front of us. There was nothing.

Instead of the civilization we had expected to find, we were standing in a small clearing on the top of a cliff, next to a small waterfall. Looking down from the cliff's edge, we could see the Andean Sea below us. Several miles down below us and off to our left, we could see a deserted beach. A huge house sat on the tree line at the far end of that beach. Near the house a long dock reached into the clear blue sea. At the end of the dock, a large boat bobbed tranquilly in the water.

"There it is, civilization!" Barbie erupted with excitement.

"Great, how do we get down there?" I frowned over the edge of the cliff at the house below us. It was a long way down.

"Hell if I know. I need to sit down while we figure it out. My feet hurt. They keep getting poked by twigs and who knows what else," Barbie grumbled.

"I told you not to wear those shoes," I said, lowering myself to the ground beside her.

In silence, we watched the setting sun light up the Andean Sea below us, both of us lost in our own thoughts.

"It's really pretty up here," I said, more to myself than anyone.

"It is." Barbie agreed. "I'd take a picture, but," she frowned, "Bessie has my camera."

At that, we began to giggle uncontrollably.

"This really has been an awful day," Barbie said, between fits of giggles.

Bursting out in another fit of giggles, I added, "Now we can add 'lost in the jungle' to our week of mishaps. It can't get any worse."

Barbie smiled, "Nope."

To our right, the trees rustled softly, giving way to a group of local men, dressed in varying types of camouflage, with big guns held out in front of them. With minimal sound, they stepped imposingly into the clearing, their faces stoically unreadable. One look at the intruders and our giggles evaporated, just as suddenly as they had appeared. The situation was now beyond funny.

The band of soldiers stepped forward, provocatively waving their guns in our direction. One of them spoke to us. Unfortunately, it wasn't in English, and the only Taiwanese phrases we had learned were, 'No', 'How much', and 'Another'. Desperate for a way to communicate that we were not a threat, I strove unsuccessfully to recognize at least one word. Pointing his weapon toward us, the speaker barked another garbled command. That I understood. As if prodded by an electric jolt, Barbie & I jumped to our feet, holding our hands high in the air, so that the men could see we weren't armed.

"We're saved! They must be local guards for someone nearby," Barbie smiled.

"Funny, I don't feel saved. It might have something to do with all those guns pointed at me," I retorted, smiling for our audience.

"Let me take care of this," Barbie whispered to me.

"Gladly." I couldn't help but wonder what she expected to accomplish. Then again, this was Barbie. She might actually get us out of this jam.

"We got separated from the elephant safari," Barbie explained loudly to the gun-toting soldier of fortune who had spoken.

The men aggressively pointed their guns while angrily barking something at us in Taiwanese.

"We're lost," she responded, loud and slow.

"They're not deaf," I grumbled.

"No, they are not." The words, spoken with a heavy European accent, seemed to come from everywhere and nowhere, all at once.

"Who said that?" I whispered in a small voice.

The small army, who had by this time surrounded us, began to close in, pushing us farther back toward the cliff face. Once the escape routes were fully defended, the voice said something in Thai, effectively pausing our assailants.

"It appears that you ladies are in a...difficulty," said the voice.

Barbie and I looked at each other. At the same time, we said, "No."

"No? You do not see this as a difficulty?" he asked, stepping from the trees to pass through the wall of guns and camouflaged men.

Our mouths fell open as our brains registered this new situation. The words *'deadly'* and *'stay away'* reverberated through my brain in Greg's voice. It was the Albino.

"If I wasn't afraid before, I am now," I hissed at Barbie.

"Do not be fearful. As long as you give me what I seek, no harm will come to you." His eyes rested on my, the smile on his face anything but reassuring.

"What is it that you want?" I asked, with confidence that I wasn't feeling.

"The jewel. I am wanting the jewel that Ivan trusted to you." The ends of his mouth turned up, distorting his face into an eerie grin.

The jewel again? Barbie gave me a look that confirmed my suspicion. He wasn't going away without it this time.

I smiled disarmingly, before saying, "I told you the other day, I don't know any Ivan."

He shrugged, then said, "Sometimes, he is not calling himself Ivan. Sometimes, he is calling himself any number of names. The name is not of consequence. What matters is that you give me the jewel, now."

I shook my head, "I don't know what you're talking about. You have the wrong redhead."

His face contorted in anger, as he unobtrusively signaled the men behind him with a twist of his head. As one, they began to close in, brandishing their weapons.

"You leave no option. Since you will not give it to me, I will take it, by force. Do not worry, it will not hurt…much," he said, with a sickly smile that made my stomach twist into knots.

Barbie shot me an alarmed look, "So help me, if I find out later that you have that jewel…"

"Run for it!" I grabbed Barbie's hand, before she could finish her sentence, and ran, heading for the only spot not heavily covered by the gun toting Taiwanese army.

"Where are we going?" she yelled.

"That way," I called back, pointing to a small open spot in front of us.

"Even if we get past them, we'll never outrun them in the jungle," Barbie screeched.

"We don't know that!" I shouted behind me.

Moving quickly to cut us off, the men began firing their guns above our heads. Before we could slip past, they had closed the hole, blocking our escape. Desperate to avoid both the men and their bullets, we turned back toward the only area that wasn't blocked by our assailants, the cliff face. As I turned, a hand grabbed at my arm, spinning me around. Twisting out of his grasp, I shoved the tip of my walking stick into his stomach as hard as I could and pushed, knocking him off balance. Once I was free, I ran after Barbie. I caught up to her at the edge of the cliff.

Our attackers had closed off all exits to the jungle, and were assertively waiting for us to realize that there was no way out. It was a game of cat and mouse, and we had been served up on a platter.

"Jessie," Barbie whispered conspiratorially, "We're going to have to jump."

"What?" I looked past my cousin at the chasm below us, with wide eyes.

"It'll be just like Jamaica." She smiled encouragingly.

"Jamaica?" I looked at her in disbelief. "In Jamaica, we were with experienced divers who were willing to rescue us if anything went wrong. If this dive goes wrong, all we can expect from these guys is a bullet storm."

"Don't worry, it'll be okay," she reassured me.

"Okay?" I gave her an incredulous look. "We don't know how deep it is, if there are rocks under the surface, what kind of tides we're dealing with..."

"Trust me." Barbie cut me off. "We'll back up a little, then take a running jump. Unless you can hand over the madman's jewel, it's our only way out of this mess."

With wild eyes, I shifted my gaze to the Albino and his army before dipping my head in agreement.

"Sure." My voice was infused with a calmness that I wasn't feeling. "It always works in the movies. We'll be alright." I was babbling now.

With casualness we didn't feel, we slowly stepped towards our assailants. In mock surrender, we held our hands high, smiling agreeably at the group of armed aggressors surrounding us. With relief, we watched smiles take the place of frowns on our foe's faces until, assured of their victory, they lowered their guns.

Once the danger appeared less imminent, Barbie and I exchanged glances. With a quick turn, we sprinted for the cliff. Shots screamed out behind us as we raced, barely ahead of a stream of bullets, for the cliff's edge. Thought had completely left my brain by the time Barbie and I leapt into the emerging sunset.

"This is not the movies!" I yelled, as sapphire skies replaced the emerald turf beneath our feet.

The echoes of the Albino howling in some unknown language, while his mercenaries responded with another volley of gunfire, followed us into the void. After an endless moment, where we were suspended in nothingness, those sounds were replaced with the vibration of the wind rushing through my ears. I was flying. Then, I wasn't.

They always say, *'Whatever you do, don't look down'*. They are right. Everything was fine, until I looked down to see the cerulean sea racing towards me. At that moment, panic took over. Like the cartoon character that I had wanted to be in elementary school, I foolishly attempted to climb back up into the sky. Falling farther, despite my pitiful attempt at self-rescue, my life flashed before my eyes.

"That wasn't nearly as glamorous and satisfying as I would have liked. I hope I don't die," I said, to no one in particular, just before hitting the water.

Twenty Three

It felt like I had fallen through a brick wall. Pain shot through my body. Then, I was submerged. Water was everywhere. Too quickly, I became confused and disoriented. I knew I needed to swim to the surface. The problem was, I wasn't sure which direction was up.

After several attempts to find the way out of my watery prison, I could feel my muscles fatiguing. In a panic, I suddenly realized the eminent danger our haste and confusion had placed us in. With renewed determination, I once again pushed towards what I hoped was the surface.

My spirits sank as I grasped handfuls of heavy water, instead of air. I could feel myself sinking further into the dark waters below when strong arms wrapped around my chest pulling me up, up, up through the liquid barrier that had been holding me in its clutches. Dark spots shifted across my vision as I greedily tasted the ocean damp air.

"We did it," I finally managed to choke out.

"Yes, you are lucky to be alive," my rescuer agreed, dragging me out of my watery prison and onto the sun warmed beach.

Barbie was waiting for me, looking fabulous as usual. With a glare, she said, "I'm glad you're alive. When I get my strength back, I'm going to kill you."

"Why?" I somehow managed to croak out the question, while coughing up sea water.

"Why?" she asked. "Because you got us lost from the safari, in this cursed, gun-toting-weirdo infested jungle. That's why." She flicked sand at me, emphasizing her displeasure.

I only nodded. It was too difficult to speak. I had swallowed too much seawater.

While we weren't looking, a small group of men had gathered around us. They must have come from the house. The two men who had rescued us were kneeling on the sand checking our vitals. Gingerly, I sat up, pulled off my right boot, and proceeded to dump out the water. Once it was empty, I did the same with my left boot. Barbie nodded, pulling herself to a sitting position to begin freeing her feet from what was left of her sandals.

"I changed my mind about killing you. These guys are smokin'. Which one do you want? Because, I like them all," Barbie whispered in my ear.

I took a moment to gage this new situation. My rescuer was a vaguely familiar looking blue eyed blonde, with a hard eight pack on his chest. He was wearing small, tight, white European style swim trunks and a deep tan. The other men gathered around were similar in build and dress. She was right, our rescuers were almost too good looking.

"Barbie, I think we're dead," I said in a whisper.

"I'm Nick. You're lucky George and I were out here securing the boat. If we hadn't been nearby, you might have drowned." My rescuer said in a heavily accented voice that was simultaneously deep and soothing.

"Thank you." I smiled gratefully. "I'm Jessie. Where are we?"

"You are at my beach house, off of Cape Panwa." A familiar voice said.

I looked up just, as Barbie grumbled, "Fuck me!"

"You!" I exclaimed angrily, shakily stumbling to my feet. It was official, we had died and gone to hell.

He didn't even blink. "This time there are no bodyguards to whisk you away, and you can bet that I won't be turning my back on you." He rubbed the back of his head gingerly. "Up until now, you've made things difficult, but the hard part is over. I must have finally done something right to have you literally fall out of the sky, like a gift from heaven." He held out a hand to help Barbie up, and said, "Ms. Jons, I would appreciate it if you, and your cousin, would be my guests."

"I am so sorry. We are going to have to decline." She crossed her arms. "On account of you being an asswipe."

He pursed his lips, showing a hint of anger. "I'm afraid that I must insist."

Barbie and I surveyed our options. We were surrounded by a group of capable looking men, an empty beach, and the jungle. We were out of options.

With an angry frown, I said, "It doesn't look like we have much choice."

As the men walked us into the house, Barbie whispered, "I really do wish you had a way to signal the Wolfman, so he could come and rescue us."

"I think the bat signal is being used." I rolled my eyes. "Create a distraction. I'll pull out my super powered dog whistle. He should be able to hear it with his superior wolf ears."

"This is no time for sarcasm," Barbie chastised.

"You're wrong Cuz, this is the perfect time for sarcasm," I insisted.

Barbie frowned at the men surrounding us. "I think we're in serious trouble this time, cousin. This guy is a certifiable sociopath."

I gave her a quick smile. "We'll think of something. As long as we stick together, we've got a chance."

"Boys, take Ms. Jons to the east wing, while I take Ms. Hart upstairs."

Barbie and I traded worried looks. Focusing on Random, I firmly said, "I don't want to go upstairs. Take me to the east wing, with her."

Random shook his head. "You and I have unfinished business. Besides, you'll be a lot less trouble separated." He turned to the men, speaking too softly for us to hear.

Barbie leaned forward to whisper in my ear, "We should have taken our chances with the Albino. This guy is a nut."

Nodding my agreement, I began to mumble to myself, "Why can't I figure these things out when I first meet a guy? I have got to be the worst judge of men ever." My gaze fell on Barbie, reminding me of her history with men. "No, you are definitely a poorer judge than I am. Greg was right, what were we thinking going off together? That's always an invitation for disaster! When will we learn?"

"Pull yourself together! It's going to be alright," Barbie attempted to console me. "Just don't panic."

The men had finished their pow wow and were indicating to Barbie that it was time to go. With confidence that I knew she couldn't possibly possess, she followed her captors. Outwardly, she gave no indication of distress. A deep worry formed in my gut as I watched Barbie flirtatiously link arms with her captors. The way she was carrying on, you would think that she was out on a date.

Random impatiently indicated that I was to follow him. I stood rooted to the spot, watching Barbie disappear from sight. Random pulled out a gun, waving it menacingly. Briefly, I envisioned myself grabbing the gun and wrestling it from his hands. Shaking my head, I reminded myself that there were three of them, they were in better physical shape, and bigger than me. I heard my daddy's voice saying, *'Pick your battles, girl.'* With no other practical options, my feet took the rest of me upstairs.

The ominous sounds of our footsteps echoing up the stairs fueled my imagination. With each step, horrible scenarios flitted through my thoughts. Desperate for a distraction, I asked Random, "Who are you, really? What's going on? And, what do you want with us?"

He smiled a creepy smile. "I'm a businessman with a business opportunity. You should never pass up a good opportunity, Jessie."

I narrowed my eyes at him. "When I met you at the airport, you seemed like such a nice guy."

"I am a nice guy." He smiled. "A nice guy who enjoyed your help, and your company, on that tedious trip. Long flights can be so wearisome, without good company. Wouldn't you agree?"

I frowned at him. "If you're really a nice guy, why are you being like this?"

"Like what?" His confusion appeared to be genuine.

"You drugged us at the club, accosted me at the hotel, and now you're keeping us here, against our will," I retorted angrily.

He shrugged, then said, "I didn't want to drug you. You were such a darling to help me out in the states, then just as things were about to get interesting, you left me alone at the bar. After I had bought all those drinks, too. I couldn't let that happen again, not before I got what I wanted. The drug was a little harmless insurance, just to be sure you didn't wander off. Somehow, you still managed to leave me hanging, just as things were getting interesting. You should know, I was very disappointed. I was looking forward to enjoying more of your company. I know women think men like a tease, but they don't. It's not nice to make promises you don't intend to keep. Then, when I came to find you at the hotel, your cousin hit me over the head. I was almost arrested by the security guard. Thankfully, my grandfather was very popular with the locals and I was able to talk my way out of it." He frowned his disapproval at me.

"I never promised you anything. You just assumed I would sleep with you. That's not my fault," I protested.

He shrugged, "Your actions made me believe otherwise."

I stopped walking, "What actions? *You* hit on me in line. *You* switched seats on the plane. *You* followed me to the cab. *You* invited me out to drinks. All *I* did was accept your company."

Waving the gun towards me, he prompted me to keep moving. "Yes, but accepting was an indication of your interest. Besides, I saw how you kept looking at me in the security line. That's why I let you help me."

"What? I looked at you because you were signaling to me." I shook my head. I had met guys like him before. There was no use arguing, and I knew it. "You let me help you with what?" I gave him a confused look.

"Don't act like you don't know." He gave me an impatient look.

"I'm not acting. What are you talking about?" I asked.

"You know, the jewel."

"The jewel again? Why is everyone so insistent that I know about this jewel?" I asked.

"Don't play dumb. I know you have it. I slipped it into your purse, while we were in line for the security check in Oklahoma City. Now, I need it back."

"You slipped something into my purse? I didn't see you." I frowned up at him.

With a shrug he explained, "You were busy removing your jewelry. I slipped my necklace into your purse, then I helped you put your jewelry in with it. It was perfect."

"So, our meeting was planned?" I gave him a startled look.

"I would say it was more orchestrated than planned. When I saw you, I knew that you were perfect. An innocent like you would never raise suspicion. You had your boarding pass in your hand. I could see that we would be traveling to the same destination. I just needed to get close enough to slip the jewel into your things. Then, I could arrange for us to meet on the plane to New York and retrieve my jewel from your purse, without you suspecting that I was anything other than another passenger." His smile faded to a frown as he said, "Then, you sat with it tucked behind your back, up against the window, denying me my jewel."

"What is it with my purse?" I protested. "Do you men ever stop to think that a girls purse is private and not for other people to be putting stuff in?"

"Ah…you were perfect, so unsophisticated," he said, tenderly stroking my cheek, "wearing your casual summer clothes, with the expensive earrings and matching necklace around your neck. When you took off your own jewelry, putting it into your purse beside my necklace, I knew that you were helping me. You carrying a necklace or two in your purse raises no suspicion. Me they would suspect. I couldn't have planned it better," he explained.

I shook my head. "I don't understand why you would need me to carry your necklace through security."

"Of course you would not. So innocent." He chuckled. "Let us just say, it would be a difficult situation for me to have to explain. I knew that you would not have to explain. You would not be questioned, and you were not."

My eyes widened as I realized what he was saying. "It was stolen? You put a stolen necklace in my purse? At airport security? I smuggled a stolen necklace out of the airport? Out of the country! If they had found it, I would have gone to jail!" My voice had raised a couple of octaves, betraying the anger welling up inside of me.

He nodded in agreement, saying, "Yes, that would have been unfortunate."

"Unfortunate?" I shook my head in disbelief. "Wait a minute. You traveled to Oklahoma City just to steal a necklace? The Crown jewels were too much of a challenge for you? So, you broke into the Governor's mansion instead?" It was just my luck to get stuck with a second rate thief for a stalker.

"Of course not." He laughed at my indignation. "The jewel, which you so cleverly helped me to smuggle out of the states, is The Black Orlov. It was sold at auction two weeks ago. The previous owners were having it delivered to the new owners, in California. I was able to intercept the delivery, merely hours before the necklace switched hands, and charter a plane, before anyone realized that it was missing. I was on my way out of the country when my plane had to make an emergency landing, in Oklahoma City. It was the next day before I could get a flight out. By that time, news of the missing jewel had saturated the television and radio networks."

I thought back to the morning I had left home. The bartender had been saying something about a stolen necklace during my layover. I hadn't thought much of it, at the time. Now, not for the first time, I was wishing that I paid more attention to the world around me.

"I remember hearing something about that." I frowned at my captor.

"Airport security had been tightened, everywhere. I was afraid that it would be difficult to get through, with the jewel. So, I found someone to take it for me," he smiled at me.

"Lucky me." I rolled my eyes.

He laughed. "When you told me that you were traveling to Phuket, I decided to let you bring it with you. Then, you left the club without saying goodbye. You didn't give me your number, or tell where you were staying in New York, and you hadn't told me the name of your hotel in Phuket."

"You should learn to take a hint," I growled.

"I called all of the hotels on the island. You weren't registered anywhere, but, as you can see, I am nothing if not persistent. I walked three beaches before I found you." He smiled, "Persistence always pays off. When I did find you, I was presented with a new business opportunity."

Unsure of what to say, I just stared blankly at my captor.

Staring deep into my eyes, he reached out to stroke my cheek. "You, Jessie, are my lucky charm."

Fear kept me from ducking away. It kept me from doing anything. He had those wide crazy eyes that you see on the mug shots of criminals. Once he broke eye contact, I glanced around in desperation. There had to be a way out! The stairs were behind me. To get to the stairs I would have to push by the overly muscled Tweedle Dee and Tweedle Dum blocking my way, then outrun them down the long hallway. If, by some miracle, I made it to the stairs, what then? I couldn't leave Barbie.

Putting his hand down, Random opened a door, gesturing for me to step inside. "After you, my lucky charm."

A new fear settled into my stomach like a pound of lead. "I'm pretty sure that I know what you plan to do in there. I'm sorry to have to let you down like this, but," I paused, wandering just how unstable

Random was. With a small shake of my head, I added, "I'm not feeling it. You see, I'm on my period. And, I've got a raging case of herpes, warts, gonorrhea… It's really disgusting down there. Take my word for it. Anyway, I'm not doing the sex thing these days."

"I'll bet I can change your mind," he said, with a creepy smile.

With a shake of my head, I said, "You don't seem like the kind of guy that would use force."

He was giving my breasts a look that made me think I'd misjudged him. I looked to my guards for help, but they seemed to be sharing a brain cell. Words nervously spewed from my mouth, as I desperately worked to keep him talking.

"Then again, you didn't seem like the kind of guy who would steal a necklace and use me to smuggle it out of the country, either."

Random smiled, and said, "I make an excellent first impression."

Edging away from the door, I looked for an opportunity to escape. "Yes, you do." If I was going to get out of here, I needed to keep him talking about anything other than making use of the bedroom on the other side of the door. "There's one thing that I don't understand. You keep talking about a business opportunity. What could I possibly have that you would want to steal?"

He gave me a serious look. "Your cousin."

My heart stopped as his words reverberated in my head, "My cousin?" My voice seemed to come from someplace far away.

"Your cousin is a world famous actress. I will contact her agent and ransom her. She is worth billions. Perhaps, they will pay for you as well."

"You want to ransom us?" Shit! We were in big trouble. I bumped into Tweedle Dee, bouncing off of his eight pack. "Umm...no. I don't think your plan is going to work. You should just let us go. Tell you what, since you guys rescued us, we'll just call it even." I smiled what I hoped was a friendly smile.

He smiled back at me. "I do like you, Jessie. You are a funny girl."

I frowned as he took my arm to pull me through the doorway. "Really, you should just let us go. I mean you have the jewel. You don't need me, and," I hesitated, afraid of how he might react, "they aren't going to pay the ransom."

"Of course they will pay, and you know that I do not have the necklace, yet." He closed the door behind him. "I had planned to retrieve it the other night, but you failed to bring your purse to the club, and once again, you left me at the table without saying goodbye. When I came to your hotel to retrieve it, you left me with a concussion. I'm going to have to teach you some manners if this relationship is going to work."

"Relationship? What relationship?" I held up my hands. "You used me to smuggle your stolen necklace, drugged me, and now you're holding me prisoner, at gunpoint. We don't have a relationship."

"You will change your mind after a night with me." He ran his hand down my cheek.

I stepped back, rolling my eyes. "Yeah, that's not gonna happen. I told you about the herpes. You don't want herpes. It's bad stuff."

He laughed. "You don't have herpes, or any of those other diseases."

I pursed my lips. "Sure I do. Anyway, you don't want to find out."

"We can get to know each other later. Here, we have all the time in the world." He smiled. "Is the necklace still in your purse?"

"I don't know." I shrugged. "I never saw it. Until now, I didn't know there really was a jewel. It seemed like a case of mistaken identity or maybe a prank. Barbie would so do something like that to me."

He gave me a strange look, then asked, "Barbie?"

Widening my eyes into my most innocent look, I said, "A friend. A crazy friend."

With a shrug, he said, "So, it is still in your purse." He looked at me, "Where is your purse? I will be very disappointed if you tell me it is at the bottom of the cove."

I shrugged. "Bessie has it."

"Bessie?" He blinked his confusion.

"Bessie. That's what we named our elephant."

"Elephant?" He repeated.

"Yeah. That's why we were lost in the jungle. That stupid elephant took off without us. Our purses and Barbie's cellphone were still with Bessie when she ran off. She left us to find our way back through the jungle, unable to call for help. Stupid elephant," I grumbled to myself.

"What!" He gave me an incredulous look.

"After walking for hours, we were surrounded by armed men in camouflage, who didn't speak English, but looked really mean. The Albino wanted the necklace, too. Just like the Irish Mafia, he didn't believe us when we said that we didn't have it. Our only option was to jump off of the cliff to escape. That brought us to our current situation. As you can see, we've kind of had a rough day. Why don't you give us a break and not hold us for ransom." I widened my eyes, letting the slightest bit of moisture collect in the corners. It was a trick that had worked for me before. With an obviously forced smile, I softly added, "Please?"

"So, you're telling me that my jewel is on an elephant, somewhere in the jungle?" He looked angry.

"She has some of my stuff, too," I retorted.

He stood quietly, contemplating the situation. Staring unseeing out the window, he asked, "The Albino is there? Looking for my necklace?"

Knowing it probably wasn't the time, I couldn't help but add, "Don't forget the Irish Mafia, some weirdo whose name I didn't catch, and a tiny blonde with a wicked left hook."

Frowning down at me, he said, "Perhaps, you're not such a lucky charm. If you have herpes, I may just have to kill you."

My eyes widened. "Whoa, don't be hasty now. Why don't you just let us go? We'll go back to the safari agency, where I'm sure Bessie has returned by now. She seemed pretty smart," I lied. "We can pick up our stuff, and you can get your necklace. What do you say?" I nodded my encouragement.

"I have a better idea." He looked at me. "I'll go to the safari agency to collect your things, then I will have the jewel and you. When I return, you and I can spend some time getting to know each other, while I ransom off your cousin."

"But, what if they don't pay the ransom?" I asked, afraid that I already knew the answer.

He shrugged. "Then, we'll have to kill you both. Tell me which safari you used."

"Elephant Safari or was it Safari Elephant?" I asked myself. "Or maybe it was Island Safari…no that's not it."

He grabbed me by the throat, lifting me until I could look him in the eye. "You'd better remember, quickly."

His thinly controlled anger coursed through his arm and into his fingers as he slowly put more pressure on my windpipe. All I could think of was, I don't want to die. Spots swam before my eyes.

Painfully, I choked out. "I don't know, the name of the safari. B…Jennifer made the arrangements. The shuttle picked us up, and drove us there. I didn't pay that much attention to the name."

At that, he released his hold, allowing me to drop to the floor, clutching my throat. Fear and anger coursed through my veins, along with the withheld blood, filling my head with life preserving fluids. I sat, gasping for air. Random had pulled a Jekyll and Hyde before my eyes. I didn't know whether to be angry or afraid. Before I could speak, he leaned down, lifted my chin with his finger, and focused his crazy brown eyes on mine.

"I'll be back for you. Try to improve your manners by my return."

My vision was still cloudy, but I could hear his footsteps echo down the hall. Strong hands lifted me by the armpits, carrying me into the room, and depositing me on the bed, without a word. I didn't bother to look up as, moments later, the door clicked ominously shut.

"Jessie, how do you manage to get into these messes?" I asked myself. The silent room seemed to mock my fear, spurring me to action. "Okay Jess, you can do this. Maybe, he forgot to lock the door when he left." Great, I was talking to myself, again.

I mentally rolled my eyes at the suggestion, but I was desperate. I didn't want to be here when Random returned. Expecting the worst, I headed for the door. A quick check confirmed my suspicions. It was locked. Nervously, I walked around the room, studying my prison for a way out.

It was a large room with a huge bathroom on one end and a large walk in closet on the other. The bathroom held only a single toothbrush, toothpaste, shampoo, conditioner, comb, towel, and a wash rag. The closet was empty. In desperation, I spent a few moments trying to pry loose the clothes bar, to use as a weapon. Someone had taken pride in their workmanship when they built this place. It wouldn't budge.

Heading back into the main room, I looked for possible weapons. It was opulently furnished with a four poster king sized bed, matching dresser, a makeup table, and divan. Large, heavy rugs covered the floors while beautiful landscape photographs of the island hung on the walls. I searched through the drawers for weapons. They were completely empty. There wasn't so much as a bobby pin to be found. This was obviously an unused room.

I walked to the large picture window. The view of the setting sun over the deserted beach was stunning. Shaking off nature's trance, I tried to open the window. It was stuck.

"If you can get it open, you can jump." I encouraged myself.

"You're on the third floor. If you jump, you'll break your leg," I reasoned.

Taking a deep breathe, I took a moment to consider my options. I could picture myself stealthily landing on the ground, crouching low, and running into the forest for help. In my mind, I came back with an entire police force. Barbie was safe and all the bad guys were arrested. I could hear Random cursing me as they led him away in cuffs. Then, I bumped my already hurt knee on the window sill. In a flood of pain, reality came crashing back.

"Come on Jessie, how far do you think you'll get, at night, in the jungle, with a broken leg, and a bum knee?" I asked myself.

It didn't matter anyway, the window wouldn't open. I flopped down on the bed in defeat. Our only hope was for Random to bring back my purse. If we were really lucky, Eric would realize we were missing and use the signal to come find us. I smiled at the thought of Eric beating Random up.

"I'd like to see that," I said to the empty room.

I frowned. I was worried about Barbie, downstairs with all of those horrible men. I hoped she was okay. Sometime later, I heard an engine outside of the window. I looked out, just in time to see a truck driving down the dirt road that led to the house. I could only assume that it was Random, going after the necklace.

"Maybe he took his men with him, leaving just the locked doors to keep us prisoner," I said hopefully, to no one.

Suddenly, I had renewed hope of finding a way out. An hour later, I had to admit to myself that there was no way out. I was securely trapped. All there was for me to do was wait. With growing despair, I lay down on the comforter, closing my eyes. Hopefully, Eric would get here before they realized that Barbie wasn't Jennifer Jons, the famous movie star.

Twenty Four

It was dark in the room. Something had woken me. I lay still, listening. Someone was in the room with me. Pretending to be asleep, I planned it all out. Once he got close enough, I would surprise him and take his gun. Then, I would march him down to wherever they were keeping Barbie, and we would make our escape. It would work. It had to. Anyway, it always works in the movies.

He stopped at the edge of the bed. I could feel him reaching for me. Swallowing my fear, I jumped up, grabbing his arm. He quickly jerked it out of my hand. I reached for him again. He hit me, lightly. I was disappointed. He hit like a girl.

"Jessie! Quit it. It's me."

That was weird, he sounded just like Barbie. I stopped with my fist in mid-air. "Barbie?"

"Yes, now be quiet. We need to get out of here, before they get back," she hissed.

"How'd you find me?" I whispered.

"The guys told me where you were. Come on," she whispered back.

"The guys? As in Random's thugs?" I asked, with surprise.

"They don't work for Random. He's just a two bit hoodlum, in a lot of trouble. You see, Random stole a necklace for a guy, a really bad guy. That guy sent his men here to pick it up. When they got here, Random didn't have it. The guy he stole the necklace for gave Random a week to get it back. His guys stayed to make sure he finds it."

"What will they do to Random, if he doesn't find it?" I asked.

She shrugged. "They didn't say, but I don't think it's good. Their boss really wants that necklace. The stone in the necklace is a huge black diamond, called the Black Orlov. It's cursed."

"Cursed?" I asked, incredulously.

Barbie nodded seriously, "They said that the owners of the Black Orlov have a bad habit of turning up dead. The stone's curse brings bad luck to whoever has it. The guys believe that's why Random lost it, the curse. They really aren't excited about having to take it to their boss."

I felt lightheaded. "Dead? How do they end up dead?"

"I don't know," she shrugged. "I forgot to ask."

"Barbie, this is important! I have the necklace. I'm the new owner. ME! Random slipped it into my purse at the OKC airport. And, think about it, my luck has been catastrophic since then."

"You have the Black Orlov!" She shook her head slowly, in disbelief. "I don't know how they died. It's just a superstition. The guys mentioned it during poker. Later, Nick was telling me the story. And, well…that Nick is a great kisser, among other things," she smiled.

"Oh my god!" My mouth dropped open. "He raped you!"

"Shhh…keep it down. No, I wasn't raped, sicko." She wrinkled her nose. "What is wrong with you?"

I regarded her closely. "Are you saying that you slept with him, willingly, after he forcefully held you hostage?"

"Hey!" She looked down at the keys in her hand. "He's a nice guy. He spotted me for poker. Anyway, I haven't had any in days. He was worth the wait." She gave me a conspiratorial wink. "I would have been here earlier, but that man is a machine. He has skills in other areas as well, if you know what I mean," she added.

"How long have I been asleep?" I demanded crankily.

"Shut up," she grouched.

"So, you slept with your captor, then he told you where to find me, and let you go?" I asked.

"No. The guys told me where you were much earlier. They'd tell Jennifer Jons anything." She grinned. "After we played a couple of rounds of poker, I tired Nick out, waited until he fell asleep, handcuffed him to the bed, stole his keys, and his boots, and came looking for you. The boots are way too big, but better than walking through the jungle barefoot."

Against my better judgment, I was impressed. "Where'd you get the handcuffs?"

"They were Nick's." She shrugged.

"Good job, cousin. They said we couldn't take care of ourselves." I rolled my eyes. "So, how do we get out of here? Do I have a guard?" I wondered aloud.

"Don't worry. I took care of him, too." She opened the door.

My mouth fell open. "Really, how long was I asleep?"

"I didn't sleep with him." She glared at me. "I hit him over the head, with a table lamp that I found downstairs. By the way, you're welcome, for sacrificing myself to save your ass."

"Sacrifice? It sounds like you enjoyed it," I quipped.

She grinned. "You have no idea."

"Ewww!" I made a face. "TMI!"

Barbie laughed as she led the way out of the room.

"How many guys are here? Do you think they'll try to stop us from leaving?" I asked quietly.

"A bunch, and I don't know. Probably," Barbie answered.

"Okay, what's the plan?" I asked.

"We sneak out the front door, and hide in the jungle until daybreak, then we try to find our way back to civilization."

When we reached the bottom of the stairs, I responded, "I'm not sleeping in the jungle, waiting for Random to come find me. Remember, I'm cursed to die a horrible death. That means either he'll find me and kill me, brutally, or I'll get eaten by a huge snake while hiding in the jungle."

"Fine by me. What's your plan?" Barbie asked.

I bit my lip. "I don't have one," I admitted.

"That's what I thought," Barbie retorted smugly. "So, we follow my plan. Don't worry about the snakes. I don't believe in curses and neither do you."

We reached the front door, without being caught. This was easier than I expected. I quickly unlocked the door, slowly easing it open, to hide the sound.

"Leaving so soon?" The Albino said, from the doorway. His translucent skin radiated in the moonlight, like a ghost.

Speechless, I felt myself take an involuntary step back.

"Mother Fucker!" Barbie growled behind me.

Getting my courage back, I whispered behind me, "I'll take him high, you take him low."

"What about them?" she asked.

"Them?" I looked past the Albino, and my heart sank. "Shit!"

"Let us step inside, shall we?" The Albino urged us back into the house.

Once the door had been firmly shut, he glanced around the hall. "Where are your new friends, Ms. Hart? Are they asleep in their beds?" His smile sent cold shivers down the back of my neck.

Barbie and I traded fearful glances.

With a clicking noise, the Albino sent his armed militia to check the house. Turning his attention back to us, he said, "We will make ourselves comfortable, whilst we wait for your friends to join us." He smiled, ushering us into a large sitting room.

Sometime later, we were sitting in the room, staring at each other. It seemed like we'd been doing this for a really long time. I checked my imaginary watch, again. Still half past a freckle. Time was moving way to slow. It was late, we were all showing signs of fatigue.

Finally, the noise of an engine sounded outside. Barbie and I strained to hear, hoping it was a rescue. Lights flashed through the windows, followed by the sounds of men yelling.

The Albino smiled a sickly smile, then said, "It appears that our host has returned. I must go and meet with him."

Looking at one of his men, armed with a small canon, he said something in Thai. The man nodded, hefting his gun.

The Albino smiled a sickening smile. "Adul will entertain you, until my return."

Keeping his eyes and gun trained on us, Adul nodded. The Albino motioned to the other men. Silently, they followed him out of the room. A moment later, we heard the front door shut loudly. Adul stared unblinking at us, cradling his canon. I stepped towards the door. Adul lifted the gun, shook his head, and barked something in Thai that I couldn't understand.

Barbie and I looked at each other. Barbie shook her head, slowly. I took a step back, next to my cousin. Adul smiled and lowered his gun.

"So, that's how it is," I muttered.

"Looks like it," Barbie agreed.

The loud voices outside intensified.

"We've got to get out of here, before crazy eyes and the psychopathic hottie finish duking it out," Barbie whispered.

I nodded my agreement. At this point, I wasn't sure which one was crazier, the Albino or Random. I was pretty sure I didn't want to find out. "What about the sentinel?" I whispered back.

"I have a plan. You distract him, and…"

Adul started making grunting noises while waving his canon in the air. Once he had our attention, he shoved the barrel between us, barking orders at us in Thai.

I rolled my eyes, and said, "Fine! We get it."

He glared at us while pantomiming that we should stand on separate sides of the room. I looked at Barbie. She was jerking her head up in quick bursts. It looked like she was having a seizure. She opened her eyes wide and jerked her head again, as if to say, come on. Adul and I were both staring stupidly at her.

She wanted a distraction, maybe a small seizure would work. I took a step toward the door. Adul barked at me again, frantically waving his cannon. Barbie gave me a look that said, *'stupid'*. Yeah, I had to give her that one. I stood staring at Adul, trying to think up a good distraction. One that would make him forget about emptying tiny pieces of lead into our bodies.

Barbie was mouthing something at me. I sighed, shaking my head. She knows I can't read lips. She rolled her eyes at me, fingering the buttons on her blouse. Sometimes, I wonder about Barbie. I really do.

Gunfire erupted outside. Adul turned slightly towards the window, craning to see into the dark. Barbie slipped closer to me, stopping when Adul slid his cannon up and shook his head. The gunfire stopped, giving us Adul's attention again.

Barbie stage whispered, "Show him your boobs."

"What!"

"Your boobs. Show him," she insisted.

"No!"

"Come on. Just pull up your shirt and give him an eye full."

"You have a problem. You know that?" I whispered.

"To distract him," she said, rolling her eyes toward the gun cradled against his arm. "Trust me. He'll forget about everything else."

"Maybe your boobs would make him forget about everything else, but mine aren't that impressive. I'm sure he's seen bigger."

"It's not about quantity, it's about boob. Just do it."

I glanced down at my boobs, then at Adul. I didn't want him to see my girls. They didn't want to see him. There had to be a better way.

"Jessie!" Barbie hissed.

I shook my head. "What's plan B?"

Barbie gave me a look designed to wilt flowers, muttered something under her breath, and quickly scooted next to me. I gave her a warning look as Adul, already agitated by the gunfire outside (which had started up again) lifted his gun to aim. The gunfire and yelling stopped. Everything seemed to go in slow motion as the world around us fell silent. Adul's trigger finger was in place, his gun aimed at my head, when Barbie's hands flew up. Adul's eyes' widened as he watched Barbie grab my tank top, and roughly pull against the fabric of my shirt.

"Rrrrrrrriiiiiiipppppppppp…" The sound was deafening in the silence.

Adul lowered his gun. We were both staring at my wonder bra. He took a step towards me, a silly grin on his face. As his hand reached out, I took a step back. At the same time, Barbie took a step to his other side. In disbelief, I watched her sucker punch Adul in the back of the neck with all of her strength. For a moment, nothing happened. Then, Adul's eyes crossed, and he slowly sank to the floor in front of me.

"What was that?!" I looked at my cousin with disbelief.

Barbie shrugged, "Twelve years of martial arts."

In awe, I asked, "Why did I have Junior teaching me self-defense in high school, when you can do that?"

Barbie shrugged, "Honestly? I've always wondered about that."

From the other side of the wall, angry voices followed by gunfire interrupted us.

"Quick, tie him up," Barbie hissed as she retrieved the cannon from the floor.

"Tie him up? With what?" I asked.

"Find something!" She snapped.

My eyes rested on the large curtains hanging over the far windows. I ran over, grabbed the curtain ropes, then rushed back to Adul. Kneeling next the unconscious form, I took a moment to pull his shirt off.

Barbie laughed, then said, "I didn't think you were into old, short guys."

Rolling my eyes, I said, "I'm not! I want his shirt, not his body."

Shrugging her shoulders, she nodded, and said, "Well, hurry up!"

Once I had his shirt, I juggled the ropes trying to decide on the best way to secure him. With a loud sigh, Barbie grabbed a piece of rope from my hand and quickly began looping it around the unconscious man's hands. Moving to his feet, I pulled the rope around his ankles, mimicking my cousin. I was concentrating hard, brows furrowed, biting my lip, when Barbie impatiently snatched the ropes from my hands.

Shaking her head at my incompetence, she said, "Someday, I really need to teach you how to tie someone up, quickly."

In a flash, the man was all trussed up like the Thanksgiving turkey. I couldn't even tell how she did it. Her hands were a blur of ropes and fingers. I was still admiring her handy work when Barbie signaled to get my attention. She had opened a window, away from the lights and noise, and was motioning me to come. Pulling the pilfered shirt over my head, I ran across the room, quickly slipping through the window behind Barbie.

Once outside, we took a moment to assess the situation. We could hear the pop of gunfire and see shadowed fighters in the near distance. All I knew was, I didn't want to go that way.

"Over here," Barbie whispered loudly to get my attention.

My eyes followed her pointing finger to an old Jeep, sitting mere feet away from us. Following Barbie at a running crouch, we reached the jeep without bringing attention to ourselves. Peering inside, Barbie clapped her hands in glee. The keys were in the ignition!

Rushing around her, I jumped in, scooted behind the wheel, and started the engine. I wasn't about to let Barbie drive. Barbie drove like it was the Indie five hundred when she was just on the way to the mall. With the headlights off, and Barbie riding shotgun, we headed for the driveway at breakneck speed.

"Where are we going?" Barbie asked, once I slowed down.

"This way," I answered.

"That's what I thought. Let's hope those assholes left us a map."

Moments later she was staring at a map with glee. "They even circled the house for us! I know where we are!"

"I'm more interested in how to get back," I retorted.

"Turn here," she said, just as I was passing the road.

Turning sharply, the Jeep tilted onto two wheels, but I made the turn. Barbie and I grinned at each other.

After about five minutes, Barbie said, "I wish we had some money, I'm starving!"

"Me too," I said, with a frown. "Too bad our money's back at the house."

A low buzzing interrupted our thoughts. It was coming from the backseat. We looked at each other. At the same time we asked each other, "Was that a phone ringing?"

Without warning, Barbie vaulted into the backseat. A moment later her head popped up beside mine, a huge smile on her face.

"You're not going to believe this! It's here! All of our stuff from Bessie, our purses, my phone, and money!" Barbie squealed with delight.

Grinning back at her, I said, "Let's stop at the next town and get some food!"

Fifteen minutes later, we pulled up to a shack full of people, music, and the smell of food.

"You order, I'll go across the street and get us a room," Barbie said.

"A room? We can't be that far from the hotel."

"Yes, but I don't think we want to risk going back."

"I guess it could be dangerous to go back, tonight," I agreed.

"Tonight, tomorrow, ever," Barbie said, with a straight face.

"Ever!" I exclaimed. "What about our stuff?"

"Our passports are the only important things. I have mine in my purse. You have your passport in your purse?" She asked.

"Yes," I agreed. "So is that cursed necklace."

"You don't believe in curses, remember. I'll have one of those yummy mango drinks if they make them," she called over her shoulder as she crossed the street.

Twenty Five

"Jess!" A sharp whisper and jab to the ribs startled me awake.
"Wh…"

"Shhh, we have company. Get on the floor."

I listened carefully as the door slowly creaked open. A shadow could just be seen, slowly creeping into the room. My heart rate shot up. The tense atmosphere had jolted me to full awareness. To my right, I could faintly make out Barbie. She was lying flat at the end of the bed, Adul's stolen cannon in hand, ready to shoot. One look at the situation and I dutifully slid off the bed, hunkering down beside it. A moment later, I heard Barbie let a shot out. The bullet whizzed across the room, reaching its target.

"Good shooting!" I congratulated her.

"Shhh…watch for the others," she cautioned.

As if to emphasize her words, a shadow briefly blocked the moonlight to our right.

"The window," I whispered to Barbie.

"On it," she whispered back. I could feel, more than hear, her rolling off of the bed to the other side.

Peering around the bed, I could faintly make out a dark shadow as it soundlessly stepped through the window. A moment later, there was another and another. They were silently streaming through the window, like roaches running from the light. To my right, I could hear Barbie carefully trading shots with our invaders. I knew we didn't have many bullets. Things were about to get ugly. I needed a weapon.

Without thinking, I inched towards the lank form on the other side of the room. I was mere inches away when the dark lump moved, ever so slightly raising his gun arm. Damn! I wanted that gun. I needed that gun. The dark form in front of me looked me in the eye, silently daring me to come within his reach. My blood ran cold with fear.

"Guns down." It was a familiar voice. "You too, Barbie."

"Where the hell have you been?!" Barbie exclaimed from under the bed.

"Looking for you two," he said, as someone flipped on the light switch. "Are you all right?"

"We're fine. No thanks to you," Barbie grouched.

My eyes took a moment to adjust, as the room was suddenly bathed in cheap fluorescent light. Barbie was squirming out from under the bed. Several of our attackers were assessing their wounds.

Eric stood in the middle of the floor. With confusion, I looked from Eric to the unknown man in black bleeding at his feet.

"You okay?" Eric asked the man on the floor.

"Just a flesh wound," he grimaced.

"I'm billing you for that." He glared at Barbie.

"He should have knocked." She glared back.

"We didn't know the situation. We still a ways form the house when the GPS fled the Coulthurst house. We thought you'd been kidnapped, again," he responded. "How were we to know you'd escaped?"

"Three kidnappings in one night is a little much for anyone, even us," I answered flippantly.

Eric's eyes took mine hostage while he silently considered my words, as if he couldn't decide what he wanted to say. The seconds crept by, feeling like minutes, then hours. Still we stood facing each other, eyes locked, neither breaking the uncomfortable silence. Finally, he shook his head. I shrugged my shoulders in response. He let out a deep sigh before ordering his men down to the street. It wasn't until Barbie channeled her inner Florence Nightingale, and helped the wounded men outside, that Eric spoke to me.

"Trouble, you really are trouble," he said, wrapping his arms around my shoulders and pulling me close. "I was worried sick."

"Yeah, me too." My words were muffled by his shirt.

"No more elephant safaris for you. It's too dangerous," he said into my hair.

"Okay lovebirds." Barbie rolled her eyes at us as she stepped into the room. "All of the other superheroes are tucked in and on their way back to the Hall of Justice. So, if you're not too busy," her voice raised an octave, "would you mind telling us where the hell you've been, and why you shot up our motel room at two in the morning?"

Eric shrugged, "You want the long version or the short version?"

"The short version. I'm tired," she grumped.

"I got a call from my man saying that you had gotten on the safari, but since no one bothered to invite him, they were booked up." He shot me an accusatory glare. "He couldn't follow the tour."

Barbie shrugged, saying, "You were very clear that we were not to interact with *your* men." She rolled her eyes, adding, "It's not our fault he couldn't keep up."

Choosing to ignore Barbie, Eric said, "Since he couldn't get on the safari, I told him to wait at the main building and monitor the GPS until you got back. By the time anyone realized that you were missing, it was getting late. Once he notified me that you hadn't returned. I called my men off of our target, redirecting them to look for you two, and leaving your guard at the safari, just in case you turned up there." He gave me an apologetic look. "We were off the island checking out a property off of Ao Luk Bay. So, it took a minute for me and my men to get over to this end of the island. When your abductors showed up for your things, my man at the safari followed them. He was able to radio the coordinates, but without knowing where they were keeping you, I couldn't risk my man going in, during the firefight, and without backup. We rendezvoused at the road to the house towards the end of the firefight. In case you were wandering," he grinned down at me, "my team won."

Barbie huffed her impatience at Eric.

"A room by room search gave us confidence that you weren't on the premises. None of the survivors seemed to know where you were, but we didn't know how many had fled the premises during the skirmish. We had to assume that your captor had moved you during the fight. With nothing else to go on, we pulled out the GPS, followed the signal to this hotel, and belatedly came to the rescue," he finished his explanation.

"Why didn't you just knock on the door?" I asked.

"I would have, if you had gone back to your hotel. But, a cheap motel seemed out of character, especially for your cousin." He gave Barbie an inquiring look.

Barbie shrugged in answer.

"I had to assume that you were still being held against your will."

"So, because you thought a seedy motel was 'out of character', you broke in and began shooting the place up? You could have killed us!" Barbie exclaimed.

"Actually, you did most of the shooting. My men were under orders to shoot only as a means of defense, until the situation could be further assessed. That is why so many of my men were wounded, but you two came through without a scratch."

Barbie and I exchanged glances.

"Oh…"

"Okay…"

"Why didn't you go back to your rooms at the resort?" He asked.

"It seemed like a bad idea, under the circumstances," Barbie snapped.

"Don't mind her, she's just cranky," I assured him.

"He'd be cranky too if he'd been ditched by an elephant, walked an entire jungle in strappies, had an army threaten him, jumped off a cliff into the arms of a psychopath, got locked in a basement, and finally escaped, just to have a bunch of idiots scare the shit out of him by invading his hotel room in the middle of the frickin' night. My hair is a mess. I don't have on any makeup. My clothes are ruined. And, just look at my feet! My feet are never going to recover from this!" Barbie wriggled her cut up toes at us.

Eric was trying hard not to smile, and doing a poor job. "Would you like a ride back to the resort?"

We both hesitated, looking at each other.

I shook my head. "There are a couple of guys we're kind of avoiding right now."

Eric raised an eyebrow in question.

"You wouldn't know them." I waved off the unspoken question.

"I may surprise you," he disagreed.

Barbie rolled her eyes, and said, "The Albino, he's a really pale guy with a weird accent, an army of Asian mercenaries, and a mean streak."

Eric nodded, "I don't think you need to worry about him."

"He's dead?" Barbie and I asked in unison.

"No. The local police picked up someone matching that description on the other side of the island."

"For kidnapping and shooting at people?" I nodded my approval.

Eric shook his head, laughing, "No, speeding."

"Speeding!" Barbie squealed. "There is no justice in this world."

Eric gave Barbie a look before shaking his head, and saying, "He won't bother you again."

"But, you just said he was speeding," Barbie glared at Eric. "In case we weren't clear. He's a scrawny albino man with a bad case of short man syndrome. Which is it, arrested or dead?"

"No, *you* said he was dead. What *I* said was that you don't need to worry about him bothering you," he expounded.

"So, what you're saying is that he's not dead?" Barbie clarified.

"What I'm saying is that he was arrested, for speeding." There was just a hint of irritation in his voice.

"Speeding! That's like getting Al Capone for tax evasion," Barbie muttered angrily. "Why didn't you shoot him, arrest him for kidnapping, or something more acceptable?"

"We are not the police." Eric's tone had grown cold with aggravation. "We had to let them go. We didn't have any authority to detain the survivors from the firefight."

"Who said anything about detaining them? You had guns, it's your responsibility to shoot the bad guys," she insisted, looking to me for support.

"Once my men had cleared the area, we did the only thing we were legally able to do, notify the local police that there had been a firefight and that many of those involved were either dead at the residence or traveling away from it. The police have had a busy night rounding up the stragglers."

"What about Random?" I asked. I was curious, but mostly I was hoping to move the subject along while acting as a buffer between Barbie and Eric.

"Random what?" He gave me a confused look.

"Random Chance," Barbie answered for me.

"What about it?" Eric looked completely baffled.

"Him, Random Chance is a him," Barbie explained.

"Have you been drinking?" Eric asked.

"Obviously not enough!" Barbie frowned.

Rolling my eyes, I explained, "Random Chance stole the cursed necklace that was all over the news the day that I met him in Oklahoma City. In order to bypass security, he slipped it into my purse, cursing me."

"Wait. You had it, this whole time?" he asked, surprise in his voice.

I nodded unhappily, adding, "Random Chance made me the owner of the cursed necklace. Now, I'm going to die a horrible death." I could feel the tears gathering in the corners of my eyes.

"No, you're not," Barbie insisted.

"Yes, I am." I answered.

"Random is…?" Eric asked, trying to make sense of it all.

"Random is the one who was holding us prisoner, in his house, until he could ransom us to Jennifer Jons' agent. Those other guys weren't actually with him. They just came for the necklace. Then, the Albino showed up with his mercenaries."

"The Albino wanted the necklace?" he asked.

"Yes, him and everyone else," I agreed. "Anyway, when Random got back from the safari office with our stuff, the Albino met him outside. That's when they started killing each other. We didn't want to be killed. So, we slipped out the back, borrowed a jeep, and somehow ended up with the cursed necklace, again. Now, I'm doubly cursed." I looked at Barbie, adding, "And, the curse says that I will die a horrible death."

Barbie rolled her eyes at me, whispering, "Drama queen."

Eric gave us a look that questioned our sobriety. All he said was, "And, Jennifer Jons, the actress, also wanted the necklace?"

Pursing my lips, I shook my head, then clarified, "No, they thought Barbie was her."

Eric turned his attention to Barbie who gave him her best movie star smile. Shaking his head as if to say he shouldn't be surprised, he asked, "Random Chance, is he about six foot, dark hair, dark eyes, with a tan?"

"That's him." Barbie frowned. "A hottie with horns." A moment later she added, "Random is a psychopath, and he knows where we're staying. Between the Albino and Random, we decided to get some sleep here tonight, then go straight to the airport in the morning. Our flight leaves at eight."

Eric nodded, "I don't think you'll have to worry about him anymore."

"Did he get arrested, too?" I asked.

"I'm pretty sure he's dead," he said.

"How sure?" Barbie asked.

He gave her a blank stare.

After a moment she shrugged, and said, "Good enough."

"The curse!" I exclaimed.

"Good riddance," Barbie approved.

"What!" I gave her a shocked look. "You can't speak ill of the dead."

Barbie shrugged. "He was a bad guy. Anyway, all I said was good riddance. I could say a lot worse. He tried to ruin our vacation."

Eric shook his head at us, and said, "Get your stuff. I'll give you a ride."

Barbie and I exchanged glances, before nodding our agreement.

As I reached for my purse, Eric said, "Do you have the necklace, now?"

I nodded.

With an incredulous shake of his head, he held out his hand, and said, "Give it to me."

"Not you too!" I exclaimed. "Why does everyone want this cursed necklace? It's bad luck!"

"It's worth a lot of money. Last week, it was sold for one million and ten dollars. The man you know as Random almost caused an international incident when he stole this necklace. I was hired to bring it back." Eric held out his hand. Shaking his head in disbelief, he said, "I've been searching everywhere and all I needed to do was ask you for it."

"Yeah, let's see the necklace that's caused us so much grief over the last few days," Barbie said, stepping in front of me.

I had to admit, I was curious. Reaching into my purse, I dug around until something black and shiny caught my eye. Slowly, I pulled it out. The gunmetal black diamond was the size of my palm, encrusted with smaller white diamonds, and set in a platinum backing that was attached to a delicate platinum chain. It was breathtaking.

"Over a million dollars?" Barbie asked, in a breathless voice.

Eric nodded, reaching out his hand.

I took a long look at it before gingerly placing it in his palm. "Be careful, it's cursed."

Eric gave me a strange look.

"All of the owners, including Random…," I paused. "Did Random die a horrible death?" I asked, but I was pretty sure of the answer.

Eric grimly nodded. "Someone shot him. He bled out."

"All of the owners, except for me, have died a horrible death," I finished ominously.

We stood, quietly staring at the black diamond resting innocently in Eric's hand.

"I don't believe in curses and neither do you, remember?" Barbie announced, breaking the silence.

"I do now," I answered. "Look at all the bad luck I've had since this thing was put in my purse, making me the owner."

"You didn't know that you had it. So, technically, you were never the owner. Anyway, you always have bad luck, the worst," Barbie said. "Really, this trip hasn't been that much worse than your normal luck." Barbie grinned at me.

I watched Eric place the necklace in a small velvet covered box. Where had that come from? Once it was secure, he slid it into a small black bag. I cursed my poor observation skills. I hadn't even noticed the bag.

"Sure, I didn't know I had it, but that doesn't matter. The Black Orlov knew I had it. I'm next. I'm going to die a horrible death." I frowned. "Do the owner a favor and get rid of that thing," I said to Eric.

"You're not going to die any kind of death. Let's get you back to your room. You'll feel better in the morning."

I let Eric lead me outside, but I still couldn't shake the feeling that something terrible would happen to me, and soon. "It is the morning," I grumbled. "Our flight leaves in just a few hours."

Twenty Six

By the time we picked up our bags and raced to the airport, we had all but missed our flight. The only reason we didn't was Barbie. Sometimes, I think it would be nice to be Barbie, then she hooks up with some weirdo, with a flat nose, and no eyebrows in the bathroom...eww! Fifteen minutes into our plane ride was an eww moment.

By the time she came back I was asleep. I think I slept most of the blissfully uneventful ride back to New York. Stepping off of the plane, Barbie ran into an old *'friend'*. It only took a few hours for me to realize that I was a third wheel and jump on a plane to Boston. Yes, Boston!

I hadn't seen Greg in weeks. I needed to thank him for his help, and... Okay, I wanted to see Eric. We had parted with a long sweet kiss that I'd been dreaming of the entire trip back. I wanted another.

Before I had left New York, Barbie had found me the address to Wolf, Inc. in Boston. Once my flight landed, I caught a cab to Eric's office. Stepping through the front doors, I had a feeling of déjà vu.

"All of his buildings really do look the same," I marveled.

"Excuse me, you can't go back there," the man in black sitting behind the desk said, in a firm voice that left no doubt in my mind that he would shoot me if I ignored him.

I smiled my most innocent smile, then said, "It's okay. I'm here to see Eric. I mean Mr. Wolf. I'm a friend."

"What is your name? I'll buzz him," he answered.

"Jessie," I muttered thinking this would never happen in the Seattle office. There I was treated like a member of this member's only club. This guy was ruining my surprise. With a roll of my eyes and a grunt of disapproval, I sat down beside my luggage to wait. A moment later the elevator dinged, and the doors began to open.

"Sir, I was just buzzing you. You have a visitor."

Eric looked at me with surprise, then said, "I thought you were in New York."

'I thought you were in New York?' Of all the scenarios that had run through my mind, this was not one of them. He was supposed to say, *'Jessie! I missed you so much. Come, let's get married, and live happily ever after.'* He was supposed to grab me and kiss me like I've never been kissed before. He was supposed to be happy - no, ecstatic - to see me.

"Eric, who is this?" A melodic voice came from behind him.

I looked for the owner of the voice. She couldn't have been more than five feet tall, without the five inch heels on her tiny feet. Her expertly coiffed hair was the color of midnight, and there was a lot of it. Her features were delicate. Her wardrobe was flattering. She was perfect.

Jealousy flared deep inside me as I frowned across the room at the dark haired beauty standing beside *my* Eric. My cheeks burned with betrayal as the seconds ticked by. Still, Eric hadn't answered. Why didn't he answer? I shifted my burning gaze to him. He was giving instructions to the desk guy while paying me, and the harlot at his side, no attention.

Without my heart's approval, my feet turned and walked out the door. Seconds later, I was crying my eyes out in a cab, on my way to the airport. It was time to go home.

Pulling out my phone, I made a call that I never thought I'd make again. Momma and daddy are right, I thought. It's time to settle down, with a nice local guy. Time to grow up, and start a life.

"Hey woman!" I could hear him smile through the phone. "I was just thinking about you."

This was more like it. Sure, we've had our share of problems, but we have history. We're connected to each other, always there for each other, when it matters. And, we're older, more mature now. Those problems are in our past.

I took a deep breath, "Mike, I only have a minute. Is that offer to pick me up still good?"

"What time?" He said it without hesitation.

Yeah, this was the right answer. We've known each other our whole lives. We understand each other. Despite all of our past troubles, there is still an attraction, an electric current running between us. I felt it that day, heading to the airport. I could feel it now, coming through the phone.

"I'm on my way to the airport. I'll send you a text as soon as I get my ticket."

"I'll be there," he assured me.

I knew he would be. That was the only thing I knew.

Epilogue

Three months later, Barbie was lying on my bed, at my parent's house, while I shoved clothes into an overnight bag.

"Tell me again why we're running out into the cold, on Thanksgiving night, to catch a plane to someplace in Canada that even the Canadians have probably never heard of," Barbie insisted.

"I already told you. Greg got a call, and…"

"And, you're afraid somebody else is going to buy up all the prime igloo building spots?"

I shot her an irritated look, and said, "You and I both know that Greg isn't a real estate agent."

"He's not!" Barbie gave a fake gasp. "I had no idea!"

Tilting my head to the side, I raised one eyebrow at my melodramatic cousin.

With a grin, she said, "It's about time somebody let me in on the family secret. I was starting to feel unloved."

"Unloved?" I questioned.

She shrugged, "So, what *does* dear cousin Greg do for a living? Let me guess...superhero, detective, gigolo...oooh," she crowed, clapping her hands with delight. "Super villain?!"

Pulling a shirt out of the closet, I said, "FBI agent."

"FBI," she repeated. "What is the FBI doing sending an agent to Canada? That is definitely outside of their jurisdiction."

"That's what we're going to find out," I said, with a smile.

Squinting her eyes at me, she asked, "Why are you suddenly so interested in what Greg is doing?

I shrugged, "No reason."

With a frown, she said, "I'm not buying what you're selling."

Rolling my eyes, I said, "I don't know. I mean, I need to get out of town, after the Mike fiasco."

"Uncle Bill was telling me about that," she grinned. "Did you really douse him in gasoline and set him on fire?"

"NO! Is that what they're saying?" I asked, horror on my face.

"So, you didn't set him on fire?" She asked, disappointment in her eyes.

"It's complicated," I evaded. "Anyway, I'm pretty sure that the engagement is off."

"I get that," she nodded her agreement. "What I don't get is what your kinky sex life has to do with following Greg to Canada."

"It doesn't, and my sex life is far from kinky. I just, I don't know." I shrugged, "It's like you said, why would the FBI send Greg to Canada? It's got to be big," I hesitated before adding, "Wolf Inc. is involved."

Barbie's face brightened, "The Wolfman! I like him!"

Rolling my eyes, I said, "Of course you do. He's a lying, cheating, scumbag; just your type."

"So, you still don't want to talk about it?" She asked.

"There is nothing to talk about," I growled.

Barbie nodded, "Just so I've got this straight, we're going to Canada, because you think your old boyfriend is meeting up with your brother to hunt down the big man himself, and you don't want to stay here and face your old/new boyfriend after yet another really BIG fight where you may or may not have set him on fire."

I pulled a pair of jeans out of my closet, moved to put them in my bag, nodded, and said, "Pretty much."

"I'm in."

"You are?"

"I always was. I just like to know what I'm getting into," she said. "You don't think I'd let you run off half-cocked without me to save your ass, do you?"

"I was really hoping not. Besides, you're paying," I said, with a grin.

"You have got to get a job, or a rich husband," she said. "I'd give you one of mine, but they're all broke."

Curling up her nose at the shirt I was shoving into my bag, she shook her head, and said, "That one makes you look fat."

"Fat?" I eyed the shirt in my hand. "I thought the stripes were flattering."

She curled her lip. "I'm sure they are, on someone else, and in a different color. Take the green one in the back. That color makes your eyes pop."

Tossing the striped shirt into the bottom of my closet, I reached for the green sweater that Barbie had pointed out. With a sigh, I slid it back into its place.

Barbie raised an eyebrow in question.

Rolling my eyes, I answered her unspoken question. "Mike gave it to me, a couple of weeks ago, just because." With a sniff, I brushed away a tear.

"Let's get this straight, he picked you up at the airport, after you caught the Wolfman with some skank, with a great big shiny rock. You moved into his house, started picking out curtains and flatware. Everything was love and roses last week when I left for Bora Bora. I get here and all you can tell me is that you've moved back in with your parents, and you're *pretty sure the engagement is off*."

"Do you think this jacket will be warm enough?" I held up a brown faux leather jacket lined with green polka dotted silk.

"What happened? I need to know!"

"Nothing. It just…"

"Don't you dare tell me that it just didn't work out," she glared across the room at me. "I invented that lame excuse."

I took a deep breath, then said, "Fine. If you must know."

351

"I must," she insisted.

"He picked up the phone the other day, and went psycho."

Raising a suspicious eyebrow, she asked, "Who was calling that would make an otherwise sane man go psycho? An ex-sane man?"

"Yeah." I frowned. "He's called a few times, but like I told Mike, I have nothing to say to him."

"Uh huh," Barbie pursed her lips. "And, Mike?"

"Didn't believe me. He accused ME of cheating! ME! He's the one who cheated on ME. I can name names!" I paced the room in anger.

"I see." Barbie watched me pace. "You can't blame him, Jess. The Wolfman is super yummy hot. You come back from Thailand, all distraught over him, and you won't talk about it. He calls, and you still won't talk about it. You obviously have unresolved feelings for the Wolfman."

"You've been spending too much time with your therapist." I glared across the room at Barbie.

Barbie shrugged, "I'm not seeing him anymore."

"Of course not. What happened in Bora Bora?" I asked.

Barbie grinned, "I found someone much more enticing, if you must know." She frowned, "But, we were talking about *your* man drama."

"Right," I said, flopping onto the floor beside my bags. With a loud sigh, I rolled onto my back, staring up at the ceiling.

"And?" Barbie prompted.

"And, we fought, and fought, and fought, for four days. We fought about Mike and Traci Lee. We fought about me and Jim. We fought about Mike and Heather. We fought about me and Eric. We fought about me and Mike. Then, we fought about my wanting to move, see the world, and do something fun with my life, and Mike wanting to stay here, in Tish, forever. It was somewhere around that point that that Mike said I was lucky to have him, that no sane man would even consider marrying me, and that Jim had dodged a bullet."

"Ooooohhhh!" Barbie said. "So, you gathered your stuff and moved back home?"

"Not exactly," I murmured.

"What did you do?" Barbie asked suspiciously.

"It was an accident. I'm not even sure how it happened," I said in a small voice.

"OMG! You did set him on fire!" Barbie's eyes were wide.

"I found a matchbook, to a motel. He doesn't smoke. He said Bubba left them there. How convenient," I frowned, reliving the moment.

"Jessie!"

"I took a match out of the matchbook, lit it, and tossed it at him, then another, and another. He was backing up, yelling that I was crazy. I just followed him, throwing matches. About halfway through the matchbook, he tripped over a paint can, splashing paint on him and the floor. The match was already in midair. It hit the paint on his pants leg." Guilty tears filled my eyes, as I said, "I didn't expect him to catch fire. They were just matches!"

Barbie shook her head, "Only you would accidently set a man on fire, just after he told you that no sane man would want you, proving his point."

I nodded, and said, "I know."

About the Author

Once upon a time, in a life far far away, Jenn Brink was a mental health counselor. Now, she's an Army wife. No, it's not at all like the television show. She spends her days taking care of the untwins, teen, and the mutt, all with her phone close by, just in case her smoking hot soldier calls. When the planets align properly, she even gets some writing done.

Now that 'Cerulean Seas' is finished, Jenn is focusing on 'Nail Polish, Push-Up Bras & Pirate Ships'. A fun, YA, paranormal, pirate adventure. Be sure to check it out in the spring! But don't worry, she's still working on the next Jessica Hart book, 'Silver Bells', and a thriller that she's calling 'Tabula Rasa'.

Jenn welcomes your comments through email, Twitter, Facebook, Goodreads, and on her website. She LOVES hearing from readers, and reading their reviews of her books, so post those reviews!

You can find the social media, and email links, for Jenn on her website, along with chapter previews and a few short stories, at www.JennBrink.com.

24394211R10208

Made in the USA
Charleston, SC
23 November 2013